CONSTANTINE SAW IT THEN: A DUN-COLORED GUNSHIP, COMING IN LOW OVER THE FIELDS, ITS ROTORS A GLIMMER IN THE FIRELIGHT.

It slowed to hover over what remained of the camp, and in a flash of gunfire from below, Constantine thought he saw a small glassy something thrown from a window of the chopper. A moment later there came an upburst of yellow smoke or powder, spreading out in the rotor wash.

What was it? Constantine wondered. Gas warfare? Smokescreen?

Then he saw a curious thing. The billowing smoke—visible in the light from a burning tent near the chopper—was forming into a specific shape, an enormous head that kept reasserting its shape on the smoke, as if the head were made of a clear crystal and the smoke was filling the transparent vessel from within. The head—bigger than the helicopter—turned this way and that, a face like a viciously feral Neanderthal, but with spikes in place of fur on its head, and great interlacing tusks. Hadn't he seen that face somewhere—in some temple painting? He didn't think so. Yet it looked so familiar. Strangely familiar. . . .

JOHN CONSTANTINE™ HELLBLAZER™

WAR LORD

A NOVEL BY JOHN SHIRLEY

BASED ON CHARACTERS FROM THE VERTIGO/DC COMICS SERIES

POCKET STAR BOOKS

New York   London   Toronto   Sydney

An *Original* Publication of POCKET BOOKS

A Pocket Star Book published by
POCKET BOOKS, a division of Simon & Schuster, Inc.
1230 Avenue of the Americas, New York, NY 10020

This book is a work of fiction. Names, characters, places and incidents are products of the author's imagination or are used fictitiously. Any resemblance to actual events or locales or persons, living or dead, is entirely coincidental.

ISBN-13: 978-1-4165-0343-9
ISBN-10:   1-4165-0343-9

This Pocket Star Books paperback edition February 2006

10 9 8 7 6 5 4 3 2 1

POCKET STAR BOOKS and colophon are registered trademarks of Simon & Schuster, Inc.

www.dccomics.com
Keyword: DC Comics on AOL

Cover design by John Vairo
Cover illustration by Tim Bradstreet

Manufactured in the United States of America

For information regarding special discounts for bulk purchases, please contact Simon & Schuster Special Sales at 1-800-456-6798 or business@simonandschuster.com.

For Micky

Special thanks to
Jamie Delano, Charles Kochman, Steve Korté,
John Morgan, Paul Mavrides, Perry Shirley
and all the mad blokes at the
Voices From Beyond Hellblazer forum
(http://hellblazer.ipbhost.com/index.php)
who gave me lots of much needed advice.

It's inside me. I keep trying to kill it. But it just won't die.

—Jamie Delano, *Hellblazer* #34

From the Servants of Transfiguration

Dossier on John Constantine

Top Clearance: Eyes Only

John Constantine, a working-class British magus, is rumored to be a magical adept by some, a con man by others. He may or may not be problematic to the SOT. He was born in 1953 in Liverpool (making him a "Scouse") to a family that can be charitably called "working class," and this class association has marked his personal style. According to hospital records he was a twin, but his brother was born dead, asphyxiated by an anomalous loop of umbilicus. The magical symbolism of this seems ambiguous, to say the least. Additionally, Constantine's mother died in childbirth. His father, Thomas Constantine, apparently blamed the infant JC for this. Thomas was incarcerated for stealing women's underwear, at which time the boy and his sister were sent to live with an aunt and uncle, a rather troublesome pair, in Northampton. John Constantine's relationships with family members have been rocky at best.

In 1967, he was expelled from school. Eventually he moved to Portobello, London, where he was involved in some of the more extemporaneous "rock and roll" scenes extant at the time. Constantine is reported to have had scores of occult adventures—possibly *misadventures* is a better term—but our researchers find it difficult to separate out fact from legend. It does appear that Constantine had a particularly nasty interaction with a demon invoked at Newcastle, leading to an extended sojourn in Ravenscar mental hospital. Despite the notorious sadism of Ravenscar's staff, he seems to have emerged from the hospital with his sanity largely restored, all things being relative.

Constantine seems to be almost entirely without conventional financial support. We have no record of his taking money for an occult investigation or activity. He appears to make some of his very modest living through supernaturally enhanced gambling.

Our researchers are unable to discover precisely when and where Constantine learned about the Hidden World and gained a proficiency in ritual magic. We note a number of Constantine's ancestors with a reputation for the supernatural (see SOT files, *The Inquisition*), hence he may have inherited some magical ability. He also seems to have actively explored the supernatural from fairly early in childhood, quite on his own initiative. As an adult, he may well have had inspiration from some other well-known figures in the uncanny realm, including the voodoo priest known as "Papa Midnite" (see dossier entry, "Papa Midnite: An authentic personage"). There are rumors that Constantine was involved with the (mythical?) elemental known as the "Swamp Thing."

His abilities are not known for certain, but John Constantine is understood to be capable of limited telepathy, precognition, astral projection, and the successful invocation of elementals, demons, and angels. There are persistent tales of his having visited Hell itself, somehow walking away more or less intact. However, he does not seem to have been allied with Hell's supervisory denizens, nor is he regarded as a diabolist. Indeed, in recent years Constantine has been known to seek out white-magic spiritual adepts in a bid for improved control over his abilities.

Constantine has his weaknesses, including bouts of drunkenness, but is to be regarded as a dangerous adversary. He is not without allies and is influential amongst aficionados of so-called "chaos magick." E.g., there are at least two "alternative Tarot" decks which include an image of John Constantine as one of the face cards.

SOT operatives interacting with Constantine should keep in mind that he is cunning and treacherous. Our psych profile on him suggests that he is not without loyalty and some peculiar code of ethics evolved according to his own lights. Unfortunately we have no reason to believe his loyalty could ever extend to the SOT. He must be regarded as a loose cannon, at best.

If the opportunity arises, John Constantine's elimination would be advisable.

1

THE FOXES HAVE HOLES AND
THE BIRDS OF THE AIR HAVE NESTS . . .

London, England

Good to be back in London—especially on a Friday night: a crisp night in April, it is, near the Thames. I feel people streaming through the city, coming up from the Underground like bubbles in a boiling teapot; they're joined by people moving singly from shops and office buildings, to become part of a living torrent that breaks into thousands of rivulets finding their way to parties and computer cafes and nightclubs; people migrating to the cinema, people going to watch a match on telly with their friends—most important, people going down the local for a pint.

That's where I'm headed. It's a relief to be a faceless part of the stream, just another one of the excited particles in the solution, volatile with social chemistry, economic heat. But not much economic heat, me. Not sure I've got the dosh in my pocket for a drink—I reckon

*one of me mates will buy, at The Cutter—they'll stand
me a pint and something decent in the way of a smoke,
Bob's your uncle. Someone I know's sure to be there. I
can feel them there—though I'm still a block away. I
can feel a couple of old friends and others I know who
never trusted me, rightly so.*

*Must lock down the old intuition. If I let myself feel
too much I'll start to see things—those other things.
Glimpses come: I see people from earlier times, in Ed-
wardian dress; in Regency; in the togs of King James's
time and Elizabethan too; pasty white or apple-
cheeked they are, all mingled, now, with a modern
crowd. Round here there're as many dark-skinned
blokes from Pakistan and North Africa as the old
Anglo-Saxon-Norman-Celt genetic hodgepodge. . . .
Dogcarts and carriages translucently overlapping with
delicately off-gassing smart cars and big black exhaust-
flatulent taxis and great hulking chrome lorries . . . an-
tique tarts mingling with modern: is that James
Boswell leering at a tom as she lifts her dress in a
reeking doorway?*

*Don't know if the anachronisms are ghosts, or a gan-
der through time. Don't care, don't want to see them at
all.*

*I twitch my attention back onto the impulses from this
time: John Constantine's twenty-first-century London. . . .*

*But sometimes I miss London 1979, strutting in punk
regalia on Carnaby Street, telling the old Swinging London types to sod off—now there was energy, there was
life, because life doesn't sustain itself without rebellion.
But this, now, this twenty-first-century polyglot parade,
this'll do. It's full of vital cultural crosscurrents and it's*

what the big kaleidoscope of time has shifted me to and you've got to just look at the kaleidoscope and fancy them colors. . . .

Not sure how I decided to come over here today. Not sure where I was yesterday. More than that: feeling a little fuzzy about the last week or so. Must've gotten pissed, blacked out . . . must've been one fuck-all of a piss-up . . .

Passing a doorway exuding curry smells; passing a frock boutique, doomed to fail like most of them; passing a chippie with its smell of deep-fried fish—and here's The Cutter, with a painting of a cutter, all sails set and billowing, on the swinging wooden sign over the door. Hope someone's got a Silk Cut. . . .

✦⊶⊙⊷✦

John Constantine was about to push through the door into The Cutter when it burst open and a couple of compact, short-skirted girls came bouncing out, their laughter tumbling together. Trying to keep in practice with the fairer sex, Constantine smiled coolly at the little blond with the heart-shaped face and said, "What's so funny, then, love? I could use a laugh."

The girl's gaze slid past him like he wasn't there, her expression unchanging, the stream of giggling chatter unceasing. The two girls flounced off down the street, arm in arm, helping each other walk and laughing at their own drunkenness.

Slipping through the door before it closed, Constantine felt a bit down at the snub. He was getting older—was he so old it was like he wasn't there, for the young ones?

Grow up, John, he told himself. *The bloom's off the rose and that's that. No new rose in town for you.*

It felt good to be here anyway. He gazed contentedly at the teeming pub; at the dark, crowded wooden booths, floor going slanty with age, signs extolling ales, walls displaying banners for football and rugby teams. Good to be in his own local. Peculiar thing, a pub, how people are focused on whoever they're talking to, or just there alone, drinking—but they're with all the other people in the pub, too, people they don't know and won't say a word to, all night long. Not that there aren't social boundaries. But on some level, you're *with* everyone there.

Still, it seems some will walk right by you like you *weren't* there even though they've known you for decades. Because there went Rich—skinny, lined face, hair dyed magenta, spiky atop, long in the back, dressed in whatever had come handy—walking by as if he hadn't seen Constantine.

Rich was an old friend, clueless and yet peculiarly connected to the very heart of Britain. A fellow veteran of punk rock and devilishly improvisational was Rich—Constantine had known him since the era of his own band, Mucous Membrane.

"Rich!" Constantine called as his old mate, sloshing pint in one hand, roll-mops in the other, whipped by him in the crowd, shouting at someone over the noise. True, Rich was half deaf—maybe he hadn't heard Constantine. He wasn't blind, though. He had to have seen him. "Already sozzled I see. . . ."

Or is it some kind of social freeze-out? What've I done now?

Trouble was, Constantine couldn't remember how he'd come to cock things up. Really was blurry, the last few . . . hell, the last few *weeks*. He might've firebombed a day care for all he could remember. . . .

But there's someone at the bar who won't ignore me.

"Chas!" Constantine called. More like an extension of himself than a best friend, was Chas. Cabbie and reluctant factotum. Chas claimed to be sick of the Hidden World—but always had to see what was hid.

Constantine slipped past a big weeping drunk in a football T-shirt—Manchester United—and a long-necked, probably French female in a black pinafore and heavy eye shadow, and found a spot at the dented oaken bar next to Chas. He looked Chas over as if he'd never seen him before—as if he were watching a stranger through a secret window.

With his short dark hair receding, Chas was not markedly younger than Constantine. The outline of his face was softening, thickening with middle age, the lines around his eyes etched with cynical humor. Just now he was telling a story to a stocky, bald bartender in a rugby jersey and matching braces. Took Constantine a long moment to remember the bartender's name—Addy, wasn't it?—which was strange in itself. Constantine rarely forgot a bartender.

The bartender was pretending to be amused as Chas rattled on, both of them ignoring Constantine. "Not again, I says! Stone me! You 'in lurve' again, I says! Woman's allergic to sarcasm—all bug-eyed at me, she says, 'Oi yeah I'm in love, 'e's a god!' Yeah he'll be god of her fanny soon enough!"

The bartender grinned and caught up a cloth, swiping a lager spill off the bar directly in front of Constantine. "Pint of the usual, Addy," Constantine said. "This wicked wag here'll be buying. Eh, Chas? Can't spare a greeting for your old mate, you can bloody well spare something wet and a fag."

Chas kept chuckling, staring into his porter. There was a sadness behind it, Constantine saw. Chas was married—but could he have a thing for this girl he was talking about? Midlife crisis?

"Right, Chas, carry on as you like," Constantine said, disgusted. "Just saw Rich. About as observant as you are. Unless you gits are playing at a snub. What'd I do, mate, get on a piss-up and summon your mum back from Hell? Let's have it."

Chas ignored him. Constantine shrugged. "Well you can bog off then. Oi, Addy—how about that pint?"

The bartender did set a drink down in front of him. Gin over ice. Constantine reached for the glass, thinking the bartender had heard him wrong, but sod it, gin would do the trick—and then he stared at the glass . . . as his fingers passed through it. He tried again to grasp it, again his fingers passed through it. He felt the cold of the liquid very faintly—but he was unable to really touch it. The girl in the black pinafore paid the bartender and took the drink.

"Strewth!" Constantine burst out, watching his gin and ice depart.

"You can't pick up a glass, John Constantine," said

a voice at his elbow. "And you can't talk to living people."

Constantine turned to see a man who wasn't quite there—he'd appear to be solid enough one moment, then someone would walk through him and he'd shimmer like a television image when a storm's shaking the cable. Constantine saw ghosts fairly often—he'd seen some on the way here after all—and was not terribly surprised. "Your picture's not coming in proper, mate," he said, looking the ghost over. The ghost was a military figure, a British Army colonel in tropical-issue khakis and shorts. Hair slicked back; flaring, curled mustache; red scowling face.

"You escape from a David Niven movie?" Constantine asked. "Kind of chilly for those short pants."

"Haven't got time for whimsy, recruit," the ghost said. "We've got a campaign to wage. No time to be swanning about bars. Just wasting your time trying to talk to the civilians. They can't see ghosts."

"Ghosts . . . plural?" It came home to Constantine then. The penny not only dropped, it clattered, and spun around in the coin box. No one was snubbing him—they simply couldn't see him. Not many can see a disembodied spirit. "Bloody hell! Who did for me? Who killed me?"

"No no no no, you're not *dead*, recruit!" The ghost slapped a quirt on his hip impatiently. *"I'm* dead! I'm a ghost as much as old Henry the Eighth still bumming about his castle. But you, you're just missing your earthly vehicle! You're traveling out of body. A good ways out of body—some thousands of miles! Your body is still alive—or was last I checked."

Constantine snorted. This wasn't adding up. "Now look here, you git—ghosts are confused, right enough. The dead take a while, sometimes, to realize they're dead. But if I'm only temporarily disembodied, well, mate, I've been disembodied many a time. At least as often as Tony Blair tells the truth. You know—now and then. I'd *know* if I was traveling out of body. I wouldn't have forgotten it."

"You don't know if something's gone amiss. That is precisely what has happened. You got lost, Constantine. And the truth is, while you're not dead—you're *not far from it.* Wandering off like this, you're in danger of being dead—and soon!"

"Am I now? Where's my body, then? Someplace choice I hope. Being ravaged in a coed dormitory, is it?"

"Not sure what a 'coed dormitory' is. Your body is in a kind of trance state, do y'see, in a monastery, in Persia—they call it Iran now, I believe."

"A monastery? Rubbish. You've got the wrong bloke. I'd never go to a monastery. . . ." But his denial wasn't convincing either of them. A monastery—Persia. It did sound familiar. "Persia . . . Iran . . ." Constantine almost remembered—but the memory flitted just out of reach. Then it settled down again in the shadows. He reached for it and again it flitted away. "Fuck me! I almost had it. Don't quite remember . . ."

"That's correct, John Constantine, you don't remember. You have failed to remember yourself." The mustachioed ghost clasped his hands behind him and scowled at Constantine like a drill sergeant. "You forgot your duty. You were given a task by those you went to learn from, and you buggered it up royal. Let your appetites carry you here, didn't you, eh? Wanted a drink, wanted a smoke, see London again. Your spirit carried away by old cravings. Classic spirit-Bardo tendency, of course—heard old Swami Vivekananda warn of it once. Only *you're* not a dead soul. Not quite yet. You're just bloody AWOL is what you are! There is yet a thin kind of connection back to your body—otherwise it would die, completely, don't you know. But that connection's fading, recruit, eh? You'd best come with me. . . ."

"And who are you, then, squire?"

"Not a squire—I'm a colonel, full colonel, Futheringham by name. *Was* a colonel, I should say. Not sure if rank applies posthumously. Seems improbable: very little applies posthumously, truth be told. Only reason I remember who I was at all, don't you know, is my mission. Special privilege, and all that."

"On a mission, are you, Futheringham? I was on a mission to get drunk. And you're cocking up my mission."

"You're not attending, recruit. You *can't* drink— you're not in a body."

Looking down at himself, seeing his own form flickering, Constantine had to admit the justice of this. He could see his trench coat, his slender hands, his crooked tie, his stained shirt and trousers, and his scuffed black shoes. But they weren't quite there— they were a psychological construct. "Right. We covered that. Disembodied. I was forgetting. But look here, Colonel, why do you keep calling me 'recruit'?"

"Sent here to recruit you, was I not, eh? Indeed I am. You're to join up—become a Peace Corpse. Do your bit to stop war like a good dead soldier."

"Become a—? Sod that game of soldiers, guv, I've no wish to be recruited. Only dead soldiers I'm interested in are the glass kind. I'm off to find my body and take it to the nearest bar in Iran—"

"You don't actually expect to find a bar in Iran, do you, Constantine?"

"Right. Muslims don't do pubs. Nearest country with a bar then."

"Come now—aren't you even curious about what a Peace Corpse is?" Futheringham asked, raising his bristly, ghostly eyebrows.

Constantine waved a hand dismissively. "Call me a fantasy-prone madcap but I'm going to hazard a guess it's something to do with the ghosts of crazy bastards like you, mate, who died in war and don't much care for it."

"Not far from the truth, old boy," Futheringham said, stroking his mustache. "Died in the Bengali rebellions in 1909, I did—in Mandalay. The rebels killed me in retaliation, don't you know, for the massacre I ordered. Only justice was my death, really. At the time I thought it for the best, that massacre. I was quite wrong. A massacre—indiscriminate killing of any kind—is never for the best, not at all. Terror leads to terror, Constantine. Violence to violence. Hard for a man to learn that, when nature shapes him for killing. I knew better, and I ordered the massacre anyway. Still making up for it. I'm a Peace Corpse myself. Need your help. Come along, have a natter with the other Peace Corpses. . . ."

Constantine patted his coat for a smoke, didn't find any. If he could psychically materialize a coat, couldn't he do cigarettes? Wouldn't taste right, probably, if they had any taste at all. "I'm not interested in a cank with any kind of corpse—seen enough of them, I have—nor am I interested in *becoming* any kind of corpse, peaceful or restless, 'old boy.' Now bugger off so I can work out how to get back to that half-starved 'vehicle' I was shambling about in."

"Work it out, eh? Don't remember how to get there, do you, hm? Used to be able to, Constantine. Not the first time out of your body. Missing something are you?"

"Right, well . . . I do seem to be. Don't seem to have a silver cord about me. Short one ectoplasmic lifeline back to the body."

"That's a sign that you're amiss, you're lost, wandered off, recruit—and too far from your body!" Futheringham broke off a moment to ogle the bartender pouring a beer. "Blimey, that lager looks good. Got a taste for lager in India—you want something light and cool, there. Wish I could have a drink myself." He sighed and turned back to Constantine. "Anyhow, allow me to clarify one point, recruit: you don't have to become a corpse to work with us. Truth is, we need one of the living, preferably someone with some talent. Used to the Hidden World. Great deal to be done. Got to avert a war."

"A war, is it? Colonel there's no avertin' 'em. They get a fucking life of their own. I'll be nipping off now before you start reciting 'Gunga Din'— "

"Aren't you wondering why you don't remember

coming here, why you were so disoriented? Slipping into the River of Nepenthe, washing down to the great Sea of Soul, eh? Wouldn't want that prematurely. Got things to do, you have. Adventures awaiting."

Constantine shook his head. "I've had enough adventures, cloth-ears. Want some peace and quiet—but not your kind. A glass of bitters, something cupping me packet, a packet of smokes—and I'm happy as a clam."

"Not you, Constantine. You're the restless kind. Hunger after the secrets of the Hidden World. Think you're a great adept? Barely scratched the surface."

Constantine snorted, turned away from the dead colonel, and walked determinedly to the nearest wall. There was a dartboard on it—and a dart flew into his etheric body, right through the place his heart should be. Someone crowed in triumph as the dart hit the bull's-eye with a *thunk*. Constantine hesitated—then closed his eyes and walked through the wall, dartboard and all.

When he opened his eyes, he was on the sidewalk, watching a group of skinheads come sniggeringly his way. Crawling with racist tattoos, chanting *"Oi!,"* they seemed morally feckless—lost, confused, and under some kind of malign influence, all of it woven into one inexorable trap.

Wankers. Far too many of their sort about—more all the time, in some places. Made a man want to leave the world entirely.

But then I'm lost myself. Not supposed to be here. Futheringham is right. . . .

He suspected he had gotten lost on purpose. Trying to escape himself. Get away from the burden of just being John Constantine. He had almost managed to forget. But the memories were coming back. . . .

He was missing his physical self, but he could feel the bruised body of his life, quivering with painful memories: all the messy decisions, all the greasy gray areas, all the mistakes he'd made and all the horror he'd seen. His mother's death; the body of the murdered child he'd found in the quarry; his childhood with his self-pitying, sneering, abusive, drunken father; the nightmare of Newcastle and Nergal; his ordeal of self-punishment in Ravenscar mental hospital for the mistake that had sent a child to Hell; the deaths of good friends, who'd made the mistake of getting too close to him; his visits to the literal Hell . . . where his father had begged for his pity. It was all there with him—still a part of him.

Now Constantine watched the skinheads bowl past in their *Screwdriver* jackets and outsized black boots, and remembered a time when he'd allowed himself to become numb to the world.

A bodiless state, Constantine thought, *has its privileges.* He looked up at the sky and willed himself upward. He began to ascend like a balloon without enough helium in it, very slowly, drifting this way and that. . . .

He got as far as the top edge of the building the pub was in and stopped in midair—glaring down at the sidewalk. Where was he supposed to go now? Arabia? Someplace back east, wasn't it? He couldn't remember which country Futheringham had mentioned. He was forgetting more and more. "Fucking hell!" he muttered. And then he called, "Futheringham!"

"Thought you'd come around," said the colonel, ascending through the roof beside him. "Can't help yourself but be intrigued—as indicated in your file. Had a full report on you."

"I haven't agreed to anything yet. Who did this 'full report' on me?"

"Young lady called Mercury. Daughter of someone you were sweet on, it seems . . . but that's another story. Now see here, I've got directions, psychic map all worked out. You want back to your body, I'll lead you there . . . but you've got to give me the okay to put a directive in your mind. A suggestion, lead you to our people, in the Middle East. Brief you on the job. Mercury's there—needs your help, she does. There's someone planning to kill her. Slowly, I should imagine."

Constantine hesitated—he didn't know why he should trust this ghost. He might not be what he seemed. Might be lying about Mercury. Something else, too, was tugging.

He looked over the city and saw souls rising up, here and there, from hospitals and car accidents and lonely apartments, the newly dead like thistledown caught in a wind; he felt that wind himself.

He watched as they were swept off to join the River of Nepenthe—the River of Forgetfulness. He could just make out that etheric river's gleaming course, wending through the fifth dimension to the infinite Sea of Consciousness—where individual souls melded back into the oversoul.

Now *there* was peace. A sea of peace . . . in forgetfulness.

He felt himself drawn upward, toward the current of the dead; toward that shining Sea of Mind. Toward the dissolution of all burdens, all fears . . . Heaven? Maybe. Hell? Not likely, this time. Reincarnation? Quite possibly.

They'd soon sort him out, he decided—and he headed toward that tempting, sweetly singing river. . . .

"Hold on there, can't let you go AWOL again, recruit!" Futheringham said, taking Constantine by his ectoplasmic wrist. "You've lost touch with your survival instinct—it's mostly because you're disconnected from your body! Been tempted to go that way myself, know it's tempting, but I've got a job to do, haven't I. So have you. Your young friend Mercury needs your help!"

Mercury. She'd be an adult now. Even as a child she'd been the most powerful psychic he'd ever met. As the seconds passed, he was increasingly losing touch with his memory, his identity—but he remembered Mercury. Marj's daughter. She'd looked right into his soul. She'd been almost a daughter to him—then Marj had fallen for another guy, someone with a saner life. She'd taken Mercury off with her.

Hard to forget Mercury. Sense of loyalty, history there. She'd gotten her nice clean soul dirty, mucking about in the sewage of his psyche. He owed her. Another kind of tugging.

Just in case Futheringham was telling the truth about her, he would have to look into this. He would have to trust this ghost.

Reluctantly, Constantine let the ghost of an old soldier draw him away from the River of Nepenthe.

Let himself be drawn into the sky—but toward the East. Toward Iran.

2

SOME CAN SEE THEM

Baghdad, Iraq

"We've got to hurry," said Uncle Sabbah, "because soon it will no longer be safe."

"Are you sure it is safe now?" Zainab's grandmother asked. Both of them spoke in Arabic. They all stood awkwardly together in the shade of the high walls around the courtyard.

Zainab and her younger brother, Ali, exchanged looks mingling excitement and anxiety. Ali, three years younger than Zainab, was turning eight today. They wanted Sabbah to talk their *Jaddah*, their grandmother, into letting them go with him for the birthday trip; but then again, she had a worrying way of being right.

Barely summer in Baghdad, already it was hot. Shading her eyes against the afternoon sun, Zainab looked at the children, at the car in the small, half-shadowed courtyard, and back to Sabbah.

Zainab's Jaddah, herself in a widow's traditional black *hajib*, was looking at Ali's clothing, frowning, her black eyes hooded with worry.

Sabbah was a man in his midthirties now, and today he wore a secondhand, ill-fitting gray suit. Only his beard was traditional. "Should you not dress more traditionally?" Grandmother asked. "Perhaps a *dishdasha?* Someone might take you for an American, or British. You could be shot."

"No, Jaddah! Please!" He got into the driver's seat of the dusty old blue Ford sedan, gesturing to Zainab and her brother. Zainab got in front, Ali behind Sabbah. Only Ali's' place had a seat belt. Ali caught his tongue between his front teeth as he worked on the seat belt.

"Maybe wait till the children's father is home," Grandmother said. "He comes home soon for lunch."

"No time, the zoo is only open a few hours a day now! It's the boy's birthday present from his uncle! I must go!"

She sighed and made a hand-washing gesture, and a flutter of dismissal. "Ma-assalama!"

"Fi aman Allah!" Ali piped up dutifully, in reply, waving.

Her sad eyes softened as she looked at Ali. Sabbah started the borrowed car—two tries and it was rumbling—and they drove slowly out of the courtyard.

"Eid Milad Sa-eed, Ali!" Grandmother called after them.

"Yes, happy birthday, Ali . . ." Sabbah said, parroting her distractedly, as he nudged the car between impatient pedestrians.

"Wait!" Grandmother called, as they swung, bouncing on creaking shocks, into the street. "Wait! A moment!"

"She's calling to us!" Zainab said, looking at Sabbah. She hadn't missed the note of urgency in Grandmother's voice.

"Too late, too late," Sabbah muttered, squinting into the street. "Too much traffic, can't go back, we'll be late."

Zainab looked back at her grandmother, a dark figure in the shadows of the courtyard's driveway. Soon she was hidden behind a bus, then a U.S. Marines Humvee.

They drove through what had been Saddam City, toward the Tigris and the zoo, between high rises, some of them pocked with mortar damage, past hotels barricaded with concrete vehicle barriers and barbed wire; the terrain around the tall, sunwashed, balcony-stacked buildings was patrolled by armed men, sometimes in paramilitary outfits, sometimes in plainclothes, sometimes in Iraqi army uniforms, all of them looking both tense and bored.

She turned to Sabbah to ask a question, but he was chewing his lip, both hands clamped to the steering wheel, eyes darting about the traffic, and somehow she felt he would start shouting if she spoke.

"Are there tigers at the zoo?" Ali asked suddenly.

Zainab considered. "I have heard that most of the animals are gone, stolen or sold or died. But now there are about eighty, or ninety animals—only one tiger alive, I think."

Ali leaned forward to peer up the street, as if to help the car on its way. "Will we get there soon, Uncle?"

"Very soon," Sabbah muttered.

A jingling song, a song she had never heard before,

emanated from Uncle Sabbah's coat. He fumbled in the pocket, pulled out a cellphone and flipped it open, driving with his other hand. He murmured a greeting in Arabic. She couldn't hear much of what he was saying. She saw him glance at her and say, "Yes, I have them with me." After a moment he glanced at his watch and added. "I am watching the time. Yes. Yes . . . I will be there." He broke the connection and glanced at her again. There was sweat running down his temples, though a breeze came in the open window. "Why do you stare?" he asked.

"You are too hot. Doesn't the air-conditioning work?" As she spoke, Zainab reached for the air-conditioning knob.

"No!" He slapped her hand down. The slap stung, and Zainab felt her eyes moisten.

"Why did you hit me?" she demanded, rubbing her wrist.

"I am sorry. But this is not my car, Zainab."

"I know you borrowed it, but—"

"This is . . . it belongs to a friend of mine. And it is quite fragile; things are mostly broken in it and I don't want to make it worse. Do not touch anything. Not anything."

"Yes, Uncle . . . did your friend loan you that cellphone? You never had a cellphone—"

"Yes!" Sabbah interrupted. "Yes, he loaned it to me. Be quiet now!"

They stopped at a corner where a traffic policeman held up a sign. A group of women in scarves and long dresses passed together in front of the car, going to their left, and Zainab turned her head to watch them, admiring their scarves, and that's when—out of the corners of her eyes—she seemed to see a man sitting very quietly in the backseat of the car, beside Ali.

Startled, she turned to look—but he was gone. It must have been a reflection in the back window, she decided.

Sabbah let out a long breath and looked at his watch.

"Does the zoo close soon?" Ali asked, leaning forward anxiously. "You are looking at your watch."

"No, no, it does not close soon," Sabbah murmured, chewing his lip.

He took a pack of cigarettes out of his pocket, shook it, lipped one out of the pack, reached toward the car's cigarette lighter—then froze, staring at it. Slowly, he drew his hand back. He took the cigarette from his mouth and tried to tamp it back into the pack, but his hands were shaking and it wouldn't go in straight; it crimped up, until finally he threw it into the street.

The traffic policeman waved them through, and they went on, approaching the Tigris. Zainab remembered a story she had heard one of her father's friends tell, of how American soldiers had taken a car from some young Iraqi men traveling through the city, and how they'd made the young men jump into the Tigris, and one of them had drowned; and a week later an American military truck had gone into the Trigris, off a bridge, and trapped men had shouted for help as the truck settled, but the people on the bank, remembering the young men forced to jump into the Tigris, simply watched the soldiers drown.

She became aware of something strange: her heart

was beating loudly in her chest, though she was just sitting there quietly. It was as if her heart sensed something that she couldn't see.

"He is not Iraqi, really," said a voice she did not know. She turned and glimpsed the man in the backseat again. He was a white-bearded man, who looked rather like her father, but he wore a robe, and he had faded blue eyes and a nose almost as prominent as the beak of a bird. The car moved through an intersection and the light shifted as they drove from a shadowy block onto a brightly lit one, and the man vanished when sunlight glanced through the window.

"What's the matter, Zainab?" Ali asked, almost laughing at her expression.

She turned back, her heart thudding. She heard the man's voice again, soft and low pitched. "He comes from the Jordanian side of the family, and he has been in Pakistan until recently. He came here with a Pakistani company to work. And why?" She looked in the backseat again and saw the old man's eyes, floating against the rear window, then they were gone. "Why?" asked the voice again. She turned sharply to the front of the car. She'd been ill with a fever a few days before. She must still have something, giving her delirium, she decided.

Her heart jumped like a frightened animal as the strange tinny song came again from Sabbah's coat.

Sabbah chewed his lip, and looked at his watch, and reached for the cellphone.

⇥◈⇤

As Private Paul Gatewood walked up, Lance Corporal Binsdale and Specialist Vintara were standing together on the overpass, their assault rifles in hand, watching as the driver of the supplies truck, an Arab guy subcontracted by Halliburton, tinkered with the engine. Gatewood stood with them, looking at the Arab. The man wore glasses and a turban; he tugged at his clipped white beard as he puzzled over the engine.

"Now I wish I spoke that fucking language," said Corporal Binsdale, a young black man sweating in khakis and a Kevlar vest. The others were sunburnt white men in fatigues. "What the hell's his name again?" Binsdale's own first name was Kaytel, something about a TV commercial on when he was conceived.

"I don't know, Kaytel," Vintara said. "Abdul or something."

"Man, you think they're all named Abdul."

Gatewood hesitated about speaking up. He'd had a hard time getting these guys to accept him already. When he'd transferred in from South Korea, they'd found out he had a B.A. in English. *"Fuck,"* Vintara had said. *"A fucking English major. That'll help."* And Binsdale called him "Major English," even though he was an enlisted man like the rest of them.

Finally Gatewood said, "His name's Fahad. I think."

"You think, Major English, or you know?" Binsdale asked.

"I'm pretty sure."

Binsdale glanced along back at the troop truck behind them, where seven soldiers were sweltering in the rear. He could see cigarette smoke drifting out of the back, a violation of regs. Gatewood had the same thought: the corporal was going to have to get them out of the truck soon, what with the heat, but that would constitute unnecessary exposure of troops in a high-target area, namely on this overpass, and that was bad ju-ju, as Vintara liked to say. They could back up, go by another route, but there was a lot of traffic waiting behind them—stopped four car lengths behind them, not wanting to be close to potential targets—and it'd be hard to get past them.

Binsdale muttered, "Fuck!" and, putting on his sunglasses against the glare at the front of the small convoy, walked to the materiel truck blocking their way off the overpass. After a moment, Gatewood followed, thinking that he might be of help, but he only knew a few words of Arabic, so he hung back a pace. While standing there, he thought he saw someone out of the corners of his eyes. He turned and just glimpsed an American soldier he didn't know. Army. He was a young guy, skinny, with thatchy brown hair and a sad smile, and he didn't have his rifle; he had his hands in his pockets. He was walking by, looking at Gatewood, nodding to him, and Gatewood was going to ask who the hell he was—he sure hadn't come with them—and where was his weapon, but the guy slipped between the vehicles and was gone, almost like he blinked out. All this in a second, as Binsdale called, "Hey—uh—Fahad?"

"Yes, soldier officer?" the man said, not looking up from the engine.

"I'm not an officer, blood. Listen, if you can't get

this thing started we're going to have to push it out of the way. Maybe with the truck behind."

"You are making to leave me behind here?" The man looked at him in alarm.

"No, man. The truck's almost empty, nothing much in it, it's going to pick shit up, so we can leave it. We'll send some guys around."

"Looters will take it, soldier."

"Well maybe, I'll call in for someone to watch it. Maybe get the local cops here."

"Local cops are looters, too, soldier."

"Mostly not, blood. Don't trip, we got it covered. You start it or not?"

"Maybe it is start." Fahad looked at his watch. Glanced over his shoulder. "I will try. . . ."

"You do that."

Binsdale walked back to Gatewood and Vintara. "Well he—"

"The fucker's running off, Kaytel!"

"What the fuck?" Binsdale ran toward the truck, aslant across the road and blocking their way out of Saddam City. He stopped, staring after Fahad—then looked at the truck engine.

Gatewood stepped to the other side of the truck, and saw Fahad sprinting down the farther side of the narrow overpass, toward the road paralleling the Tigris.

"Holy shit," Binsdale said. "He cut the distributor wires. I think that fucker was planning this all along. . . ."

⊷≡◉═⊷

"Why did you stop?" Ali asked, as Sabbah pulled up at the curb, half a block from the overpass. "Have we not enough petrol?"

"Yes, yes, we have enough, we—it's just too soon," Sabbah snapped looking at his watch.

He looked pale, to Zainab. She remembered her Jaddah speaking of Sabbah with a mixture of pity and contempt. *"He has nothing. Look at him, no woman, no job, everything he tries has failed. Always bad luck. Now he is with those fanatics. . . ."*

"He *is* one of them," said the man in the backseat. Zainab didn't turn to look, but she knew he was there. "And he has vowed to give his life. You must try to get out of the car. You must survive, so that you can find a way."

Zainab squeezed her eyes shut, opened them, and looked—

"What?" Ali said.

She shook her head. No one there. Except she thought she felt the man looking at her still.

Her breath whistling loudly between her teeth, Zainab looked at the American soldiers, who seemed stuck somehow on the overpass, waving their arms and pointing at the engine of their truck. One of them was setting up orange cones a little distance in front of the stalled vehicle. That meant keep back or else, she knew. People who approached a stalled American vehicle without permission were often shot, whether they intended harm or not.

She looked at Sabbah. She thought about the car that he had never had before and the cellphone he had never had before, and she could feel the fear rolling off him with the sweat. He began to murmur prayers then, traditional prayers. They seemed to be pressed out of him like the fear and sweat.

"Oh," she said. The man in the backseat was right.

Sabbah looked at her.

Zainab turned to Ali. "Come, we'll get out and wait in the shade."

"No," Sabbah grated. "You will stay in the car."

"I am too hot, Sabbah." She unlocked her car door, started to press the handle to open it.

Sabbah grabbed her by the upper left arm and squeezed, and she whimpered in pain. "I said no! You will wait—we're going—"

The cellphone chimed from his pocket again. He let go of her arm and clawed at his coat, his motions frantic, till at last he got the insistent cellphone out. "Yes, yes . . . yes we—yes. Now. Yes."

She turned to look at her brother and mouthed, *Run. Run!*

Ali stared at her, blinking, not comprehending.

❖───◎═══───❖

"Okay, this is what we're going to do," Binsdale was saying.

Vintara was staring at a car driving up toward them, a dusty blue sedan. Three people in it. "That fucking car—coming out of park there—it's coming up here, and they can *see* those cones, man. They see we're fucking blocking the way!"

He unslung his rifle from his shoulder.

Gatewood put a hand on Vintara's shoulder. "Wait,

Vintara, Jesus—there's kids in that car. Two kids—"

"I don't fucking care, that scraper is not coming up here."

"Vintara, we have orders; you don't light up a family car with kids in it, unless you see a weapon."

"And Lieutenant Mayfield said fuck that, he said if they won't stop you light them up—they're Ali Baba, man. And fuck, here they come—!"

Time seemed to slow then, becoming like a dead leaf drifting slowly down, and Gatewood felt as if someone was calling him.

He turned from Vintara, and saw the young soldier again—the guy just appeared at his elbow. "Hey bro, huh-ah. Listen, Vintara's going to hit you—move! And get the kids out of the car. . . ."

Then time sped up to normal, the same time as the car coming at them sped up; Gatewood moved, and the blow hit him only glancingly. But he fell to his knees. . . .

✦✦✧◎✧✦✦

"Sabbah, don't!" Zainab shouted.

"Shut up!" Sabbah shouted, tears rolling down his cheeks.

She knew what he was doing. The soldiers had sometimes shot at cars approaching a checkpoint too quickly. Families had been killed, and now they'd been ordered not to shoot at cars containing women and children. But Sabbah and those who had sent him were using her and her brother as camouflage, to get them near the trucks. The car was a bomb.

"You are martyrs, we are martyrs, *Allah Ahkbar!*"

"No, Sabbah, my brother is so little—no!"

"This is all I have, this I will have!" Sabbah shouted, stepping hard on the gas pedal.

Zainab reached over and grabbed the steering wheel and jerked it hard to the right so the car swerved, turning broadside to the soldiers just twenty-five feet from the cones.

Sabbah slapped her so hard that her eyes were filled with blue sparks and she lost her grip on the steering wheel. He shouted a prayer and opened the glove compartment and as her vision cleared she saw wires attached to the sort of switch used to turn on a light, the whole fixture sitting crookedly on a sheaf of dusty papers.

Ali was screaming and trying to open his door. Sabbah was pawing at the switch, trying to set off the bomb. The car spun to a stop. . . .

⇥◉⇤

Gatewood was sitting on the ground, holding the side of his head, hearing gunfire just above. It came to him that he'd been trying to stop Vintara from shooting up the car, and Vintara had hit him with the butt of his gun. Now the gun was firing; brass was clinking on the asphalt.

"Oh fuck, Vintara, don't shoot that car, not this time. . . ."

He felt strong hands lifting him up by the armpits. Binsdale. "That's a bomb car, you know that, man."

Vintara stopped shooting, and, a bit unsteady,

Gatewood ran to the car, looking for the kids—the driver was shot to pieces but he was alive, still fumbling with something on the dashboard. "This is a sucker move," Gatewood told himself, as he helped the little boy drag the girl free. He dragged them both skiddingly away from the car—then the blast came, spinning him around like he was on a turntable. He felt the scorching heat of it; he heard shrapnel singing past his head. He heard Binsdale shouting with pain—but everything he heard was through a blanket of ringing. He fell, lay there stunned a few seconds.

Shaky, he got to his feet and looked down at himself—no blood, no torn clothing. Binsdale was clutching his side, but it looked superficial from here. A piece of metal from the wrecked car; the stink of gasoline and blood from the twisting pillar of smoky flame. He could make out oozing pieces of the driver, smoking to one side of the wreck.

There were two small, slender figures lying near the overturned orange cones nearby. The smaller one, a boy, stirred—and suddenly sat up, holding his head and wailing. The other, his sister maybe, lay still, blood pooling around her neck, her shoulders.

"Vintara," Gatewood said loudly, not even looking toward him, "did you fucking light up those kids?"

Vintara was sitting against the bumper of the truck, staring at the bomb wreck. He nodded. Then he shook his head. "I was shooting at the driver. . . . I think I hit one maybe; I don't fucking know. . . ."

Gatewood wobbled over to them, his head aching in distinct throbs that went with each step, and saw that the girl's eyes were fluttering.

Gatewood sat down next to her and took her pulse. It seemed more or less regular. The wound was just under her collarbone. He found a compress in his belt pack and pressed it to the wound; she twitched at the touch. The little boy, close beside him, had stopped crying. He was staring with his mouth open at Gatewood.

Hearing ambulance sirens approaching, Gatewood felt the girl's pulse. He smiled at the boy. "She'll live, kid."

He glanced up, and saw two men standing together nearby. An Arabic man with a white beard and the young soldier. He knew they were there and not there, at the same time. He could feel it. The others never glanced at them.

Both men nodded to him. Gatewood heard the young soldier's voice in his head. *"You must survive, so that you can find a way."* Then the old man and the soldier vanished into the smoke from the burning car.

⋆⇌◉⇋⋆

They vanished for Gatewood; they were fully aware of one another as they rode the smoke upward, letting it carry their subtle bodies into the air, up and up into the sky over Baghdad.

They were aware of the people below, trying to get on with their lives. Children studying the Qu'ran, parents selling coffee and sweets from little booths, young men agonizing over whether they should risk taking a job as an Iraqi policeman—a death sentence to a sizable percentage of police trainees—and people simply trying to get home to their families.

A car bomb went off south of the city at the opening ceremony for a new hospital. Sixty-seven souls were broken free of their physical moorings and went spiraling up toward the River of Nepenthe—the River of Forgetfulness—wailing with disorientation and loss.

The ghost of the old man and the young soldier were aware of all this as they, too, ascended. Both of them felt a longing to join the drifting procession to the river; to let it carry them into the shining Sea of Mind.

But they could not go with the other souls drifting through the sky. They had both taken vows, on dying, the young soldier and the old man, to ease the suffering they had seen in life; the suffering that both of them had helped bring about. They had taken a renewed vow to avert the great black spiritual cloud that hovered over the horizon of this plane of Being. But it might be too late. It was difficult to tell. The future was balanced on a razor blade. . . . It might fall either way—or slide out of control, falling to be slashed in two.

"Where to?" the ghost of the young soldier asked.

"East. Afghanistan," the ghost of the old sheikh said.

"Did they find someone?"

"I found him, gentlemen," came a third voice, echoing to them etherically, in English. The speaker, invisible to them just now, was somewhere far away. But a spirit can be distant and nearby at once. They knew just who he was; neither was surprised at the telepathic contact. *"I haven't a great deal of confidence in*

him. He may abandon us at any moment, eh? Indeed he might."

"Who is it, Colonel?" the white-bearded ghost asked.

"A man named John Constantine. I'm afraid he'll have to do. There's no time to find another."

"Did you say John *Constantine?"* the white-bearded ghost asked, his heart sinking.

"I did."

"And—he's an Englishman? Neither old nor young? A mocking tongue about him? Hair the color of dried straw?"

"His hair looks like it bloody is *dried straw. A mocking tongue? Bleeding smart-mouthed little prat, more like. That's him, all right. Best we can do. You know him?"*

"I know of him. And if he's the one we have to work with . . ." The white-bearded ghost then used an expression in Arabic that roughly translates as follows:

"We're totally fucked."

3

I THOUGHT I WAS SOMEONE ELSE, SOMEONE GOOD

The Elburz Mountains, Iran

"Not sure I can eat now without spewing up, Bakky," Constantine muttered, as old Bahktiar pressed the bowl of soup in his hands.

"You eat, the Abi Sheikh, he says you eat. Good goat's meat, fresh," the old servant Bahktiar insisted. He was a small, gnarled, nearly toothless man in a dirty yellow robe and turban. He had never approved of Constantine and disliked being called "Bakky," so of course Constantine called him that pretty much always.

All too firmly back in his body, sitting on the edge of his cot in the chilly old mountain monastery, the robe itching him as usual, Constantine looked at the soup and thought of the cover of an old Rolling Stones album and almost threw up. But he took the wooden bowl in shaking hands, closed his eyes, and made himself sip some broth. It went down surprisingly well. He had slept on returning to his body, and it was now just dawn. Most of the monks had been up an hour and a half already, meditating.

"*Salam Aleikom*," said the Abi Sheikh in Farsi, stepping through the doorway of the little cell. Bahktiar instantly fell to his knees before the monastery's master. The sheikh was a tall gangling man with a thin, silver-streaked black beard, a beaklike nose, deep brown eyes filmed with age, a frayed blue robe and a faded blue hat like a truncated cone. Known only as "the Blue Sheikh"—or simply *Xodavand*, Farsi for "Lord"—the old magus had once revealed to Constantine that he was in fact not natively Persian; he had been born in Egypt, but after two hundred years in Iran, the locals thought of him as one of their own. Constantine knew him for an expert on both Persian and Egyptian magic, and the teachings of both Zoroaster and Hermes Trismegestus: teachings that merged into one, if you went far enough back.

The Abi Sheikh patted Bahktiar on the shoulder and waved him away. A Zoroastrian monk himself, the old servant stood up but lingered, glaring at Constantine because, as usual, this Brit interloper had failed to fall to his knees in the presence of the master of this monastery. Bahktiar made a "get down, kneel" gesture with his hand, which Constantine ignored.

"*Koda Hafez*, Bahktiar!" the Blue Sheik prompted, seeming amused at the servant's indignation.

Bahktiar ducked his head, sent a final fierce look at Constantine and slipped out past his master.

"*Hali shoma Kub-e?*" the Blue Sheikh inquired.

"Not bad," Constantine replied. "How's yours hangin', mate?"

The Blue Sheikh chuckled. He had long ago accepted Constantine's unwillingness—or inability—to demonstrate submissive devotion. He did not regard Constantine as an equal—the Blue Sheikh had few equals amongst mortals—but being almost four hundred years old, the sheikh was too wise to suppose the trappings of submission to be of real importance. What mattered was the life of the heart. "I see you've learned to understand a little of the local language, John, if not speak it. Please continue to eat your soup. You have fasted enough."

Constantine took another sip and put the bowl aside. "You know about me getting sidetracked to London, eh? I was hoping to slip in before anyone noticed I'd been out all night at the pub."

The Blue Sheikh grunted and looked Constantine over. "You wear the robe of goat hair; you have eaten little and slept sparingly and sat in meditation much: you have struggled with your appetites, I can see that. You would have drifted away into the River of Nepenthe, were it not for the light you have kindled in yourself. Even so, forgetfulness was coming upon you—but I believe you were called back by someone. . . ."

"You could call it that, O Sheikh. An old geezer—died some time ago in India, he said—he led me back. Don't know what became of him. You send him along?"

"No, I did not. But I permitted him to go when I perceived what he was about. He works with those who have taken the peace vow."

"You haven't got a . . . a smoke about you, have you, Sheikh, eh? I mean—at this point, I reckon I'm in Dutch here already . . . no, I don't suppose you'd have one. Didn't notice a cigarette machine in the monastery."

"You have been here some months, you have never before asked me for tobacco. Has someone been giving it to you?"

"Ah, well, O Sheikh, can't be a bloody tattletale, now can I?"

"But I *do* have tobacco—in a hookah. At my age, I no longer smoke it. It's a great deal of work to restore the body after the damage tobacco does, and I become addicted so quickly. Still, if you'd like . . ."

"I would, yeah, that'd be brilliant!"

The Blue Sheikh, walking in long strides, hands clasped in front of him, led the way through corridors carved of naked rock. In occasional niches were rechargeable lanterns that made it look a bit like an archaeological dig. As they went, the sheikh remarked, "You know, this part of the mountain is from an ancient time before Mount Damāvand proper— Damāvand is an old volcano which rose up and overwhelmed the old mountain, of this hard stone. The old mountain contained a temple, in the time of Atlantis . . . some of the chambers still exist, far below. But all the tunnels you see are new—only a few thousand years old. . . ."

After a winding trek through a maze of damp time-darkened stone corridors, Constantine had to duck his head to push through silken curtains draping a low doorway into a lushly furnished chamber he'd never seen before.

Must be the sheikh's apartments, he supposed. If he was being brought here, he reckoned he was either to be elevated to another level of initiation, or given the old boot in a polite kind of way—he suspected the latter, since he'd bollixed up the out-of-body assignment.

The air smelled of incense; of frankincense and myrrh. The stone floors were covered in thick, ornate rugs, dark blue and purple set off by red and yellow borders; the walls were swathed in hangings in the same colors, intricate patterns suggesting energy forms. Electric lights were strung at intervals on wires, some filtered by scarves of blue and purple, glowing near the low ceiling. A fire burned in a trim wrought-iron stove in the corner, its rusty chimney pipe curving through a hole in the stone wall.

Bahktiar came in, scowling, with a wooden bowl of perfumed water in which floated shreds of blue flower blossoms. He held the bowl between Constantine and the sheikh, who made a hand sign over the water and softly intoned words in a more ancient language than Farsi. Constantine dipped his fingers in the water, sprinkled it on his head, murmuring certain words himself. It was a purification ritual—typical of Zoroastrianism.

This done, the sheikh indicated crimson pillows heaped on either side of a hookah and the two men sat across from one another, legs folded. Bahktiar reappeared from the shadows of an adjoining room carrying a carafe of tea and two small glass cups. He scowled again, but seeing that Constantine was obviously a guest, kept his moodiness to himself, never looking at them. The old sheikh found a leather pouch of tobacco on a low wooden table beside the pillows—a highly lacquered black table, looking like it had come from China, originally—and poured some into the hookah. Bahktiar brought him a small burning twig, holding it to the tobacco as Constantine lipped the wooden mouthpiece and gratefully puffed the tobacco alight. The teacup, tiny and filled with boiling-hot tea in the Middle-Eastern manner, was more difficult. He inevitably burned his fingertips.

"You were drawn to your own death, you know," the sheikh said, after Constantine had ingested enough tea and nicotine to make him feel more comfortable.

"Drawn to me death? How's that, O Sheikh?" Constantine asked, savoring the feeling of smoke accompanying the words across his palate. "Not something I take to, in normal circs, me death."

"Why do you think you were in London? Because once out of your body you had felt yourself drifting toward death. Something in you *wants* to die—something else wants to live. You are not yet inwardly unified. But very few are."

"You got me right on the unification, mate. I'm about as unified as a gin bottle post hammer, I am."

"No, John Constantine, you're not so bad as that. But you are divided. The survivor in you drew away from death and fled toward London. You wanted to—what is the expression in English about the ground . . . to be ground yourself or . . ."

"To ground meself?"

"Yes. Like with electricity. To stay here on Earth, you needed to find comfort in the familiar. So your soul, confused, flew to London. It wasn't really drink or smoke you sought."

Constantine chuckled. "How little you know me, O Sheikh."

"How little you know yourself, John," the Blue Sheikh responded gravely. "Your burden has been great. You have lived more than fifty years—not so much to me, it's true, but with all that you have experienced, it might be said you've lived enough for five men in the last fifty years. The burden was beginning to be too much. And the guilt—you have tried to let the guilt go. But you have not quite succeeded. If you wish to ease your . . . your karma, as they say . . . now perhaps is the time in India."

"How am I to do that? You mean that business with Mercury and a war that the old geezer with the walrus mustache was on about?"

"Yes. I do not know the details. No more than you know."

"And it just happens to coincide with me buzzing off? You've had enough of me, I reckon . . ."

"It does, as you say—happen to coincide."

Constantine puffed the tobacco pensively. It was stale, but not bad. "Going to give me my walking papers, are you?"

"You came here to learn how to control the Great Energies. To learn the wisdom of those you call 'the magis.' To be able to send your soul where you will— too often in the past, your soul, once out of body, was buffeted about. You have learned these things to the extent that we can teach you. You knew much already. Much was . . . I believe the expression is, 'second nature' to you—because this is not your first time in this world. You are an 'old soul,' as we say . . .

you learned more than you realize, with us. No *conscious* effort is wasted. You can teach yourself after this. To learn seriously here takes years—there are more important tasks for you."

Constantine blew a smoke ring at the ceiling and watched it turn purple as it neared a colored light. "Sure you don't have a little more on my friend Mercury? Young woman, she is. Like a daughter to me. Could do with an inside track. . . ."

"You mistake me if you think I know all, John Constantine. I see only that you are called for a task . . . that task is masked in cloud. Someone does not *wish* me to help you, I suspect. Remember that Angra Mainyu—the one you call Lucifer—he will be setting traps for you." The Blue Sheikh smiled as if savoring an amusing anecdote, a story he was remembering, and poured Constantine another cup of hot, sweet tea. "You have made him furious with you many times." He tilted his head, looked at Constantine with narrowed eyes. "I seem to see you—differently. I hear a name. Konz."

"Konz? Don't think anyone had the nerve to saddle me with that contraction—though Rich calls me Con Job, it must be admitted. . . ."

"This was long ago. Many lives . . ."

Constantine puffed on the hookah thoughtfully. More than once he had become aware of previous incarnations. The teaching of the Blue Sheikh's sect—an order that was sourced in Zoroaster and the Magi, but with a strong Sufi affinity—held that the afterlife was a mixed bag, depending on the growth of your spirit. Some, trapped in psychological states of identification with negativity, consigned themselves to dark, dangerous regions, Hells of various kinds, until at last they reincarnated; some drew closer to the source of life, their expectations creating paradises, until a need for spiritual evolution induced them to move on; others were reincarnated immediately. Some had created for themselves a strong existence in the afterlife; others were just echoes in the Sea of Consciousness.

"Which past life is going to rear its ugly head this time, O Sheikh?"

"Ah—I see an entanglement with a dark spirit, with the heart of rage—from millennia ago. But how it will emerge—this is obscured from me."

"Well then—any advice at all . . . Xodavand?" Constantine asked, raising his teacup in a toast to the Blue Sheikh. Best to use the honorific "Lord" with this spiritual toff, he reckoned, if you want some advice from him. Not that he didn't feel some genuine humility around the Blue Sheikh. But humility was something he hated *showing* anyone. Where he'd grown up, it'd always been a mistake to let anyone lord it over you.

The sheikh took the second hose from the hookah and had a few puffs himself before answering. "I advise only this—remember the path we're called to by Zoroaster: 'Good reflection, good words, good deeds.' The simplicity of this formula is its greatness. Cleave in simplicity to these three principles and the good road will be shown you."

Constantine smiled sadly. He had never noticed goodness to be rewarded—not in this vale of tears.

Anyway, he felt he had very little virtue to bring to reflection, words, and deeds. Maybe he'd come to the monastery in search of some deeper good. But he suspected he was too tainted to find it. Someone good could do it. . . .

Long ago he'd tried to send his darkness, his sickness, to Hell, with a spell that had created a kind of Constantine golem. The spell had worked a little too well—he'd had to couple with a demoness to get back some of his edge, his balancing darkness. But he lost the balance easily. Slid easily into the dark side of himself: there was always more darkness in a man—because it arose freshly out of anger and out of the choices he made. And there is always more to be angry about; there are always more choices to make.

He had sharpened his skills here. But the desire he'd nurtured in the back of his mind to become a good man like the Blue Sheikh—

Wasting my sodding time with that one.

Hadn't he seduced that girl who'd come to the monastery selling milk? Hadn't he paid her to bring him beer? Horrible piss-water that beer had been—made in the huts of some local shepherd, piss might've been one of the ingredients, in fact—but it'd gotten him drunk, all right.

He had tried to make up for it by working harder: by sitting longer in meditation, by fasting more, by struggling more with his lower self. But he'd only become weak and confused and his soul had drifted off to London.

"There is, as it happens, very little I could do to help you," the Blue Sheikh went on calmly. "That is why I am smoking—it does not matter now, as I have to be killed this afternoon."

Constantine choked on his tobacco smoke—which was not something he did often. "What?"

"Yes: I have what one might call 'an appointment to be murdered.' You are the first to be told, as it happens. I will be killed this afternoon by an assassin. The mullahs of this country have sent someone to do it—they believe me a heretic. We are not particularly Muslim here in this retreat, after all—not as the Ayatollah understands the teaching. A Muslim will pull the trigger, but there are those who wish the assassination to look like the Americans did it." He said "did it" as if it had already happened. As if, to him, it had. "If they arrest me, my followers will be troublesome."

"But . . . if you know that it's coming . . . must be some way to stop the bastard."

"I believe you once saw your own death—so you told me. Do you now concern yourself to avoid it?"

Constantine shrugged. He'd had a vision of one death that might come to him, of drowning. "It was a long time off. Wasn't like a certainty, either. It was like it *could* come that way—and likely would, but . . ."

"Nothing is certain until it comes to pass," the Blue Sheikh said, putting his teacup down with exacting attention. "It is a matter of likelihood, merely. I *could* avert this death. But I choose not to. I have outlived many wives, many children. I have only one son alive—he is two hundred years old himself, and busy in Nepal. I will see him in the Hidden World. I will see them all there. I am ready for another stage now."

"Look here, O Sheikh, you can't check out now—this world's a mess. Needs your help, it does."

"There are others who will help. And there are ways we can help from the Hidden World. In truth, my time has come. . . ." The Blue Sheikh looked up at a naked lightbulb overhead, as if somehow it were showing him something only he could see. After a moment he said, "I can feel the assassin approaching. I feel him—and now I *see* him. He is driving a large American vehicle up the mountain pass. He stole this vehicle from an American intelligence agent, after murdering the man. He knows that at this hour I walk in the garden of stone outside the monastery. He is getting out of the vehicle now . . . he conceals himself behind a boulder. He loads his rifle . . . I have asked the guards of our retreat to stay away from the garden today. No one sees him. He waits for me . . . he waits to liberate me . . . I must go to him. . . ."

Constantine shook his head. The Blue Sheikh didn't show his true nature to people most of the time. But Constantine had seen it once—and he was sure the world needed the Blue Sheikh. "Bloody hell," he murmured.

Standing up from sitting cross-legged on the floor is difficult to do with grace, but the Blue Sheikh did it. He gazed down at Constantine—and his eyes grew to fill Constantine's vision. . . .

Constantine looked away.

"I cannot help you with what you must do, John Constantine," the Blue Sheikh said, his voice softly hoarse, "and I must go. You will take the road back down the mountain, toward Rasht. There is someone for you to meet on the shores of the Caspian. I cannot see who. I see only that you must go to the Caspian Sea." He broke off, as if listening. After a moment he added, "Perhaps there is something I can do for you—I can give you a warning. It is whispered to me that when you see a man who cuts the throat of a bird, watch for your enemy—he is within reach. And remember, John Constantine: reflection, words, deeds."

Constantine nodded. Feeling he wanted to say a great deal and for once unable to speak.

"And John . . . say nothing to the others here about where I go now."

The Blue Sheikh went to the doorway, walking with simple deliberation. He stopped for a moment, turned back with a mischievous smile on his face. "Oh, by the way, I am glad you didn't tell me who gave you the cigarettes. I believe the expression is, 'No one likes a fucking snitch,' eh?" He tugged meditatively at his beard. "And as for that girl delivering the milk, don't feel bad—she had a good time. I almost took her to bed once myself. But she was too young for me." He winked, and then he slipped through the curtained doorway and was gone.

The old servant returned, dropping Constantine's clothes, laundered and folded, on the floor beside him. "Now," Bahktiar said, snatching the hookah hose from Constantine's mouth, "he tell you, you are here enough. You can make dressing in those, and you get out. You have brought bad things here. You go."

Constantine stood up, feeling awkward as he shrugged out of the robe, and began to pull on his clothes: boxers, white shirt, black tie, black trousers, black shoes, trench coat. It had been a while since his trench coat had been so clean. "You hear where your master's going, Bakky?"

"My name is not Bakky!"

Reaching for patience, Constantine buttoned up his shirt, and repeated, "Did you hear him say where he was *going?*"

"No. He does not tell me where he goes."

So it's true. The old bastard doesn't know his master is slated to be shot dead in a few minutes.

He had been asked to say nothing about the assassination. But he couldn't just stand by. He could interfere with the assassination himself. Could be the Blue Sheikh might change his mind, given the chance. . . .

Constantine danced into his socks and shoes, elbowed Bahktiar out of the way and headed for the door.

"You leave this place! Do not come back!" Bahktiar called after him.

"You can kiss my arse," Constantine growled at him, pausing in the doorway. "You're just a bloody hanger-on here, Bakky. Hanging around for fifty bloody years. Never learning a fucking thing."

Bahktiar looked crushed—Constantine had struck a nerve. And he regretted it. Reflection, words, deeds. He'd already cocked up one of the three.

"Oh Christ, forget it, Bakky." And he set off to find the Blue Sheikh and the road to Rasht.

❖═◎═❖

The monastery of the Blue Sheikh was almost indistinguishable from the mountainside. It was an ancient warren of tunnels and ventilation shafts cut into a cliff of Mount Damāvand, overlooking a misty valley laced with attenuated waterfalls. Constantine hurried out the wood-and-brass front gate and stopped in the cool gray dawn, looking around for the monastery's master. He picked out the familiar blue robe almost immediately against the dull backdrop of stone fifty yards down the hill, the sheikh strolling along the graveled path into the "stone garden." Constantine saw no cars, though the sheikh had predicted one, and no gunmen.

More like something you'd see in Japan than Iran, to Constantine's eye, the stone garden was made of rubble from hundreds of years of tunneling, set up along a gravel trail meandering down the terraced slope. Some of the stone sculptures, of stone chips roughly mortared together, were shaped like man-sized poplar trees in full leaf; some were fashioned like flames; another resembled a frozen fountain of water; and one was a pillar of smoke with a woman's face. The Blue Sheikh was said to have made them himself, around two hundred years before. The sculptures were artfully spaced between shapeless boulders of gray stone streaked with cinnabar. There were almost no plants in the garden; the Blue Sheikh strolled to the single tree, a Persian hornbeam on a craggy terrace halfway down the garden path. He stopped there, waiting in dignified expectancy, at the base of the gnarled, nearly leafless tree. . . .

"Xodavand!" Constantine called out. He didn't know the man's real name and he'd have felt stupid shouting *Blue Sheikh!*

There was no response from the magus—or none spoken aloud. But as the monastery's spiritual master stood there, calmly awaiting death under the hornbeam tree, Constantine seemed to see him in some greater context. He understood the significance of the blue robe and turban: it was the exact color of the "blue current," the discharge of power glimpsed when a great adept transfers energy from himself to someone he is healing. Constantine had once seen the Blue Sheikh emanate a pulse of this blue light when laying hands on an ailing monk. The man had been near death; the next day he was on his feet, sweeping out his cell and singing.

Now the garden itself seemed to have a fuller meaning to Constantine. Its images were of fluid, changeable objects—flame, water, smoke, women, growing trees—but captured in stone, the symbol of the cessation of movement, of the static. The garden declared that what seems firm is fluid, is part of an energetic change, and what is fluid is also, in some way, forever; the transitory is preserved at the place where a single consciously sensed instant connects with eternity.

And the only lively color in that garden of the changing and the unchanging was the robe of a conscious man: the blue of the energy of life itself.

Constantine stared, then shook himself out of his reverie and started down the path, into the stone garden. "Sheikh! You can't—"

Inevitable as the cymbal clash in a symphonic composition, the gunshot rang out—and the Blue Sheikh staggered back against the tree. He slumped down, knees drawn up, gazing across the valley, at the sun rising between the hills.

Constantine found himself running down the path—stumbling in his haste across the uneven ground, and it was a stumble, perhaps, that saved his life. A bullet struck chips from a low boulder beside him and he looked up to see a man with a smoking rifle in his hands, poised behind another boulder, near the road. Constantine could just make out a red-streaked black beard and deep-set eyes. Someone shouted at the man, he turned to reply, and Constantine, heart hammering, took the opportunity to jump behind a sculpture of a rising flame. A car horn honked and the gunman drew back, gone from sight. A dusty blue Ford SUV roared out from behind a screen of boulders and went bumping down the dirt road, into the valley.

Constantine ran to the sheikh and knelt beside him. His eyes were glazed; his chest, red with welling blood, barely moved. A breath. A breath. And . . . a final breath. And spoken with that were a few words in some language Constantine didn't understand. It wasn't Farsi or Arabic. An Egyptian dialect perhaps—maybe Coptic. But what the words meant, Constantine didn't know.

And then the Blue Sheikh was dead. Constantine looked around, thinking to see his spirit, perhaps to have a chin-wag with the sheikh's ghost. But he saw nothing but the rustling of dead leaves, the last leaves from the previous year, tugged from the branches of the tree to spiral away into the garden.

Constantine sat beside the body for some minutes, trying to feel the acceptance, the rightness of this death that the sheikh had evinced. He was trying for "good reflection" on what had happened. But all he felt was the bitterness that always came in contemplating a pointless death.

He watched the mist curl and dissipate in the valley below them.

After a while he heard footsteps, clattering gravel. He was aware of Bahktiar standing nearby with some other men, talking in Farsi.

"Did you tell him, the Abi Sheikh, he must come here to the garden?" Bahktiar said.

It took Constantine several moments to realize this was a question directed at him. "You wot? No I didn't bloody tell him to come here, you daft idjit. Who tells the Blue Sheikh where to go? Didn't you see that car?"

"We come out, a car drove away. . . ."

So that was why the gunman had left before dealing with Constantine: he'd seen the others approaching. "Well they didn't need any help from me. The sheikh saw it coming. . . ." He realized his voice was breaking. He shook his head.

Stupid, he told himself. *You hardly knew the guy. He gave you maybe a total of thirty hours of direct instruction. Rest of the time you were in the back of the class, trying to figure out what they were talking about.*

But the Blue Sheikh had let him come into this monastery. Him, a guy prone to going on drunks and chasing women; the sheikh had taken a chance on a man who had Lucifer himself perpetually angry with him. Constantine was not exactly a lucky talisman.

He took a risk having me here. He took a chance on me. He tolerated my vanity, my bad attitude. . . .

Could it be that the sheikh's death was somehow Constantine's fault? Lucifer might well have decided to stop Constantine from learning any more at the monastery. He might've whispered a suggestion into some human's ear:

Kill the Blue Sheikh. . . .

The limp-brained human getting the suggestion would make up his own reasons for the murder. The Devil wouldn't bother to tell him it was to keep Constantine from learning too much.

But there was no way of telling if Lucifer was involved. People were capable of generating their own evil without the Devil's help. Constantine was sure only of his own sense of loss. He'd felt a kind of gut-level acceptance from the sheikh that he'd gotten from no one else, ever.

The monks were weeping now as they picked up the body of their master. Two of them, bearded, robed, and red-eyed with grief, glowered balefully at Constantine.

"You can just drop that whole line of thinking," Constantine said, getting to his feet. "I had nothing to do with it."

Not that I know of.

He started across the garden, picking his way, heading for the road. One of the younger monks came after him, tried to hold him back.

Constantine tore his arm free and whirled, raising a hand—not a fist, a hand. An incantation trembling unspoken on his lips.

But the monk was looking into Constantine's eyes. He saw grief there—and turned away.

Bahktiar said something in Farsi, and then in English added, "I tell them let you go. We have called the chieftain of the valley, we have radio—he will take you and find the truth. . . ."

"Chieftain! Local gangleader you mean," Constantine muttered, heading down the hillside.

⊷═◉═⊷

Constantine had been trudging along the dirt road for four, maybe five miles. He'd walked through the little valley and a ways beyond it. With any luck, he was heading toward the sea. But his feet were aching, stomach complaining, making him nostalgic for an out-of-body experience. It occurred to him that he was in a place where the Caspian tiger yet roamed—and he had no idea how far he was from Rasht. Might take a couple of days to walk there.

He'd come here in the dark of night, months ago, sleeping in the back of a sheep rancher's truck. He had almost no sense of the lay of the land. "Here is monastery," the farmer had said, and that was that.

The road was edged with outcroppings of volcanic rock, the occasional stunted tree; from time to time, small streams from snowmelt dashed by, sometimes crossing the road. Apart from the streams and the distant brown form of a wild burro cropping a patch of grass, the only movement came from a pair of vultures, wheeling far overhead. He was increasingly hungry—daydreaming of coming upon a farmer, perhaps carrying some of the local cheese and olives for lunch. There was a pomegranate tree, and that one might be a pistachio, but neither was fruiting.

A wild gerbil scuttled under the arching root of the pistachio tree and peered fretfully out at him. "I've heard the local people eat gerbils," Constantine told the animal. "I didn't ask what was in the stew at the monastery. But I'm not one for raw meat. So relax . . . crikey, I'm reduced to talking to rodents . . . i'll be the hermit who lives with the wild gerbils. . . ."

The gerbil stared at him with beady eyes, then looked down the road, and ducked back into its den.

Constantine strode broodingly along, his emotions in turmoil. He'd made a kind of specialty of adapting to unexpected situations, to sudden changes—but after a long stay at the monastery, he'd seen his spiritual master shot dead, had been shot at himself, accused of complicity with murderers, and now he was afoot in a country where his legal status was extremely dicey. He felt like a cat tumbled about in a clothes dryer. Could things get worse?

They could: a U.S. Army surplus jeep pulled around the curve ahead. It looked to be Vietnam War–era in its green cammie paint, and it was brimming with armed men. It started past, then braked, wheels screeching, and backed up beside Constantine, pluming dust that made him cough. Five large, bearded, turbaned, and bristly browed men in paramilitary togs got out and pointed their AK-47s at him.

"You gents lost?" Constantine asked. "Need directions?"

"English, get in this jeep," said the biggest one. "You will come and answer questions."

"Always preferred to ask the questions," Constantine said. "Never good at answering them. C-average at best. Any clue as to the topic?"

"I do not know what is questions." The man grinned, his teeth brown from *kif*, and pointed his rifle at Constantine's head. "If you are preferring, I can kill you now."

Constantine got into the jeep.

Tel Aviv, Israel

"Did you arrange for the old sheikh to be eliminated?" Morris asked, looking at the hazy Tel Aviv morning. A fine view from up here.

"Which sheikh would that be, Phil?" Trevino asked. His Italian accent was slight but unmistakable. "Ah! The blue one? I did, yes—I did. It was reported to me just before you came—he is dead. One shot. Muhadar is very good."

Trevino poured Morris some more coffee, being careful with the delicate white china. A tall man with a thick head of white hair, dark, bruised-looking eyes, and a receding chin, Alfonse Trevino was a defrocked Roman Catholic bishop, at ease with Morris, whom he'd known for some years. The two men were seated at breakfast on the penthouse balcony of Trevino's Tel Aviv hotel—the costliest suite in the costliest hotel in town. The Servants of Transfiguration paid for the hotel, after all, and the SOT had accumulated nearly forty billion dollars, counting the Krugerrands, the platinum, and the diamonds, and not counting the uranium mine.

Morris was a little younger—an American, as always in a cream-colored Brooks Brothers suit. A former televangelist, Morris was short and wiry, his black hair slicked back, his gray eyes flat, his lips a straight line in a tanned face marred by a wine stain. He was a wealthy man; he could have had the wine stain removed, but the port mark on his cheek was shaped roughly like a scimitar, which had significance to Morris. His tie tack was a single gold Christian cross.

He sipped his coffee and gazed out at the humming city. The sparkling blue Mediterranean, palm trees pacing the beach; a group of synagogues with gleaming white domes; nearer were the hotel highrises and the architectural bristle of business eminence: Microsoft, Cisco, AOL, IBM all had imposing facilities here. Amusing to think that these graceful, proud skyscrapers would all come crashing down, probably to fall one into the next like so many dominos, when the Great Disclosure came about.

"We embellished the event quite skillfully, I believe," Trevino said. "The sniper's car was stolen from an American embassy in Turkey. Eventually it will be traced back there. The mullahs will be able to blame the CIA. Of course, they wanted the Blue Sheikh dead for years; only his support amongst the local people, and his avoidance of politics, kept him safe."

"And the CIA," Morris observed, "will blame the

mullahs. The man we used, after all, was with Fedayeen-e-Iran, before he was expelled."

"Yes. It's all but a small part of the design, of course. But one likes everything neat. It will be necessary to have the assassin killed, I think. Perhaps we will make it appear that the Mossad did it. . . ."

"Did anyone see the shooting?" Morris asked. It was indeed a small matter. But he was detail oriented.

"Yes—some sort of British spiritual seeker. We don't have his name yet. Someone at the monastery radioed to the local warlord. As this warlord is in our pay, I have asked him to pick the man up. He could be MI6, after all. We have a number of projects in that area that MI6 would be interested in. The sheikh may have known about them."

"Someone British. Well. Have him interrogated. Thoroughly." He toyed with a slice of toast and chuckled. " 'Local warlord,' you say. Funny, the people who get that title. Like mistaking a lion's flea for the lion."

Trevino cleared his throat warningly. He instinctively shied away from mentioning the great powers, except in a ritualistic context. Morris saw it differently. It was not as if the War Lord would come before he was ready. Every piece would have to be in place, every proper note precisely sung, before he would be set free again. That was God's will.

"I wonder if it was not a waste to kill the Blue Shiekh," Morris remarked, after some moments of listening to the honking, the rumbling of the city. "Such power. If he could have been brought to heel . . ."

"That one—never. He was a rogue agent of the Ground of Being. He would not understand what we're about. He would have been brought into opposition against us. He had to be removed from the board. And in the Hidden World, he will be occupied with bliss."

Morris looked up from spreading marmalade on a triangle of toast, but decided not to reproach Trevino for the use of diabolic terminology. The "Ground of Being," the "Hidden World"—to Morris, anyway, this was the language of occultism, ergo the language of Satan. There was only Heaven and Hell after death, as far as Morris was concerned. "This orange marmalade with the little bits of peel in it—it's so bitter. I can't get used to it."

"It comes from England. The British like things bitter or bland. Little in between." Trevino looked at his watch. "I expected to be called to the meeting by now."

"Adverse winds," Morris said, dabbing his lips with a napkin. "Coggins's plane was delayed. But he'll be here. Is everything arranged in Carthaga? Any problems with the CIA? They have a station in Carthaga. . . ."

"The CIA? No. 'The Company' is totally fuddled. They have no idea what we're about. The president tells them as little as possible, of course—they know nothing about the great plan. Nor the British. 'The Firm,' at any rate, has almost no operatives in Carthaga. . . ."

"A shame we can't use a ready-made war, like Iraq."

"Not for the consecration of the seed-heads. No. We need something fresh."

"By the way—this table, this balcony—it has all been swept?"

"I have antibugging devices about me always. Don't worry, Phil. Even the Mossad is without a clue what we're about. They have almost no one in Carthaga—there is no one to oppose us there. Scarcely anyone has even heard of that little postage stamp of a country. The first stage will come off immaculately—ah!" His cellphone was chiming. He took the tiny instrument from a pocket and put on a pair of glasses so he could read the text message on its even tinier screen. "I see that Coggins has arrived. The meeting is called; we're to be there in an hour and a half. I have time to shave and change. I see I also have a call from our man in Iran. Probably asking what to do with the Britisher."

"The Brit?" Morris yawned. Jet lag was a bitch. "Once they wring him dry, see that they kill him. And see to it they do it fairly soon."

4

MERCURY RISING

A little south of Rasht, Iran

The smoke-wreathed minarets of Rasht were just in sight when Constantine, sitting between two gunmen in the backseat of a jeep, made up his mind to do something highly risky, quite possibly stupid, and with a good chance of being fatal.

He was fairly used to making that kind of decision. This time it came when the guy with the brown teeth, nattering to his heavily armed pals, used the Farsi word for *kill* while looking at Constantine. Not a good sign.

Constantine was still feeling weak after days of fasting—and after journeying so far out of body he'd nearly been unable to come back. His latent psychic abilities had grown somewhat over the years, but his capacity to read minds was still uneven at the best of times—local conditions, his own condition, and the mental ability of his subjects affected it. Right now he wasn't picking up much from these thugs, maybe because they didn't do much thinking. You can't read what isn't there. He sensed only a general air of malevolence. The rifles and their seizing him were no proof of anything—people in this part of the world carried rifles the way people in Manchester toted umbrellas, and suspicion was a way of life here. But Constantine was sure of it; he had to escape from these bastards before they got him behind locked doors, or he'd never come out alive.

It wouldn't be long before they got to those locked doors. They were roaring down a potholed two-lane asphalt road at about sixty-five, top speed for the old jeep. "Only some minutes more, Little Satan," Brown-teeth said. He was driving, turning to leer over his shoulder at Constantine. "And we are there. Special warehouse we keep for just such as you. Not crowded. Plenty room for you. Some bars, a chair, some concrete floors, some bloodstains, eh? Good for Little Satan! You have made this kind of questioning many times, with your MI6."

"What's this Little Satan stuff, then?" Constantine asked.

"You are from England, no?"

"Oh, that's right. America is Big Satan and the UK is Little Satan. And we think of Syria as Little Asshole and Iran as Big Ass—"

He didn't get the rest out—the man on his left cracked him on the side of the head with the muzzle of his gun.

Constantine's head rang with the blow, and a little blood started down from his temple, but in a way he had needed the wake-up call. Pain called up strength in Constantine—and he had to get some strength back into him, to carry out his plan.

Me risky, stupid, probably fatal plan. What the hell. Nothing's perfect.

Weakness or not, he was going to need to tone up his psychic energy field for this. He closed his eyes, sat up straighter—difficult to maintain the right posture with the jeep bouncing around on the bad road—turned his attention away from the throbbing in the side of his head, extended his focus first to his body as a whole, then to the body's energy channels. He used his attention to tune those channels, as the pulses in light are tuned by a ruby to a consistent frequency, and then opened a channel at the top of his head, an increased receptivity to the finer energy flow from the cosmos itself. He drew power down from the cosmos—he was not able to get much of that power now, just enough—and used it to increase the strength of the energy field around his body. He was aware that the men seated on either side of him were stirring in their seats; they felt uncomfortable without knowing why.

When he felt himself ready, Constantine opened his eyes and focused them on the back of Brown-teeth's head. He consolidated his energy field further—using a technique the Blue Sheikh himself had taught him—and projected an invisible pseudopod, stretching his energy field out to encompass the driver. He saw the man shiver. Contact.

He maintained the contact with one part of his attention, with the rest focusing his mind's eye, forming a clear image, sending it through the psychic pseudopod and into Brownteeth's brain. . . .

Suddenly, two enormous lorries came roaring down the road toward them—GM semitrucks of the sort Constantine had seen when he'd visited America. They were coming right at the jeep, at top speed, looming up, about to crash into the jeep and crush it under gigantic wheels. But only Constantine and Brownteeth saw the trucks—since they weren't actually there.

Behind the wheel, Brownteeth shrieked in terror, triggering confused shouting from his compatriots as Constantine ducked down, bracing himself between front and backseat, his head between his legs—then Brownteeth jerked the wheel of the jeep hard over to the right, trying to veer from the path of the illusory semitrucks.

The jeep spun out, smacking sideways through barbed wire fence and into the muddy field beside the road, then flipping to tumble, again and again, across the muddy field, Constantine cursing himself as they went. "Con—" *bump, bang* "—stantine you blood—" *bang, thump* "—y fucking—" *crack, smack* "—berk!"

With a final crash of breaking windshield glass, the jeep came to a stop exactly as Constantine had feared it would: upside down.

And he still had his head between his legs.

He felt sodden earth pressing against his arched back. Men groaned around him—the one on the left was limp and silent. Probably dead. Constantine might die himself here, crushed into a curled potato-bug shape by the jeep and the men on either side, with his face aimed right at his own arse. The Devil would be chuckling over that one. Maybe Lucifer had given the jeep an extra flip.

Constantine pushed at the earth with his back muscles, his feet pressing the metal floor, trying to tilt the jeep a little. It didn't budge. Someone was weeping, babbling in Farsi. Was that leaking petrol he smelled?

Then the man on Constantine's right started struggling, groaning, wriggling. The overturned jeep was slanted, and there was more room on that side. In under a minute—it seemed to take five times as long to Constantine, as he was beginning to have trouble breathing with his diaphragm compressed by his curled position—the man was free, and Constantine was able to squirm to that side, pushing against the floor of the jeep—a ceiling for him now—and, almost dislocating several vertebrae, he squirmed to the side, turned his face toward the ground, and used his arms and elbows to drag himself free, choking in the fumes of petrol dripping from the cracked fuel tank. . . .

"Oh, shite of Satan," he muttered, forcing himself to stand. "Cocked up me back . . ."

Automatically, still dazed, he fumbled in his coat for a cigarette, found his old-fashioned Zippo lighter but remembered that he had no cigarettes. Jesus but his back hurt . . .

"You die for this," said the man behind him.

Constantine turned, the motion slow and painful, and saw one of the gunmen, face masked in blood, beard matted with it, one eye missing, pointing an old Luger pistol at him.

"What? *I* didn't crash the jeep!" Constantine protested, taking a step back. It was only a half-lie.

"I don't know how you make this, but you make this, and you die. . . ."

Constantine flicked the Zippo lighter and tossed it at the jeep. The bearded gunman watched it arc toward the spreading pool of petrol and shouted a single syllable of warning. Then the explosion picked him up in a fireball and flung him pinwheeling through the air to fall, burning and broken, a few yards to Constantine's left, the same shockwave knocking Constantine onto his back.

"Ow," Constantine said as he struck the ground.

But when he sat up, he found that his cricked back had been straightened out by the fall. It felt rather better now. Found his lighter intact a few feet away, too. His eyebrows seemed singed, but apart from that, it'd turned out rather better than he'd hoped, he reflected, as he started toward Rasht.

He glanced over his shoulder at the overturned jeep, burning furiously, enveloped by a great crackling orange flame striated in soot. The others had all died in the crash, or shortly after, luckily. Would have been unpleasant to hear them screaming as they burned to death.

Of course, right now, they might well be screaming in the flames of Muslim Hell.

But he hadn't lit that one.

Tikrit, Iraq

Paul Gatewood made a point of trying not to think about the ghosts he'd seen. He'd pushed them out of his mind. But sometimes they came back in.

Private Gatewood knew that the others thought he was out of it, although he hadn't told them about the ghosts—the old man, the young soldier. (Could a ghost be old—or young?)

But he had pretty much stopped talking to the rest of the squadron about anything unnecessary. He spent a lot of time staring at the shadows, half expecting to see the ghosts in there. He knew the others thought he was suffering from battle fatigue, or pretending to—some guys pretended to be losing it in the hopes of getting shipped home.

Some of the other soldiers looked at him suspiciously as he got out of the armored car. Gatewood was part of the evening's reinforcements for the push into Tikrit. The Sunni insurgents had been massacring Kurds in this town, pretty much whenever they felt like it. Gatewood's company was supposed to put a stop to it in this sector. But from the chatter on the radio, it'd seemed all they'd accomplished was to get two men shot by a sniper, one guy shot by friendly fire, a troop transport blown to hell by an IED, and two or three civilian bystanders shot dead. There was rumored to be an RPG guerilla in the area somewhere, too.

Easy to screw up in the dark. Most of the lights in this sector had been shot out. The city hereabouts was a jumble of blocky buildings, concrete and clay, with big areas of rubbled vacants lots, inky with shadow. There were a few pockets of light, cast by distant streetlights, thin by the time it got over here; a little more light stingily distributed by the quarter moon. The soldiers used flashlights and lanterns sparingly, not wanting to give any help to the snipers. When the shooting did come, you mostly couldn't see who was shooting at you. Sometimes you caught a muzzle flash on a rooftop, or in the mouth of an alley; sometimes not. Other times what seemed an enemy muzzle flash came from your own men.

Gatewood was thinking about this, and about how he could have gone to officer's candidate school and had instead signed up for the fast track to combat after 9/11, wanting to go to Afghanistan. Since it would have been smart to send a motivated soldier to Afghanistan, they sent him to South Korea, and then Iraq.

"Gatewood!" the sarge called, a voice out of the darkness, "you go with Binsdale's platoon, check out that house at the end of the street. We got intel there's a guy with an un-ID'd weapon hiding down there somewhere."

"Sure, Sarge," Gatewood said, his heart sinking. Binsdale wasn't a bad guy, but his outfit meant Vintara and Marquand, too. They'd become inseparable. Marquand had pictures of Timothy McVeigh in his room at the base.

Gatewood circled the edge of the group of men till he found Binsdale, who looked disappointed that Gatewood was coming along. He didn't like people second-guessing him, and Gatewood had a way of doing that. Also, Binsdale figured—Gatewood was pretty sure that Binsdale figured this—that Gatewood was crazy.

Maybe I am, Gatewood thought. *Maybe I hallucinated that old man, that ghost soldier.*

You must survive, so you can find a way. . . .

Kind of thing a guy with battle fatigue might hear, after all. Not that Gatewood had been in all that many battles . . .

He followed Binsdale and Muny, a stocky black guy carrying a SAW, joining the rest of the platoon toward the end of the street. He hoped Binsdale had the house right. Seemed to Gatewood that about every fourth time they were told to check out a certain house for hostiles or guns it turned out they were in the wrong house.

As it happened, there was only one house at the end of the dead-end street. The surrounds were all rubble and vacant lots; to one side was the wreckage of a small mosque. The house they were to probe had been hastily constructed in one of Saddam's abortive housing projects, a squarish two-story structure of cinder blocks and plasterboard. A light burned in an upstairs window.

"You see that window up there?" Marquand hissed. He was a man with his head shaved bald, taped-together glasses, thin lips always curled into a disapproving sneer. "Could be a sniper right there, right now. We could just chuck a grenade right through it. Report said someone was sniping from this end of the street."

"Chances are they were using that old mosque, one of these busted-up places here," Binsdale said.

"So why don't we check out the mosque?" Muny asked.

"Because orders are to check out the house. Now shut the fuck up and take Marquand and Gatewood and Vintara and go around back, see no one runs out with a weapon, tries to hide, nothing like that. Me and Norquist and Lemon'll go in at the front."

Gatewood cringed inwardly at the thought of going on any kind of mission with Marquand. Glancing at Marquand, Muny didn't seem to like the idea much either. "Shouldn't we have a battering ram, knock the door in?"

"We'll get something like that if it's locked—now get gone."

Gatewood trailed after Muny and Vintara and Marquand, his assault rifle feeling heavy in his hands.

Vintara switched on the little flashlight attached to the barrel of his rifle and they picked their way around the side of the house, over chunks of concrete, asphalt, broken glass, and patches of dog shit. The dog in question growled at them from the darkness of the lot beside the house, but they couldn't see him. Gatewood hoped the dog didn't come to investigate—Vintara liked to shoot stray dogs for fun.

There was a door around back and someone was coming out when they got there. It was a frightened-looking man in a knee-length white shirt, with three days' growth of beard, and a boy of about ten, in shorts; the boy took them in with wide brown eyes. "Not to shoot!" the man said, one hand around his son, clasping the boy to him, the other raised imploringly.

"Back in the house!" Gatewood said, stepping up and pointing at the door with his rifle. He was trying to get some kind of handle on the situation. Marquand and Vintara might do anything, left to their own devices.

The boy and his father backed into the house, the boy gaping at them in as much amazement as fear. The room, dimly lit with a kerosene lamp, contained a legless brown sofa, a threadbare braided rug, a few books in Arabic script piled beside the sofa, a small television with a wire-hanger antenna, and some half-dressed action figures—the Justice League—that could have come from an American Toys "R" Us, scattered on the floor. The room smelled heavily of cooked meat, tobacco, and some spice Gatewood wasn't able to identify.

"Found one weapon!" Binsdale said from the front room. "Was in the closet up there . . ." He came in with the others, tossed a sawed-off shotgun on the sofa.

"Sawed-off is some pretty serious firepower," Vintara observed.

"For bandits!" the man said. "Drive taxi, I am taxi drive making! Bandits, all the time bandits!"

"Everybody uses that excuse," Marquand said.

Don't say anything, Gatewood implored himself. *Go along with them for once. . . .*

"You got a coalition permit for that weapon there, Dad?" Vintara asked.

"Permit, yes! In my taxi, is in my taxi!"

"Oh right, somewhere outside," Marquand said. "I didn't see any taxi."

"Is in mosque, so no one steals!"

"We'll check it out later," Binsdale said. "What about upstairs?"

"My brother, sick there, he is sick, please, no disturb!" the man said, looking at the ceiling.

"Oh yeah?" Marquand snorted. "Maybe your brother's 'Ali Baba'!"

"No, no Ali Baba, no insurgent! Makes wood!"

Vintara sniggered at Marquand. "I'll *bet* he likes to make wood!"

"Probably a carpenter," Gatewood muttered. "I'll check out upstairs, Corporal, if you want. . . ."

"Vintara, you go with him. Yell if you see anything shady at all."

Gatewood nodded, headed for the narrow concrete stairs. He led the way, again trying to keep a step ahead of Vintara, and ascending with his rifle at ready.

Upstairs was a narrow hallway with two doors opening to the right. The first was a bathroom with a tub rusting around the edges, a toilet, a few shaving implements. The next opened into a bedroom; there was a lamp on a table that was just a sheet of wood over sawhorses, illuminating a bed on the floor where a man writhed and whimpered. But he sat bolt upright when Gatewood stepped into the room, Vintara crowding in beside him.

"Brother" was a shirtless, sweating man with sickly yellow cast, a scraggly beard, wild black eyes, matted hair.

"Hands up!" Vintara said.

The man just sat there, his lower lip quivering, one eye twitching.

"The guy is out of it, man," Gatewood said. "He's no threat to anyone."

"He's just scared he's been caught. He could be on the most-wanted list, Gatewood, you don't fucking know." He pushed by Gatewood and aimed his gun at the man on the bed. "Get your ass up! Hands where I can see 'em!"

"Vintara, I don't think he speaks English!"

"He understands me! Hands up! Now!"

"What you got?" Binsdale called from below.

"Some guy in bed—looks feverish or crazy!" Gatewood called.

"His head!" the dad said. "Please, his head! He is hurt his head!"

"I said *get up!*" Vintara bellowed—and he fired a warning shot into the ceiling.

The man on the bed screeched and snatched at something in the shadows beside the bed. He swung it around between him and Vintara—who shot him right through the copy of the Qu'ran he was trying to keep between them.

The man gave a final yelp, his back arching. He thrashed on the bed, spurting blood.

"Jesus!" Gatewood burst out.

There was a responding pandemonium from below—shouting, a thud, a sputter of gunshots.

"I got this one, he was going for a gun!" Vintara shouted. He started down the stairs.

Gatewood went to look at the dying man—gone limp now, his breath coming in fast little gasps.

There was a neat bullet hole right through the Qu'ran—and beside the bed, something else. Medicine bottles. Gatewood picked one of them up and went to the stairs.

He was stalling about going downstairs. He could tell by the sounds . . . there was something down there he didn't want to see. He made himself go down into the living room.

The soldiers were standing around, staring at the

body on the sofa. The boy's dad was sprawled face-down over the sofa, motionless, the back of his head shot away.

"He went for the shotgun," Marquand said. The muzzle of his assault rifle was smoking. "When he heard the shots upstairs . . ."

"I don't know—maybe he was going for it," Binsdale said, shaking his head.

"Maybe," Muny said, staring at the body. "Maybe he was just running by the fucking sofa."

"What, you want to take a chance, Muny?"

"Where's the kid?" Gatewood asked. The boy was nowhere to be seen.

Binsdale let out a long slow, sighing breath. "Oh—he ran off. When we . . . when Marquand shot his pops."

Gatewood shook his head in disbelief. *Little kid, alone, his father and uncle dead, running in the darkness of the city . . . of this fucking city . . .*

He looked at the medicine bottle in his hand, then tossed it to Binsdale.

"What's this, Gatewood?"

"Check it out." Gatewood working to keep the anger from his voice. "The guy upstairs had no gun. He was reaching for a book. That was next to his bed. Haldol. It's an antipsychotic medicine. Came from our own clinic. The guy was just crazy and scared."

"Bullshit, Gatewood!" Vintara spat. "You were trying to say don't light up that car that time, turned out to be a fucking bomb car! You don't know dick!"

Gatewood felt strange . . . very strange . . . like his

anger was fading into a kind of numb resignation, and as it happened the room around him was going dark. . . . Vintara and Binsdale, the others, their faces sliding into obscurity. The only light was coming from the doorway.

He turned and looked at the front door. The soldier he'd seen that day, when the guy with the bomb had tried to blow them up at the checkpoint—the ghost soldier—was standing just inside the front door. He gestured to Gatewood, urgently.

Gatewood walked to the front door, leaving the others to argue about how to report all this. Binsdale wasn't pleased with any of it. Vintara was saying maybe Gatewood hid that guy's gun; he's trying to make them look bad. . . .

Outside, Gatewood found a ghostly multitude awaiting him. It was dark here, but he could see them all quite clearly, as if each was transparent, with a small interior light, the size of a child's night-light, right where their heart should be, illuminating them from within. The man who'd been shot upstairs was there now, an apparition but no longer looking crazed or scared. Just sort of somber. The ghost of the dad was there, his face profoundly sad, staring out across the city, perhaps looking for his runaway child. The ghost soldier was there, and so was the old Muslim guy with the white beard from that day on the overpass, and dozens of others, a crowd of ghosts, all looking at him solemnly and expectantly. Fourteen, maybe fifteen children amongst them. There were whole families of ghosts here—they'd died all at once, together.

When he looked at them he seemed to glimpse the deaths that had disembodied them. Blown up by car bombers. Blown up by American bombs. Shot at American checkpoints. Shot by insurgents. Executed by terrorists for cooperating with the Americans. Murdered by Sunnis for being Shi'ite; by Shi'ite for being Sunni.

People just caught in the crossfire.

"Why are they here?" Gatewood asked. "There has to be some other place for them. Muslim Paradise or something."

"They're stuck," the ghost soldier said. "Caught here in this world, like lots of ghosts. It's the trauma does it sometimes, I guess. Me and my friend here, we're on assignment . . . and here's Colonel Futheringham. . . ." He nodded toward the ghost of the British army officer, with flourishing mustaches and a khaki uniform, strolling up to them. "The colonel and Sheikh Abdul here and me—we're on a mission," the young soldier went on. "We gathered up these people to support us. And that'll help them. . . . See, if they do something to stop the killing, somewhere, it helps them let go. You are called to help us, too."

"I need to be a ghost?" Gatewood asked, looking down at himself. Maybe he was dead. Maybe someone had shot him and he hadn't worked that out yet.

"Not at all, recruit!" the old British colonel said. "We need you alive. Part of a team, eh? A couple of others to round up. You've got to come and meet them."

"Come—with you? Where . . . ?" Gatewood didn't feel like he was having a conversation with the dead.

He didn't feel like he was taking part in a supernatural event. It all felt very natural and normal to him. Like this was what he was intended for.

"You survived, bro," the soldier said to him. "So now we're going to show you the way. You got to come with us. You're one of those who can see 'em. You look around with the heart and here we are. Now come along—you won't need that gun. We'll watch your back."

Gatewood nodded dazedly. He felt driven by an unknown momentum. He threw his rifle aside, just as Binsdale came out of the house behind him.

"What the fuck you doing with your rifle, Gatewood! Pick up your goddamn weapon!"

"You can't see them?" Gatewood asked, though he was pretty sure of the answer. "All the dead calling to me?"

"Oh Christ . . . just what I need, another fucking headcase . . . just pick up your weapon and fall in, Gatewood, you fucking—where the fuck are you going?"

Gatewood was walking on a thin path through the rubble beside the fallen mosque and into the darkness of the city's outskirts. He was being ushered along the path by the old man with the white beard and the young American soldier, accompanied by nearly a hundred dead people.

He was being ushered into the darkness by a troop of ghosts.

"Gatewood!" Binsdale shouted. "Get back here or you're on report! You want a court martial?"

Gatewood didn't even glance back at him. Watching Gatewood going AWOL, wandering off into the dark alone, Binsdale thought maybe he should go after him.

But there were mines out there, probably. And Gatewood was clearly out of his fucking mind. He might do anything.

Binsdale shrugged and turned to his men, gathering outside the house. "Fall in, you guys. Pick up Gatewood's gun, Muny. He's gone AWOL. Let's figure out what we're gonna say to the Lieutenant. . . ."

The Fedayeen fighter, watching the small group of American soldiers from the dimness of the ruined mosque's second floor, picked up his already loaded RPG-7.

"Kill him!" whispered the boy, in Arabic. The Fedayeen had found the boy running aimlessly through the ruins of the mosque.

Now the guerrilla shushed the boy with a hissed syllable. The boy watched in fascination as the Fedayeen leaned the launch tube of the RPG-7 on a broken crust of wall and aimed at the ground near Binsdale's boots. In his experience, it was best to use the splash effect of the shell hitting the ground to make sure you took out the Americans, because of their Kevlar vests. He squeezed the trigger and the antipersonnel shell flew down at the perfect angle, arcing only a little, to explode just between Binsdale and Vintara. Binsdale was flung nearly straight up in the air, flipping forward to land on his shoulder, breaking it. One of his legs was hanging by a shred. Vintara was instantly killed, a piece of shrapnel taking off the top of his head.

The Fedayeen guerilla was satisfied. One of them dead, the other desperately wounded. He gestured for the boy to follow and they ran toward the back of the mosque, the Fedayeen slipping the strap of the RPG-7 over his shoulder so he could drop down into the darkness and leave the area before the other soldiers could work out where he was.

"Will you teach me?" the boy asked, as they ran through the maze of rusted car hulks abandoned behind the mosque. Within the hour he had watched one of the Americans shoot his father down. He was eager to become a Fedayeen.

"Yes! If you do what I tell you! Starting with be quiet now!"

There might still be time tonight to get another position, the guerrilla reflected as he ran along, his RPG-7 clanking. He had two more shells. It might still be possible to kill more Americans, or Shi'ite traitors.

The night was young.

The shore of the Caspian Sea near Rasht, Iran

The Caspian was steel gray, under a sun veiled in bluish cloud the way the lights in the Blue Sheikh's chambers had been veiled by sheer scarves.

Shouldn't have started smoking again, Constantine thought, trudging down the beach. *Bloody hookah got me craving. Out of cigs for two months, since that kid got me the Turkish leaf; I was almost over it. Wonder who's got a fag?*

There were only a few people on this stretch of beach, none of them close by. A man and a woman, both in neck-to-ankle robes, walking in opposite directions, careful not to look at one another. The woman was coming toward Constantine, but clearly not looking for him. She angled closer to the road above the beach, to give him a wide berth. She wore a black chador wrapped around her head, one end tucked to veil most of her face.

Apart from these two figures, the shore at this moment was like any beach on any sea. It seemed to Constantine that he was walking along beside the English Channel; he was walking on the edge of the Indian Ocean; he was walking on a beach in California. It was all the same: the smell of brine, the crunch of sand, the water stretching out to become the signature of endlessness.

Supposedly he was to meet some unknown person here, but Constantine knew he might've come to this beach for no good reason. Not all prophecies came true; in fact, most didn't, for the average person. Not all of them did even for John Constantine, who knew where to get "the good stuff" in the way of precognition.

One time, a shining spirit had appeared to him and said, *At midnight, a crimson dragon will arise and speak to you, and your life will be transfigured!* Midnight came—no dragon. Next day the spirit sheepishly reappeared and said, *Sorry. Wrong chap.* And then vanished again.

"It's like so cool to be alive again, dude!" Constantine turned to see a man running toward him, shout-

ing, forty yards off. *"Is this tight or what?"* the man shouted.

The odd thing was, the man was wearing a gray galabiya, an ankle-length gown with a high collar common to pious Muslims, and he had a long black beard and a white turban. Staggering along like a man drunk or stoned, he kept dropping the turban and picking it up and putting it back on his head, crookedly. He had a dark face, eyes too close together, the bridge of his nose quite prominent, his lips hidden in brown-black beard. But he was behaving like an American raver on a new designer drug.

"Dude!" he shouted, skipping along. He tripped and fell to his hands and knees, crawled around a moment looking for his turban, found it, and shoved it back on all smashed. "You're Constantine, right?" He struggled to his feet and danced around, waving his hands in the air. "This is so fucking tight!"

"Right—best to keep your voice down, mate," Constantine said, glancing around.

"Wow, John Constantine! That's so fucking cool! This one guy in the third circle of limbo, man, he said you made Lucifer suck his own dick!"

"Don't believe everything you hear. And it might be best not to invoke—never mind, who the bloody hell *are* you?"

"Me? I'm Spoink Johnson, man! Just call me Spoink! Oh—the *body!* I understand why you're looking at me like that!" Spoink put his hands out in front of him like a Motown singer. *Stop!* "You don't get the bod, dude!" He put a finger over his lips and sidled up to Constantine, lowering his voice a fraction. "You like it? It was the body of this terrorist dude—he was a big planner for them and there was, like, an explosion of some bomb that he was supposed to deliver to some airport in Paris; it went off, like, early?"

"Go on," Constantine said, looking around nervously.

"Well the dude wasn't standing right by the bomb, but he was close enough that he was like, all fucked up in the explosion, right? He went into a coma, and some comas, you know, the soul hangs around—but lots of times it just goes, 'This sucks!' and it, like, cruises, and the body's just this soulless husk waiting to die, you feel?"

"Yeah, I—right. So you possessed this bastard's body, eh? What happened to *your* body?"

"Oh that. I fucked up. You know how they were saying that, like, Ecstasy, the drug I mean, MDMA, it was all, like, healthy and harmless? Well it isn't, after a few times. After you get really *up* enough times, it fucks with your brain and then you get really *down,* and I, you know, got really depressed, and I killed myself with sleeping pills; but then when you're in limbo they give you back your perspective on shit, and I was, like, all floating and in limbo and I'm going, *whoa!* And then all these angry people were coming into limbo and crying and shit and I said, Dude, what's the matter, and they said, it was war in the Middle East, like in Jerusalem and Iraq, and this angel told me, *'Dude,'* he said—"

"An angel said 'dude'?"

"Well not exactly, but that's what he meant, he said I could find a body and use it, a body that would, all, pass muster locally, because there's a big confrontation coming down, and he thought I had some gift that could help chill shit out and I'd be able to help John Constantine and I said, Whoa, I've heard of John Constantine, and not just in limbo—I was like into this occult chick in Santa Monica, and *she* said 'There's this guy in England named John Constantine, he used to be in that band Mucous Membrane that almost no one heard of,' and she said he learned how to do magic, and he—"

"You're telling me I'm some kind of urban myth in California, then?"

"You look real to me, dude." Spoink scratched his beard. Then he scratched his groin. "So what we going to do?" He became especially interested in his groin, flipping his penis about through the cloth.

"You're going to stop touching your pink oboe, first of all, before we get arrested. You see that woman walking alone now, on the beach, in the chador? She's staring at us because you're mucking about with your bloody groin. This is Iran, you berk. And number two—you're going to fuck off and leave me alone."

"What? I was sent across the universe, like the Beatles song, to party with you, Johnny C!"

"Don't bloody call me Johnny C. There's been a bureaucratic cock-up, mate. If you're my liaison, I do believe I'll just go home to London and let this thing sort itself out. Don't much believe that stuff about Mercury anyway."

"Dude! You're not going to go all British snob on me, are you?"

"Yeah, I bloody am and with pleasure. Now fuck

off, before you get me arrested—and *will you stop touching your crotch?"*

"Why—you wanta touch it? Don't be so hung up, bro, this is all, the twenty-first century! Damn it's good to be back in a body!"

He turned and leered at the woman walking along in the chador with only her eyes visible. She stopped stock-still and crossed her hands over her chest.

"Hey, baby!" Spoink called out. "What's the haps? Let's party!" He started toward her. "Take off the veil and kiss me, girl! This is the time for love to reign! Love, reign over me! Wait!"

"Christ on a bike!" Constantine swore.

The woman in the chador turned and ran.

"Waitaminnut, girlfriend!" Spoink shouted, starting after her.

"Right, I'm scarperin'," Constantine muttered. He turned to go the opposite way, thinking he had five hundred British pounds and a passport sewed into the lining of his coat, he could hire a boat, take it to along the coast of the Caspian to Azerbaijan, make his way to the Russian Caucasus, badger the British consul for a ticket to London. . . .

He turned to see the woman screaming as she churned up the sand toward the road along the beach, yelling for help, with Spoink in pursuit.

This thing is spinning out of control, Constantine thought as he hurried to the north along the beach. *Whoever is behind it is desperate, flailing about.* . . .

You're right, John, said a familiar voice from the surf.

Constantine thought, *I could ignore that voice, I could just keep heading north.* . . .

No, the voice responded, *you can't leave me when I need you, John. I was there for you. And for a while, drunken sot though you might've been, you were the closest thing I had to a da of me own. . . .*

Constantine sighed and turned to look toward the source of the voice that only he could hear: Mercury, rising from the surf almost—not quite—like Venus on the half shell. She was taking shape just beyond the lapping fringe of waves striking the beach, a wave spiraling up, spinning into its shape like a form on a lathe.

It was a slim young woman made out of sea spray, with sea foam for her hair. He hadn't seen her since she'd been a child, and this version was translucent, made of green water, but he recognized her anyway. It was Mercury, Marj's daughter, a girl he'd treated as a kind of stepdaughter while his relationship with Marj had continued. But he'd wandered off on a personal quest, and when he'd looked for Marj again he found she'd run off with a "Traveler," or so he'd heard, a British Gypsy, taking Mercury with her. . . .

Being John Constantine, he wasn't particularly surprised to see an apparition of Mercury arising from the surf. He knew her to be an especially gifted psychic, and he'd been expecting some sort of contact from her. "How you doing, kid? How's your mum?"

"Mum's drinking too much, up in Scotland. I've gone my own way, John. I sensed something happening in the Middle East, and Zed couldn't go, and I couldn't find you, and I kept getting dreams that wouldn't go away—"

"I know how that is. They just won't leave you alone."

"—so I went out to Jerusalem, and some right bastards took me prisoner, hostage like, and I read their minds and it turned out they were hypnotized or something, and now I'm fairly starving in a basement somewhere off the coast of North Africa, a place called Carthaga I think. . . ."

"Any notion where in Carthaga, luv?"

"No. I can't sustain this much longer. You've got to let this Spoink person go with you. For some reason they want him along."

"Who's 'they'?"

"I'm not sure, John, except that they're on 'the right side of the ledger.' I . . ." The figure of rippling water, constantly renewed from below, turned and looked to the right, as if at something out of view. "I've got to go."

"Don't pull a Princess Leia on me, luv—stick around and clue me in. Give me an alternative! I can't go anywhere with that plonker!"

"Got to show some faith, John! Get him out to sea! There'll be someone to help you toward Russia. . . . Help me, John. I don't mind dying, but dying like this—and knowing that a world war is going to start. . . ."

"You wot? World war? Can you be more—"

But he broke off as the misty image collapsed into the surf. She was gone, and so was the contact. He cast his psychic field out like a net into the sea, but all he picked up was a thought from a fish thinking a smaller fish looked tasty.

Constantine turned to look after Spoink and saw an

old truck with a yellow lightbar pulling up along the road edging the beach. Men were getting out, starting toward Spoink, who was still grabbing his crotch and yelling after the terrified woman in the chador.

"Oh, fuck me!" Constantine burst out. "The Morals Police."

5

WATCHED AND WATCHED
BY CROOKED EYES

Carthaga, off the coast of North Africa

"This here little country's just big enough to have a war in," said General Coggins into the headset with a chuckle, as he scanned the morning horizon from the copilot's seat of the gunship. He was a lean Texan with a pot belly and a drooping lower lip; he had those down-slanted eyes one saw amongst denizens of the Southwest who looked vaguely Asian but more likely had a few drops of Native American blood. He adjusted his binoculars but saw no aircraft out ahead at all, which was good. He didn't want to run into any Carthaga patrols; Burlington would have to shoot them down. That would spoil the illusion.

The gunship shuddered over the red-tiled rooftops of Poeni, the capital city—the only important city, in truth—on the Mediterranean island of Carthaga, fifty-three miles northeast of Tunis. It was a Blackhawk helicopter, quietly misappropriated by General Coggins, repainted in a secret hangar in the gray and yellow of the Carthaga air force. To complete the camouflage, they were all wearing the cheap dun uniforms of the Carthaga military: Coggins, Alfonse Trevino, Captain Courtney Simpson—the pilot—and General Coggins's bodyguard and persuader, Burlington, on the 16 mm gun.

They quickly left Poeni behind, heading toward the island's eastern shore, flying over rolling countryside: dusty beet fields, olive orchards. "Did our man in the Carthaga Aerial Force set up the diversion?" Trevino asked.

The thunder of the chopper made it necessary for them to speak through the headsets, though they were all sitting close by one another. Trevino clutched at the straps holding him in place with one hand, and clutched his stomach with the other when the chopper gave a lurch.

"Sure as hell did," Coggins said. "We shouldn't get any hassle from the locals on this here little outing at all."

The pilot, a tall, blue-eyed fiftyish man with sandy hair, set the autopilot, took off his headset, and leaned over to the American army general. "Best not to discuss such things over the headset, sir. This frequency's supposed to be restricted to the chopper, but there's no telling for sure. Funny things happen and transmissions get picked up. . . ." He shifted back into position with a grimace—he was almost too big to comfortably fit into the cockpit, having to slump to pull it off.

"That's an affirmative, there, Courtney," said the general. The Servants of Transfiguration were fanatics about secrecy and damned good at it. The SOT was only a rumor to the intelligence services—even the Mossad. Of course, the organization included certain CIA agents, but they would never let their ostensible employers know about their true allegiance. And neither the CIA nor the U.S. military had any idea that Coggins was here in Carthaga, nor what he was here for.

Coggins signaled the others to be careful of what they said on the headset. They all nodded except for Burlington. White-blond, florid-faced, and gray-eyed, usually silent anyway, Burlington was absorbed in checking the load on the heavy machine gun, smiling softly to himself. Strapped into the open side door, Burlington was too broad-shouldered to sit anywhere else—and he loved the big gun.

"There it is!" Simpson said, switching off autopilot and nodding at the camp of the Sudanese army battalion at the crossroads below. Date palms lined the roads up to the crossroads. There were two smaller helicopters secured to the ground just outside the camp, Coggins noted, with men loading supplies into them. He switched off his headset and relied on shouting. "Looks like they're about to pull out!"

Coggins nodded, switching off his own headset. "The dumb bastards think they're done on this island!"

Trevino was already muttering the invocations, sprinkling the sacred blood onto the small glass ball he held in his right hand. In the glass sphere, no bigger than an apple, was a yellow, swirling mist. He spoke the final words, pressed the glass ball to his heart and his groin, then hurled it out the open door,

past the gun, so that it fell into the center of the
crossroads below, shattering. The skull they'd buried
in the crossroads a fortnight before—a particular
skull, not just any skull—responded to the proximity
of the bone dust quickened to the invocation, and
awaited those emanations that would complete the
fatal circuit.

Below, about five hundred North African Arabs in
the uniform of the Sudanese army looked up from
packing their gear into the trucks the UN had pro-
vided for their pull-out from the island. They looked
at one another, wondering what the gunship was
about. Just making a show, urging them to leave the
country? Pointless! Weren't they leaving, after all?
They had an agreement with the government of the
tiny nation that they were no longer going to support
the insurgency of the island's Arab minority, they
were going to pull out so the UN could negotiate a
settlement. . . .

"Now!" Trevino shouted.

Burlington looked over his shoulder at Coggins. He
took orders only from Coggins—so definitively was
this so, he would have ignored the President of the
United States if he'd asked him to pass the salt.

"Go for it!" Coggins shouted.

Burlington grinned, his eyes glistening as he opened
fire with the chassis-mounted machine gun, spraying
the soldiers below with hundreds of 16 mm rounds in
a few seconds. Men were shattered, torn to pieces,
flung spinning about. Some of them ran for their
weapons, but few made it.

"ATS missiles!" Coggins shouted.

Licking his lips like a man about to penetrate a virgin, Simpson tilted the gunship toward the mass of fleeing men below and fired the missiles. One of them struck a truck, igniting its gas tank, making a glorious red fireball that lit reflections in Simpson's eyes as he fired the second set of missiles.

"Two missiles away!"

"Send the other two into those choppers on the ground there!" Coggins ordered.

"Yes sir!" Simpson swung the chopper around, as bullets whined from its armored underside, and flew over to hover where he could get an angle down at the choppers. He was just ninety yards above the targets—impossible to miss. Men were still leaping from the helicopters, sprinting away from them in terror, when the missiles launched from either side of the gunship. Both targets were struck, churned into flaming shrapnel that ripped through the camp and whirled human bodies through the air.

Burlington had been firing continuously—he was already on his second belt of ammo, mopping up a line of screaming, running men like an exterminator spraying ants; wherever he struck, the ants fell instantly dead.

"Die, you stupid little crawling bastards!" he shouted.

Trevino glanced at Burlington in irritation. Looking over his shoulder, Coggins didn't miss the look. He knew that to Trevino this was a Holy Mission. The men dying on the ground were sacrifices to a higher purpose. To Burlington and Simpson, it was just another chance to kill for the general.

It was a Holy Mission to Coggins, too, of course. He knew what was coming. The sword, the fire, the vengeful angels of the Lord. He was just one instrument, one part of the great plan that would call the Transfiguration down upon the world.

Still, he had to keep them all working together until the end—until the time when God would sort them out.

"That's enough, Burlington!" he shouted. "Got to leave enough alive to take the story back to their people! Courtney—take us out of here!"

"Saw someone with a home video camera point it up at us!" Simpson said.

"Good!" said Coggins. "Very good! They'll take us for those American mercenaries hired by President Mofi!"

The Blackhawk turned and headed back to the cargo ship the SOT had waiting for them ten miles offshore. Coggins was eager to get there so he could monitor the news and do what he could to encourage the war in Carthaga along. All he'd done today was strike the spark. The brushfire must be fanned to life. From little brushfires great burnings would come.

And he was confident of it; he could feel the thrum of the War Lord in the air. The great conflagration was coming.

⋯⊷⊙⊷⋯

Watching the gunship depart, coughing from the smoke of burning trucks and helicopters, smelling cooked human flesh, Major Abbide felt a strange energy rising in him. Another time he might've felt raped, disillusioned, despairing over what had happened to his battalion.

But today, he felt something else—and it was as if the feeling were rising from the earth at his feet, soaking itself into him. He trembled with it, felt drugged with it, energized by it, and before his mind's eye floated visions of carnage: the destruction of his enemies. He would take his men and he would punish the sons of whores who ran this country. He would incite the Arab majority on Carthaga to rise up and massacre the Carthagan blacks—who had power, after all, only because President Mofi's family connections gave him control of the offshore oil rigs. Mofi, in his mad arrogance, had surely sent these mercenaries in their gunship to betray the agreement, to murder Abbide's men before they left the island, to show he had no respect for the Sudan.

Abbide heard the other survivors roaring in fury, turned to see them shaking their fists at the now distant gunship, all of them burning with the same martial hatred, a hunger for revenge that was like a fever, a hot singing in their nerves—a fury more powerful than anything they'd ever felt before. It seemed to have a life of its own.

"We will give them war!" Major Abbide shouted. "And with war they will pay the price for what they have done! We will kill them all!"

And his men, as one, cheered with a sound like a hundred missiles shrieking through the air.

The Caspian Sea

"What the bloody hell are you telling them?" Constantine demanded.

"Silence, British cur!" Spoink snarled, slapping Constantine so hard that he staggered and nearly went over the side of the cabin cruiser.

Two of the Morals Police had come along on the peeling white forty-foot cruiser, one of them the coxswain piloting them out into the midst of the Caspian, the other a short man in a robe, sandals, and fez, scraggly of both beard and teeth, which he bared at Constantine as he pointed his submachine gun at his head. He shouted something in Farsi that Constantine—clutching the railing of the cabin cruiser—laboriously translated as *You will not speak or you will die!*

Awed by the famous face belonging to the body that Spoink inhabited, the captain of the Morals Police had given Spoink his .45 pistol. Spoink now waved the gun with authority, making it glint in the sunlight as, speaking in fluent Farsi, he ordered the robed coxswain to cut the engine. The pilot obeyed and the battered cabin cruiser sputtered to a slow, silent gliding in the low waves.

Constantine looked for the shore and was troubled when he found he could no longer see it. They were in deep water out here. He was in deep water in more ways than one. He figured Spoink to have been taken over by Lucifer or some other diabolic enemy from his past. He'd been set up.

Tired, hungry, and on the verge of sunstroke, Constantine was feeling magically enervated and not sure what good it would do him to use unreliable power on one of these thugs—control one and the other would top him. But he had to try. Maybe he could get the guy with the Uzi to shoot Spoink and the boat's pilot. He tried to focus his psychic energies. . . .

Then Spoink began yelling in Farsi and pointing at the water. The man with the submachine gun went and looked over the edge of the rail. The coxswain looked over the gunman's shoulder. Spoink caught Constantine's eye and jerked a thumb at the coxswain, then stepped up behind the gunman, grabbed him by the ankles and flipped him over the railing.

The boat's pilot turned gaping in astonishment— and Constantine had him over the railing before he could say Iraq Robinson.

Both men lost their weapons in the water, where they thrashed around shouting imprecations in Farsi. Constantine understood some of them.

"And your mum, too, mate!" he shouted back, tossing them a couple of life jackets. "The shore's that way! Best start swimming! *Allah Akhbar!*"

Spoink was singing a Red Hot Chili Peppers song as he started the cabin cruiser and headed it north. Something about "gorilla and cuntilla and salmonella." The shouts of the Iranian Morals Cops got fainter and fainter as Constantine joined him in the shade of the cabin. "God I need to sit down. . . . Here, was it necessary to give me that slap with quite so much verve?"

"Got to make it look good, bro." He scratched his beard. "Know how I got him to look in the water? Told him there was a mine floating out there. Damn I'm good."

"You're a fucking lunatic, mate," Constantine observed matter-of-factly.

"Doesn't mean I'm not damned good."

They continued on another nautical mile or two, till Constantine said, "Oi—switch off the engine until we know where we're going."

" 'Kay. Hey, there's a pack of cigarettes here in the little compartment under the—"

"Give me those!" Constantine snatched the pack from Spoink's hand, found his lighter and immediately lit a cigarette. He took a deep drag. "Ahh—Turkish imports. Not bad." The boat was drifting now, the sea calm. "What'd you say to those wankers, anyway, to get us out here?"

"Dude, it's so tight. I woke up in the hospital—just like ten blocks from where you were on the beach—and I had all this guy's memories and skills and shit, and none of his personality. I just got up and pulled out the tubes and walked out. I remember how to talk his lingo, I remember all the names of the *blokes* this *chap* knows—"

"The *what* the *who* knows?"

"You're English, right? Just tryin' to talk your talk. I can't say blokes and chaps too?"

"No. You can't."

"Come on, man, I love that English shit; yo, you wanta hear me do stuff from *Lord of the Rings*—I can do Gandalf—"

Constantine cringed. "Christ *no!* Don't—"

" 'Fool of a Took!' What you think? I can do Samwise—"

"Leave off that twee shite or I'll box your ears. Now just tell me, how'd you manage this? They really thought you were him, the big toff in local politics? And you told them you were gonna dump my body out here, then?"

"Soon as I found out they had access to a boat. Seems like serendipity, bro."

"What became of that girl you were chasing?"

"Came to my senses when I saw the Morals Cops. I told 'em she was showing some ankle, like a dirty damn whore. Said to just chase her from the beach—said the British son of Satan had put her up to it. Am I good or what, dude? Looks like you're stuck with me!"

"I'll decide how bloody long I'm stuck with you, mate. Might drop you off at the nearest buoy. You nearly got me arrested. What was all that rubbishy behavior on the beach, then?"

"I was dead a couple of years. I was just all hifey from being back in a body, man! I could feel my feet in the sand, the wind in my beard. I had *testicles* again!"

"Got it all out of your system, have you?"

"Totally, John, totally! I'm gonna be chilling after this, I *so* promise!"

Constantine snorted and shook his head. Funny to see the bearded, robed Muslim figure of a man spouting California patois. "What kind of bloody name is Spoink anyway?"

"Oh, you know, I was getting hifey with my boys and I always get to a point where the shit really kicks in and it's like a brain orgasm, dude, and I would always say, 'Here it comes, here it comes . . . it's going to . . . SPOINK!' I don't know why it was *spoink,* that's just how it was in my brain. So they started calling me Spoink. And I feel *all spoink all the time* right now, dude. I just feel like—Hey, I wonder if there's any tunes on this bitch. . . ." Spoink turned to the radio on the cabin cruiser control console, fiddled with it till he found something rhythmic. Turkish dance music, Constantine guessed. Spoink began to hum to himself, rolling his shoulders, snapping his fingers, doing a shuffle across the deck.

"You're getting carried away again, Spoink."

"I *gotta* dance at least once, in this body—tell you what, just one dance, and afterwards I'll be like the vocational dean at my community college. Like I've got a steel rod stuck up my butt. I don't expect to be able to stay in a body long; I got to get what I get while I can get it. I promise—I'll be cool after this. I just need to do a thizzle."

"You what?"

"I got to *thizz,* man, like Mac Dre. You get a look on your face, like this—" He contorted his face like a guy trying to win a gurning contest and began to fling himself around. "That's the 'thizz'—I get a face 'like *thizz.'* Then I *get dumb.*"

"Can't get to someplace you're already at."

"You get loose, you shake your shit, you get a thizz like thizz and you get dumb, that's the thizzle dance, bro. It's the Nation of Thizz-lam. It's about getting loose, letting go of caring what people think, let your primal impulses out!"

Watching Spoink caper about—the body of a fundamentalist fanatic doing the thizzle dance—Constantine ran his fingers through his hair, baffled. "Why you? That's what I can't bloody reckon. Any spirit would've had access to the guy's language, once they were in him. Why'd they send me you?"

"Show you later, man! Come on, Constantine, get dumb!"

"Sod off. Real question is, where do we go now?"

"Azerbaijan, dude!" Spoink said, still dancing. "That's what they told me before I came here. Don't know nothing about it except how to pronounce the name—and it's somewhere up the coast to the north. We can ask around." He flung himself sideways and almost went over the railing. Recovering, he danced about in his robe and beard and turban like a scarecrow in a whirlwind, as he went on: "Then we trade this boat for a plane ride, maybe, if we can find somebody to fly us out to the Mediterranean. Problem is—whoa, *get dumb!*—problem is, I was told they were only allowed to give us a little help. And they pretty much gave it to us already. So I don't know where to go once we get to the Mediterranean." He stopped dancing as the crackly song stopped and a deep voice in Turkish came on the radio, seeming to offer something for sale. "I don't know what the hell we supposed to do there either, Johnny Dude. Only that we're supposed to go there. That Mediterranean's kind of big, isn't it? I mean, it's not like Lake Tahoe?"

Constantine looked at him to see if he were joking. He wasn't. "No it's not fucking like Lake Tahoe." He took a long grateful drag on his cigarette. "Anyhow, I know where to go. Little island called Carthaga . . ."

The northeast coast of Carthaga

The thing in the basement with her was preventing Mercury from traveling outside her body. She was so weak now, it was just as well—she wasn't sure if she could get back in her body anymore, once she left it. But it meant she couldn't cast her mind very far either—she couldn't contact Constantine. Or anyone else. Because of the thing. The thing in the jar.

The thing with the crooked eyes.

The only light in the basement was from a dimming electric lantern sitting on the card table with the gallon jar just behind it. It made a pool of light around the jar. She tried not to look at the jar. But it was always looking at her. That's what it was there for. To keep watch on her. To keep her in check. The ropes weren't enough for a psychic.

They had her tied spread-eagled on the bare mattress of an iron-framed bed. Her wrists and ankles were tied to the posts of the bed with a soft material that held her firmly without cutting off her circulation. She knew they'd tied her that way, almost nude and with her legs apart, to make her feel especially vulnerable; to make her fear they could rape her if they wanted to and would if they felt the slightest inclination. She hated them for it and that worked for them, too, she suspected. Anything to get her emotionally distraught. They wanted to try to twist her around, to break her and use her abilities for their own, somehow. If they decided they couldn't do that, she supposed they'd kill her. She had found out just one thing too much about them.

She could feel the American coming. She felt a deep disgust for Morris, and she feared him almost as much as she feared the thing in the jar.

She tried not to look at the thing, but now her eyes flicked to it, hoping, perhaps, that it'd died in there somehow and had stopped looking at her. She could feel it looking at her, though.

It was like a huge oyster, a thing of slick gray tissue, torn from its shell and squeezed into the jar along with a clear glutinous liquid; it had two naked eyeballs, misaligned; it squirmed about under the glass at times, mucous-filmed green eyes shifting, dilating, focusing, never looking at anything but Mercury lying on the bed. She knew the thing in the jar had been parts of a human being once. She knew it had been a male—a particularly malevolent male. She knew that there was brain matter and nerves and a feeding tube of some kind in there: a throat. She knew that it fed on the other people's brain tissue—she had seen them feed it, scooping brain matter from decapitated heads and smiling at her as they did it, as if to suggest her brain would eventually feed this thing. She knew too that the thing in the jar was kept alive with both magic and perverse science, and that it was all that remained of some long-ago person. . . . She sensed all this. . . .

And she knew that it hated her more than she was capable of hating anything.

Morris, it must be admitted, seemed afraid of the thing in the jar, too—even more than he was afraid of the spiders that dangled in the dark corners of the basement. She had seen his fear of spiders in his mind.

It was Dyzigi who was the keeper of the thing in the jar. An Eastern European with his reddish hair cut into a curious zigzag pattern; eyes like black fish eggs in deep sockets; eyebrows forever arched like the caricaturish eyebrows drawn onto a clown; red, trembling lips; face pale as paper; wearing a crookedly buttoned up lab coat, this was Dyzigi. A Czech perhaps? A Ukrainian? Mercury couldn't be sure because, of all those who came to torment her, to interrogate and sniff at her, his mind was the one most closed to her.

She was so thirsty. So thirsty . . . but she was afraid to ask for something to drink. They would drug her.

She wondered if she'd really made the contact with Constantine that she had seen in her vision before they brought the thing in the jar. He had been on a beach, staring at her. She'd made herself appear to him in the water. Or had she dreamed it? She seemed to slip in and out of dreams, nightmares really, so easily now.

The thing in the jar never took its misaligned eyes from her. . . .

"She is awake, I see," Morris said, coming down the stairs. Dyzigi came down behind Morris, carrying a plastic shopping bag, humming to himself.

The thing in the jar quivered in anticipation of Dyzigi's ministrations. It flicked one eye toward

Dyzigi, keeping the other one always on Mercury.

She felt Morris's eyes on her, too. He looked at her breasts, her crotch. He intended to have her before she was killed. It was difficult to see the two men in the usual visual sense, with the only light being from the dialed-down electric lantern on the table on the other side of the dark basement.

But she had a clear telepathic impression of Morris as he approached her—a kind of psychic snapshot. It was like an image of a tree, with Morris's body as the tree trunk, and the branches spreading out from his head were all the associations of his mind. Thoughts of her led to thoughts of his daughter, and further along that branch, narrowing as it went back in time, like a branch getting smaller toward the end, was the image of some half-remembered little girl Morris had known as a child, and the girl was jeering at him. Many other branches stretched from his head; one of them led to thoughts of helicopters, explosions, marching men, missiles flying. She tried to follow that branch, further and further. She seemed to see an image of a missile, but instead of a nose cone it had a face from church paintings, Jesus Christ, wearing his crown of thorns, all sad benevolence on the tip of a nuclear warhead. Another branch formed in the tree of Morris's thoughts as he looked at her: an image of Mercury, nude, screaming in Morris's arms, his hands squeezing her throat, Dyzigi standing over her with a bone saw, the thing in the jar sitting like a parrot on his shoulder, Dyzigi leering down at her as Morris squeezed and squeezed.

Flickering images, merely. She realized then that Morris didn't know he was having these thoughts. She was seeing into his unconscious. He didn't know he wanted to rape her. He didn't know he wanted to kill her. He thought of himself as a good man making a great sacrifice for the world. He was driven by his makeup, his twisted nature, as if that nature was behind him, shoving him along—it was *behind* his consciousness, which never turned toward it, so he didn't see it driving him. He didn't know what his own desires were. He didn't know the truth about Dyzigi and the whole enterprise he had undertaken. . . . If she could just make him see himself, see Dyzigi as he really was, see it all for what it really was . . .

"Morris . . ." she began, her voice hoarse with thirst. "You think he's one, but . . ."

"She's reading your mind, you idiot," Dyzigi said suddenly, stepping in front of Morris.

Instantly the tree of telepathic imagery was snuffed out, and there was just Dyzigi's face, seeming to hang unsupported in the shadows in front of her, smiling down at her. Then the assault began.

But it wasn't a physical assault. Dyzigi had his own abilities. He was like John Constantine in a way, but he had aligned himself with the entity that Mercury sometimes called "the thinking darkness."

She had just time to say to Morris, "You think he's one but he's the other . . . you think you're one but you're the other. . . ."

Then the full force of Dyzigi's assault hammered down on her, bludgeoning her with visions. She saw a terrible angel, its face radiant with righteous fury, its eyes blue lights, its long streaming white hair merging with lightning as it flew toward her, like a hawk diving for a mouse; it struck and caught her up and carried her into the sky. . . .

"Here," said the angel, *"we can exalt you. Or we can let go of you, and you will fall into the pit of fire. Look you down below. Look and see the destiny of those who fail to serve the Transfiguration."*

She looked down and saw millions of people writhing in a lake of flame—no ordinary flame, it was a combustion of shame and self-hatred, it was self-induced pain, pain at its purest, a purely mental experience, every person thinking they were being subjected to the pain, to the flame, by something above them, and every single one of them generating their own torment.

"Some truth mingled with great lies, that's always been your method," she told the angel.

The angel looked at her in a moment of shuddering fury and she saw its face wrinkle up like a leaf going brown, crumbling, and underneath was another visage: Dyzigi's repugnant face, the face of an evil toddler, a sadistic clown. It spoke:

"If you use your abilities to serve us, you will reign afterwards beside us. If you do not, you will suffer as all the others do, and more. And all that you love will be destroyed. Look here!"

She saw her mother, Marj, then, in a tawdry squat somewhere in Scotland. Late-season snow clung to the window and smoke rose from a rooftop chimney beyond the dirty glass. Her mother, Marj, was standing there, swaying, a bottle of whiskey in her hand.

She lifted the bottle up and smashed it on the window frame.

"Mama! Ma, don't!"

But Marj raised the serrated stub of the bottle and used the broken edges to slash her own throat. Blood spurted to run down the windowpane.

"That is your mother's future if you don't help us. . . ."

"Mama!"

Mercury consolidated her own psychic force in a single desperate act of will, and visualized Dyzigi crushed, smashed into the gallon jar with the crooked-eyes thing, the two of them forced ludicrously into the same space, like a cartoon she'd seen as a child, the thing turning to Dyzigi's screaming face, its gash of a mouth appearing. . . .

It was too much for Dyzigi. There was an all-consuming strobic flash and then the image was gone, the assault—and her abortive retaliation—was ended, and she lay panting on the bed, weeping, as Dyzigi stalked over to the jar, cursing her.

"You nasty little bitch, how dare you . . ." He spoke English perfectly, his accent like cobwebs on the words. He put the shopping bag on the little table, reached inside the bag, and took out the severed head—a black man, eyes staring in horror. The top of the head was already loosened, temporarily replaced like the cap on a jack-o'-lantern. Dyzigi used a spoon to flip the bony top of the head off and dig out the brains, unscrewing the top of the jar with his other hand. He began to feed brains to the thing in the jar. It quivered and twitched and consumed the gray tissue as Dyzigi said, "I'll give you one night to think about it. Then tomorrow, you will be the one united with my friend here. He's been thinking about the taste of your mind for a long time now. . . . Tomorrow he'll know its taste, you arrogant little cow. You nasty, awful, stupid little animal . . . you empty-headed whore of a sow . . ."

6

SHE FLIES ON STRANGE WINGS

The northeast coast of Carthaga, the Mediterranean

An hour past dawn on the shore of another sea. Standing on the Mediterranean shore with Spoink, Constantine watched with relief as the splintery old fiberglass seaplane departed, its engine cutting out and restarting as it went.

"Glad they're gone," he told Spoink. "Couldn't get over the feeling they might cut me throat for tuppence."

"Dude, I was afraid the plane was gonna go down. 'Problem is not, problem is not,' he kept saying, every fucking time the engine stalled."

"The one with the big mustache said they speak a combination of French and Arabic on this island. That brain you're borrowing know any language besides Farsi?"

"He's got a lot of Arabic, too. He was a big mover and shaker in the terrorist sweepstakes, bro. Come on, man. . . ."

"Hold fire a minute. . . ." Constantine closed his eyes, consolidated his energy field, enabled his receptivity to psychic outreach.

Mercury?

He waited . . . no response. He tried again.

Mercury! It's John! Where are you?

Nothing.

He shook his head. "Can't get her. The planetary mind field's gotten as wobbly as cellphone reception. Don't know which bloody way to go. . . ."

"Road's up here, man. I think I hear trucks coming! Come on! Up the hill here . . ."

It was still soft and breezy out, but Constantine could tell it was going to be a hot day. The sun seemed to be working itself up—breathing down his neck and about to leap on his back. "Hope there's a place to get something to eat. Someplace not too well acquainted with dysentery."

And someplace cheap. He'd had to give the Azerbaijanis most of his money as well as the hijacked cabin cruiser to get here. But then there'd been two refueling stops on the way.

They climbed to the top of the rise and found themselves on a two-lane asphalt road, still black from recent construction, following the shore northward toward Poeni—just in time to meet the military convoy coming down the road.

"Oh lovely, hundreds of goits with big guns . . ." Constantine muttered.

It wasn't a big convoy; there were just nine dark green trucks and two armored cars.

"Oi, Spoink, a word to the wise," Constantine muttered, "this would *not* be a good time to do the thizzle dance."

"Right, got it," Spoink said. "I'll be cool."

The lead driver stared at the blond British-looking guy in the trench coat and stuck his hand out the window to signal a stop. The truck pulled up, the whole convoy stopping; the soldier beside the driver leapt out, AK in hand, before the truck had completely stopped. The soldier shouted something in Arabic, pointing the automatic rifle meaningfully at the center of Constantine's chest.

"Says put up your hands," Spoink muttered.

"Really? I thought he was asking me if I wanted to dance," Constantine said dryly, putting his hands up. "Here, mind that bloody Kalashnikov, mate. Keep the safety on, there's a good man-killer."

An armored car drew up beside the truck and an officer got out. He was a smartly uniformed Sudanese Arab—if Constantine rightly identified the flag streaming from the radio antenna of the armored car—and he looked like he wanted an excuse to order his men to open fire. On the way here Constantine had heard there was a conflict in Carthaga. At every fuel stop people had told them, "Don't go there, dangerous now." If these guys were Sudanese, they were part of an invading army.

"You are CIA?" the officer snapped in English.

Constantine shook his head. "Me? I'm a Brit, ah—" He looked at the bars on the man's shoulders and took a stab at his rank. "Major?"

"A Britisher? So you are MI6."

"What's all this about secret services, then?"

"You have come here very close to a battlefield, and you are from the United Kingdom, and they are not friendly to the Sudan. The tourists have been evacuated from this island, so you are not tourist. British and American businessmen also evacuated. So who else are you? MI6! They are angry about Darfur. . . ." He shrugged.

"That's not a bad guess, actually," Constantine said, looking the major's men over. Mostly small arms. No cannon towed along, nothing big. "Except of course it's all wrong, mate, all arsy-versy. I'm staying out of The Firm's way, I am. See that plane? You can just make it out, against the clouds there. Almost gone. It's a seaplane. . . ."

"Yes, I see an aircraft," the Major said, staring out over the sea, shading his eyes. "I cannot see what kind. What of it?"

"They dropped us off, just now. They were supposed to take us to Poeni—where we're supposed to meet our baggage—but they got wind that you boys were moving against the enemy. Dumped us here and buggered off before they could get caught up in the war. Afraid the Carthagans would take them for one of yours, open fire on them. Worked out, though, didn't it? I was looking for you lot. Me catalogs are in the baggage, but we can just wing it, see what your needs are. . . ."

"What? What are you talking about, this catalog?"

Spoink looked at Constantine as if he'd like to ask the same question.

"Arms and military supplies," Constantine said nonchalantly. "Where's me card? . . ." He slapped the pockets of his coat. "Bugger me, they're all in the briefcase—with the baggage. Not to worry, I'll get it to you later. My sources tell me you've got a crying need for cannon. But here, I'm not introducing myself proper." Constantine stuck out his hand to shake, smiling like a salesman who senses a big score is just around the bend. "*J. Constantine,* arms sales. We specialize in discounted American weapons and some very nice Israeli and Russian ordnance."

The major looked at Constantine's outstretched hand, then peered at the speck that was all that remained of the seaplane. He was clearly reluctant to buy into the story about arms dealers getting dropped off on the beach in the middle of a war. Arms dealings were usually done in high-tone hotels, sometimes at armament conventions, or in the back rooms of embassies. Still—there were known to be some opportunists out there. And this war was a very sudden opportunity. At last he took Constantine's hand and shook it, once. "I am Major Abbide."

"I've got some beautiful cannon for you, Major. Half regular price."

"Half? Why?"

"Because . . . we kind of fell into them. They were intended for the Iraqi army but, ah, we've got some old chums at Halliburton, steered 'em our way on the QT. . . . Need to get them off our hands quick. A little steamy they are, if you catch my meaning."

"What kind of cannon you say you get me?"

"Ah, what kind . . ." Constantine knew bugger all about weapons. "Oh you know, the big . . . Caramel . . . iz . . . koffs."

" 'Karamelizkoffs'?" Abbide frowned. "I do not know this manufacturer."

He fairly radiated suspicion. Constantine consolidated his energy, reached out with his psychic field, and gently probed Abbide's mind by visualizing cannons, stimulating an associative response in Abbide's unconscious. With any luck the answer would come in English, like most of the catalogs Abbide would've seen.

"I do not buy weapons I do not know," Abbide was saying. Then he blinked, and shivered. Muttered to himself in Arabic.

Constantine almost had it. . . .

Spoink decided he had to translate the Arabic muttering. "Says he's feeling . . ."

"Shut your gob, I'll tell you when to translate," Constantine said, as if annoyed with an underling. Wasn't hard to act that one out, neither.

"If you have nothing familiar to me," Abbide said, "I must wonder if you are truly—"

"How about a self-propelled howitzer?" Constantine said quickly, reading it out of the telepathic image that he'd harvested from Abbide's mind. He had a clear-cut catalog-style image of something like a tank but lower to the ground, slower, a portable platform for a cannon. He read aloud the text under the image: "The 155-mm M109 series, self-propelled medium howitzers. Transportable in phase III of airborne operations, don't you know. They have a cruising range of . . . of 220 miles at speeds up to 35 miles per hour, Major. Combat loaded, why, one of these babies weighs a mere 27.5 tons. More important they've got a range of 23,500 meters—98 pound projectile. Part the bastards' hair with that, eh?"

He turned to Spoink and made a close-your-mouth motion with his hand.

"Mmmm," Abbide said, rubbing his chin. "Portable howitzer. Twenty-three thousand meters, you say. Very nice. Half price. How could you get them here, though, in time to be of use to us?"

"We have a ship in the area. We can off-load the little beauties by night. Say—ten of them? Tomorrow night?"

"You have so many nearby?"

"I do. But you'll have to transfer some money by wire—a twenty-five percent deposit."

"I will speak to my government. Come, bring your man into my transport, we are about to break camp. We will have some breakfast."

"I'd love a cuppa, Major. . . ."

Southeastern Carthaga

A yellow half-moon shone down on an impromptu cemetery as Captain Simpson guided the chopper to a landing near the crossroads. Morris and his new assistant got out of the Blackhawk, ducking under the slowing blades, followed by two black North Africans in ragged caftans and sandals, carrying shovels and looking completely dissatisfied with this gig. Simpson and Burlington waited in the helicopter. All but the men in caftans wore Carthagan uniforms. None were Carthagan.

Abbide's men had improvised hasty graves for the

Sudanese soldiers fallen in the gunship's attack. Morris pointed out a grave close to the crossroads. The tall, cadaverous man the SOT had assigned as his assistant, Hanz Strucken, directed the men in caftans to begin digging. They muttered imprecations against evil, kissed the charms hanging about their necks, and set to work with shovels. Watching Strucken, with his quiet air of authority, Morris suspected the German had been assigned to him only as a kind of babysitter—a sinister babysitter—to make sure he didn't stray from the agenda. He knew himself to be expendable at this point, though he had brought certain key players into the SOT's end game with him—certain powerful American congressmen, and an oil mogul with Israeli connections—and he had a good grasp of the Prompting Ritual. He also had the necessary baseline conviction to make the invocations work. This intangible quality—"telepathically charged fanaticism" was Dyzigi's term for it—was rare.

Still, they could find someone else. And he sometimes wondered if what they had in mind for the end game was what he had planned and prayed for. The inner circle of the SOT claimed to have the same goals as Morris—but it was difficult to trust Dyzigi. He seemed to be all too comfortable with that unwholesome thing in the jar. Coggins, though, he could trust. They understood one another. He wasn't sure about the Scotsman, who went by MacCrawley.

"We are there," Strucken said, gesturing at the shallow grave. A body, with sand stuck to the blood around the chain of 16 mm wounds across its torso, lay sprawled, staring up with eyes that reflected the moon. The reek of death rose from the corpse, as if expressing the dead man's spirit wanting to retaliate for the massacre. *Smell my death. Anticipate your own.* Morris shuddered—one had strange thoughts on errands like these.

Best focus on the work at hand. "Remove the head," Morris ordered.

Strucken nodded, repeating the order to the workmen in their own language.

The two black men looked at one another and began arguing, Morris guessed, about which one would do that chore.

"Schwachkopfen!" Strucken muttered, pushing them aside. He grabbed the shovel and used its blade like an ax, handily sliced through the decayed neck with a squelching sound. Black, gummed-up blood spattered. He took a pair of rubber gloves from his coat, tugged them on, and picked up the head by its hair. Thick effluvia dripped like mud from the severed neck.

Morris thought how strange it was he'd come to take part in an undertaking like this one. But you changed, working with the SOT. You accepted strange things, dark things. You were planning for the end of the world, after all. Everyone would be done for in the bodily sense. All would become spirit. Some in Hell, some in Heaven. What they did to prepare the way really didn't matter. Spirit was above all this muck. And they'd earned their condemnation, their time in this spiritual sewer—they were all paying for humanity's original sin.

He had no serious doubts. He knew that he was doing the bidding of Spirit. He had seen the angel. He had been lifted up, and he'd been shown the future. There was simply no doubt at all. It had been such a powerful experience that he'd been spaced out afterwards, for a couple of days, almost hung over.

"Now," Morris said, "if you would put it in the box there, we will go on to the other grave."

"Are you sure this one is suitable, Herr Morris?" Strucken asked.

"I am. I don't need to do any tests. He is within the requisite distance. The old books are quite explicit. Do as I asked, please."

"Yes sir."

The head was stowed and they opened the second grave. Another corpse, another head removed. That was it. Two was all they could take from this site—except of course for the seed skull.

They found the place in the crossroads—a dirt road here—where they had buried the seed skull long before. The two workmen were set to digging it up. Ten minutes of painstaking work—they must not damage the skull with spade thrusts—and they found a lump wrapped in tanned, tattooed human skin. Strucken knelt and unwrapped the skull, just to make certain it was undamaged, and the African workmen were particularly distressed when they saw it staring up from the hole, perhaps because the runes carved on its forehead seemed to glimmer in the moonlight and a breeze sprang up from nowhere to whistle through its empty eye sockets.

Strucken rewrapped the seed skull, placed it with the other two heads in the velvet-lined wooden crate they'd brought along for the purpose, and immediately stepped back, hands on his hips, nodding in satisfaction. "Yes, you see, Herr Morris? You were right. This is the correct response, eh?"

Morris looked closer and nodded, seeing that the other two heads, with their coat of flesh still attached, were snarling, their eyes moving sightlessly, teeth gnashing. . . .

The workmen, seeing life in severed heads, stumbled backward, hands raised in signs against malevolence.

"Tell them to fill in the graves; it'll keep them busy," Morris said.

But the workmen had started running, scurrying off into the darkness. A light speared out from the Blackhawk, followed by jets of fire from the 16 mm machine gun. Burlington chuckled to himself as the two men went down, wailing.

"Was that really necessary?" Morris wondered aloud.

"Yes, I think it was," Strucken said. "Although the original plan was to drop them in the sea."

Morris looked at him. "Oh? *Whose* plan? I'm in charge tonight."

Strucken shrugged. "Shall we take the three seeds to the helicopter, sir? It will soon be time to make more. We have an appointment—the assault is to begin soon. . . ."

Farther south in Carthaga

"John! Wake up! It's after dark!"

"Whuh? Makes no sense. Supposeta shleep affer dark."

"You've been sleeping all day, dude. We've gotta

book outta here, Abbide's coming back; he thinks you're gonna sell him tanks an' shit. We gotta split before he figures out you were all fo'danglin' him."

Constantine sat up, yawning. "I was whatin' him? Were you a white American loony when you died or a black American loony?"

"I was white—but all my heroes were black."

Constantine looked around, remembering that Abbide had gone on some kind of extended recon mission around noon. He'd stretched out to have a smoke in the tent they'd been assigned, and boom, he'd fallen dead asleep. His first real rest since leaving the monastery. "Is that a cup of tea in your hand? And food?"

"Yeah. Something here made out of mashed garbanzos and some bread. I had some—it isn't bad. But it's all going through me fast."

"What d'you mean, going through you?" Constantine asked, taking the tea. He could hear soldiers moving about outside; vehicles rumbling, weapons and gear clanking, grim laughter.

"Got stomach cramps and runs from that kabob we ate on the plane."

"I fucking warned you not to eat that old muck of theirs. Smelled all wrong."

"John—you know what I'm remembering now? Not everything about being in a body is good! Oh shit, my stomach—I feel like kinda, like, nostalgic for being a freefloating spirit again. . . . Ow!" Spoink sat at the end of a cot and clutched his stomach.

Constantine took a chance on the mashed garbanzos and vinegar, wrapped in flat bread, and drank his tea.

"Been almost a year since I've had some proper breakfast. Eggs fried with tomatoes, a couple of rashers—"

"Oh fuck!" Spoink lurched for the door and, clawing at his robe, stumbled out to find a sewage trench.

Constantine located one of his last three cigarettes and lit it, trying to remember the dream he'd had. Should have written it down first thing. But with a bloody terrorist possessed by a California hip-hop skateboarder waving a cup of tea under his nose . . . Wait a mo, now. . . . He almost had it. . . .

Two eyes floating in a jar . . . move away from the jar, go up a stairs . . . At the top of the stairs, Mercury's mother, Marj, with her throat cut, reaching out for him, weeping. She takes some of the blood from her oozing throat onto the tip of a finger, and applies it like lipstick and then makes to kiss him. . . . Then he's rushing from the house, Marj, weeping, in close pursuit. . . . The house is near a marina. . . . Not a marina in the UK— he knows somehow it's here, in the Mediterranean. The houses nearby are like the ones they passed in Carthaga. A white motor yacht moored nearby. Biggest motor yacht he's ever seen . . . a name on it—"Noah"? Then . . . two eyes floating in a jar . . . an angel with a wound for a mouth . . . two eyes . . . floating . . . following him . . .

"John! Dude!" It was Spoink, capering at the entrance to the tent.

"Christ on a bike—what is it now, Spoink?"

"We're about to get killed, man. Well, killed again, in my case, I guess—"

"What the bloody hell are you—"

The explosion blew the tent up into the air, the tarp

flapping like a disease-maddened bat, Constantine and Spoink knocked down by a wave of heated air. They were on the outer edge of the blast, and neither was seriously hurt—they were mostly just rattled as they got to their feet, coughing in the smoke from the crater, to see two fighter jets roaring over. Other explosions were going off around the camp. The fighter jets had fired air-to-surface missiles at the Sudanese, and Constantine, his ears ringing from the blast, got his feet under him, but crouched, lifting his head just enough to catch a dim glimpse of soldiers coming at the camp, some of them firing their weapons. The attackers were mostly silhouettes as they came, strobically lit by muzzle flashes. Bullets slashed the air around him and Spoink. Those Sudanese not killed by the airstrike returned fire. The ground shook with mortar blasts; the air thundered.

A Sudanese soldier running by with a gun in each hand noticed Constantine standing there gaping and unarmed and tossed him a rifle. Constantine automatically caught it, as the man ran off to get into position.

Constantine looked at the gun in his hand. He looked at the men rushing toward him, firing. . . .

And he threw the gun into the dirt.

"Come on, Spoink, hurry the fuck up!" Constantine yelled, turning to run the other way. "Let's scarper!"

"I'm with you, dude!"

The two men ran between the remaining tents and leapt over hummocks of earth, expecting at any moment to feel the distinct and vivid sensation of a bullet in the spine. *A once-in-a-lifetime experience, that'd be*, Constantine thought.

They dodged into an olive orchard behind the camp. The orchard was already chewed up by mortar fire, half the small silvery green trees on fire, some of the others uprooted.

They came to a still smoking crater and leapt into it, as a spate of automatic-rifle rounds whipped through the air where they'd been a moment before. Keeping low, coughing from the sulfurous smoke, Constantine turned and peered over the rim of the crater, looking back at the battle. He couldn't make out much—mostly just flashes in the darkness, a fleeting sight of enraged faces, pockets of flame. Screams and gunfire echoed to him.

"Who the fuck is it attacking us?" Spoink asked.

"Carthagans, I reckon. The major said his men were here to support some kind of Arab uprising against a minority government. I'm guessing that's the minority's army. Don't look like the bloody minority to me. They've got the majority of the firepower around here. Abbide's been advancing into their territory—naturally they get shirty about it." He looked up as the F-16s flew over, the other way. "Could be that's the whole Carthagan air force though."

"Naw, man—look at that chopper!"

Constantine saw it then: A dun-colored gunship, coming in low over the fields, its rotors a glimmer in the firelight. It slowed to hover over what remained of the camp, and in a flash of gunfire from below, Constantine thought he saw a small glassy something thrown from a window of the chopper. A moment later there came an upburst of yellow smoke or powder, spreading out in the rotor wash.

What was it? Constantine wondered. Gas warfare? Smokescreen?

Then he saw a curious thing. The billowing smoke—visible in the light from a burning tent near the chopper—was forming into a specific shape, an enormous head that kept reasserting its shape on the smoke, as if the head were made of a clear crystal and the smoke was filling the transparent vessel from within. The head—bigger than the helicopter—turned this way and that, a face like a viciously feral Neanderthal, but with spikes in place of fur on its head, and great interlacing tusks. Hadn't he seen that face somewhere—in some temple painting? He didn't think so. Yet it looked so *familiar*. Strangely familiar . . .

The face opened its mouth, wide, seeming about to howl, but instead of sound a ripple of energy spread out from its quivering lips, as if the unheard soundwaves were visibly compressing the air. Soundwaves that were visible but not audible. The giant head vanished and reappeared, flickering in and out of visibility.

He heard a renewed roar of gunfire and shouting. . . .

He felt strange himself—a sort of heat was entering him, coming from that translucent head, spreading like a fire that raced along the branchings of his nervous system. He had mental images of going to find the gun he'd tossed away, of picking it up and firing at the men who'd invaded the Sudanese camp.

He chuckled and shook his head. *As if I was loyal to anyone's camp; anyone's army.*

He shrugged the impulse off—he'd had a lot of experience resisting psychic influences and his time with the Blue Sheikh had increased his resistance to them. It'd been an important part of his training. But he was fascinated, looking at the flickering outline of the great demonic head. Was it in fact a demon? Or something else?

It was as if the creature glimpsed in the smoke had thrust its head through a dimensional hole into the human world, with the rest of its body remaining in the Hidden World; like a man in a manhole, partway up the ladder, with only his head showing. But this thing's body was not literally underground—it was emerging from the left, the right, from above and below. Only the filters of the human mind made it seem to come from underground.

Constantine felt the old frisson, looking at the penetration of this world by the Hidden World. He once more felt the excitement, the high that he got from the clashing of those two worlds. He felt a dread, too—a dread of what this could portend, a dread of his own part in it; a fear of making it all worse, as he'd done more than once. But the dread was a component of the thrill that kept him coming back to the glimmering candle of magic, despite the foul things flapping around that flame. . . . No ordinary moths . . .

The gunship was opening fire now. It seemed to Constantine it was firing quite indiscriminately into the men below. It didn't seem to be aiming at the Sudanese in particular. Anyone was a target. It soon became evident that no wounded were to be left behind.

The brutish face of the entity—demon or god?—

took on more definition, triggering a deep, hot shudder in Constantine. . . .

A picture flashed through his mind then, a vivid image with the nagging quality of memory—but a memory of something that had never happened to him.

The light came from a natural hole in the ceiling of the cave, a rugged shaft, a vertical crack, really, that rose crookedly up to show a little sky, diffuse sunlight.

At the base of the shaft was the remains of a stone altar. On the altar was a broken skull, incised with markings familiar to Konz: the invocation to N'Hept.

But the skull was smashed; an intact skull was needed. . . .

"John!" Spoink shouted, bringing Constantine back to the crisis at hand. "They're just murdering people! People begging for their lives! Oh shit—what'd I come back to this sucky world for, dude?"

"Wondering that meself," Constantine muttered. What the hell had he just seen? An altar in a cave somewhere? When had he ever been there? Was it a memory from the past life the Blue Sheikh had mentioned?

"Fuck those bastards!" Spoink burst out. "It pisses me off! Mowing people down like that! I feel like getting me a fucking gun, man—"

"Get a grip—it's a psychic influence, you nit. And who's *this* oik now?"

A man dark as eggplant, his white teeth bared, was rushing out of the smoke toward them, armed with an M-16: American army surplus, it looked like. He wore what Constantine took to be a Carthagan uniform. He stopped with one foot on the rim of the crater, a yard away, shouted an imprecation in some language Constantine didn't recognize, and popped the rifle to his shoulder.

"Here, mate, I'm not an enemy!" Constantine said, knowing it was hopeless. He tried reaching out with his own psychic influence, but the man was afire with kill lust, and it was like spitting into a flamethrower.

But after a moment, Constantine noticed the soldier wasn't firing the gun. The soldier noticed it, too—he looked down at the M-16, gabbling furiously, shaking the weapon, slapping at the magazine to try to shake loose what he supposed was a jammed mechanism.

Constantine felt it then—a power emanating from just behind him. He turned to see Spoink holding out a hand, staring at the gun, his hand quivering as it exuded telekinetic force. He had his tongue pinned between his front teeth and looked to be struggling to maintain his hold on the M-16.

As he exerted his power, grimacing, he managed to say, "That's why they said I could help you. . . . I'm telekinetic. But . . . not strong, John—you got to grab the gun and thump him with it!"

The soldier was still trying to clear the gun, not realizing Spoink had frozen its mechanism telekinetically.

"I can't thump him, I'm not a bloody thug!" Constantine glanced at the gunship—the emanation from the giant head had ceased, the smoke was dispersed. But the soldier was still psyched to kill.

"You gotta do something, dude, I'm losing control of the gun, he's . . . oh shit, he's coming at you!"

Constantine turned to see the man had given up trying to fire the gun and was gripping it like a club, swinging it at Constantine's head. Constantine stepped back, the gun barrel swishing past. The soldier tried out the only English words he knew: "You die, fucker boy!" And he smacked the rifle butt into Constantine's breadbasket.

Constantine doubled up, the breath knocked out of him. The soldier brought his knee up, cracking Constantine on the chin and knocking him on his arse.

"Grab his gun, John!" Spoink yelled again.

"*You* grab the bloody fucking gun!" Constantine wheezed.

"What? *Me?*"

Glaring, panting, the man stood over Constantine, preparing to bring the rifle butt down on his skull— then the soldier did a sort of dance and spun around as a burst of gunfire caught him in the shoulder. Another shot took the soldier through the back and he fell over, heavily limp, facedown.

Still gasping, Constantine struggled to his feet to see Abbide, smoking Uzi in hand, gesturing for them to get into his armored car.

Spoink stared in horror down at the dead man. "Oh man. I'm not down with blowing people's bodies apart. . . ."

"A minute ago you were ready to do it yourself," Constantine pointed out. He was still getting his wind back. Black spots danced before his eyes.

"Hurry!" the major shouted as he ran back to the driver's side of the armored car. He stared for a moment at the driver—saw that he was dead, shot through the windshield by a stray bullet—and pulled him out of his seat, dumping him unceremoniously on the road. He climbed up behind the wheel. "There is no more battle, we have lost; they catch us by surprise! It's only massacre now! Come, get in, we go!"

Grimacing with the ache in his gut, Constantine climbed into the armored car behind Spoink. He settled into a seat beside Abbide, looking over at the yellow cloud where the gunship had been.

Both were gone, cloud and Blackhawk—unless that dark spot blotting stars at the horizon was the chopper, flying off—and all that remained was flame, licking up from the battlefield.

7

VENI, VIDI . . . AND I BUGGERED OFF

Not far from Poeni, Carthaga

"Has it occurred to you, Morris," Dyzigi said, "that this creature is probably still trying to contact her allies. The little whore will call our enemies down upon us if she gets through."

"Your pet in the jar," Morris observed, looking at it from the top of the stairs, "is supposed to keep her power from reaching beyond this room. So you told me." The jar was faintly self-luminous, he noted, but luminous in an unhealthy way, like burning methane.

Feeding the thing in the jar, glancing over at the bound girl thrashing in delirium on the bed frame, Dyzigi muttered, "I believe the negative ambiance from our friend Mengele here should do it—but I am not completely reassured—"

"Did you say . . . *Mengele?*"

"Yes. I never told you? The very fellow. A historical marvel we have in that jar, eh?"

"You don't actually mean—Josef Mengele? The Nazi monster?"

"Yes I did and do . . . oh, I see—you heard about his death, you feel this cannot be him. The story that was put about was wrong. This is Mengele. What remains of him. I obtained these remains, along with his soul, just as he was dying; used an ancient charm that was still surprisingly potent, as you see—"

"Never mind how he died. But—the idea of being associated with him . . . that man was . . . was . . ."

"I thought we agreed that the so-called powers of darkness were all a part of God's plan in bringing about the Transfiguration, eh?" There was a subtle quality of mockery in Dyzigi's voice, though his face, one side lit a sickly blue by the faint shine from the jar, was quite grave. "They are not the powers of darkness if they're merely gray. That would be the powers of mildness. No. The powers of darkness are as black as the pit, my friend. Like petroleum. But we burn petroleum to make our cars go. It has a place."

"Yes, well, they are part of the plan for the acceleration of time, but that doesn't mean we associate with them as if they were . . . were chums. I mean—do we really need this thing here?"

Dyzigi shrugged. "Look at the grand tapestry—it is all of a piece. Why, the book of Revelations calls for the coming of the Antichrist, before the Christ can make his appearance. The seeming triumph of the Fallen must happen first. The tapestry of God's design would be incomplete without the dark threads."

Morris seemed to hear a warning voice in his head: *A little truth mixed with great lies. . . .*

He shook himself. He must ignore that. Invasive thoughts from some diabolic source.

"Now to return to the matter at hand," Dyzigi said, "I do believe we need to kill the girl."

"What? Why? How can she be any danger now? She's quite . . . delirious. Harmless in this state."

"How can you be so naïve? She's likely in a sort of trance—a shamanistic, diabolic trance, attempting to reach those who would rescue her. Mengele may not be able to contain her forever. She meant us no good when she came poking her long nose in our affairs, Morris. We cannot make use of her. She is like a ball bearing, rolling around the floor—we will trip over her in time. She must die. I know you are . . . ah, interested in her. If you would like to make use of her body, why, I'm sure, considering the wicked purposes she must have, God will forgive you."

"Make use of her . . . ? What nonsense!"

"I can leave you alone with her. You may say your good-byes any way you choose. But she must die, when you are . . . when your good-byes are over."

Dyzigi closed the top of the jar with a businesslike twist of his fingers, put the remainders of the latest feeding head—an old Arab woman—into the shopping bag, and carried it with him as he climbed the stairs, humming to himself. He was humming "The Blue Danube." A few moments later, Morris heard him calling Strucken, to dispose of the woman's head.

Morris was left alone with Mercury.

A road along the Carthagan coast

"Yes," said Abbide, "that would be the only marina big enough for such a boat—not far from Poeni. But I cannot go there! They will see me! They will kill me! I must flee the island! I must go the opposite way—I must radio to be picked up! Or perhaps you can call your ship to pick us up?"

"Call my . . .? Oh right!" Constantine nodded earnestly, bracing himself against the metal dashboard of the armored car as they took a tight curve. He winced at the grab of inertia—and so did Spoink, both of them having gut aches for different reasons. Constantine had a big bruise from that rifle butt just under his rib cage.

He had to turn Abbide around somehow—they were driving exactly opposite the way Constantine needed to go. "Right, I'll call them. In fact, it'd help if you'd pull over here, mate, and I'll be able to use the radio here, from this spot, I reckon. . . ."

He could sense Spoink staring at him, wondering what he was up to. He hoped the fool would keep his gob stoppered.

Abbide grunted and looked around to see that no one was following them. He pulled the armored car up, stopped the engine, and turned to Constantine, frowning. "You are making some deception with me, perhaps?"

"Deception? *Me?*" Constantine looked at him in astonishment. Stanislavsky would have been impressed. "Just want to show you something, mate—look here." He drew an object from his pocket, wrapped in a tissue. He'd been carrying it for a year. Lucky it was still there. He opened the tissue, revealing a piece of jade, two inches high, carved into the shape of a bearded man: a figure of Zoroaster. "You see this lucky li'l fella here? Got an amazing property, it does. Now look . . ."

"We have no time for this!"

"Just a quick look—we can use it to barter our way out of here, if we have to." He held the little Zoroaster between his thumb and forefinger and rubbed the top of the carving's head with the index finger of his other hand—and immediately it pulsed with an inner light that began at its base and rose in a circle of shine up the figure to hover like a halo over its head.

Abbide's eyes went through the cycle from astonishment to suspicion; they widened, then narrowed. But he kept looking at the carving. "What *is* this? Witchcraft, of some kind!"

"Amazin' innit? Look closer. . . ."

Abbide did lean a little closer, fascinated despite himself—and then his eyes glazed.

"We're not going south, Major Abbide," Constantine said. He said it in his mind at the same time, with a kind of mental echo he'd long ago learned; he said it in the center of his being, and he kept his dominating intent always before him, never allowing his mind to stray from it for a millisecond as he spoke; all these factors harmonized in him so that he emanated mesmeric power. "You don't want to do that. You want to go north. See that marina. We'll get as close as we can. Might have to change uniforms somewhere. Then you'll be off to the Sudan, where you'll denounce this whole Carthaga campaign. . . . Right?"

Abbide muttered something in his own language,

seeming to feel some conflict, struggling to get free of the hypnosis.

"Spoink," Constantine whispered, "repeat what I said to him in Arabic. Keep your voice gentle, but definite."

Spoink repeated the directions as Constantine chimed in mentally, projecting his will onto Abbide as he did so, focusing his resolve through the little carving he held in his fingers the way light is focused through a magnifying glass.

This was not the ordinary hypnosis-by-suggestion. Ordinary hypnosis uses psychological suggestion; this sort uses *psychic* suggestion. Constantine was using the true "animal magnetism" of Mesmer.

"Yes . . ." Abbide said at last. "We must go . . . and find marina. . . . Let us go. Let us waste no more time. The task is urgent. . . ." He repeated the same thing in Arabic.

"Constantine," Spoink muttered, when they were back on the road, Abbide driving along like a zombie chauffeur, "you're starting to scare me."

"Me, too, mate. Me, too."

But what scared him was that brutish, demonic face he'd seen at the battle—floating above the free-associative stream of his mind. Never quite going away. And always it had that tormenting tang of familiarity.

He knew that face—somehow he knew that face was etched into his genes. Into the buried memories stored away somewhere in his very soul . . .

And he heard, again, the Blue Sheikh's words: *I seem to see you—differently. I hear a name. Konz. . . .*

Carthaga, the battlefield near the olive orchard

The returning gunship settled down on the ground near the scene of the battle. A massacre, really, Dyzigi reflected with satisfaction, as he looked around at the scattered corpses. None of the combatants moved— only human scavengers moved here, starveling locals picking over the corpses. As the chopper landed the scavengers ran off into the darkness of the ravaged olive orchard.

Dyzigi nodded to MacCrawley and the two men got out of the helicopter, with its rotors still slowly beating time overhead, a time slow as a funeral march. They had brought along three SOT operatives this time, including Strucken: a team used to dirty work. They'd had to explain to Simpson, piloting, and Burlington on the gun, that these men were not to be shot afterwards. Simpson had shrugged; Burlington was noticeably disappointed.

MacCrawley signaled Strucken to commence work on the bodies. "We must get through this, and soon; the timetable is crowded. . . ." Though a Scot, MacCrawley used no Scottish expressions and had only the faintest burr. He had been educated at Eton and Oxford. He was a shortish man with wide shoulders, a broad-seamed face in which were bristling black eyebrows, pale gray eyes, a prominent chin; he was in fact related to the sorcerer Aleister Crowley, related rather closely, but his father had changed the family name to an older form in order to avoid the association. MacCrawley wore a dark suit, double breasted and expensively tailored; he disdained attempts at camouflage. "Where is the general?" MacCrawley asked, turning to Dyzigi.

"Coggins?" Dyzigi shrugged. "Off checking the 'nukes' as he insists on calling it."

"Best keep your voice down—or better yet, use the code word. Call it 'The Blossom.'"

Dyzigi nodded, though there was little chance that anyone could hear or would care, in this place. "The Blossom is in place, but there is a problem with the launch vehicle in Paris—Coggins is looking into it." He watched as Strucken and his assistants, their faces covered in black ski masks, set about removing another head.

"Good seed heads," MacCrawley said. "I can sense it. He will groan with pleasure, and soon."

"He showed himself quite clearly to those who can see the Hidden World, at this very spot tonight," Dyzigi said. "I saw it. It was merely Its head—but I saw it clearly."

"Did the soldiers see it?"

"They saw only their own red fury."

"Then all is well."

"I worry, though, about Coggins and Morris—"

"Yes, all that bunch. They may break off from us if they suspect. . . ."

Dyzigi lowered his voice even more. "They still think we're bringing their Christian apocalypse about."

MacCrawley chuckled. "They will soon be disabused. . . ."

"But perhaps they are no longer necessary?"

"They have talents we need. They will interpret everything, right up to the end, as relating to the book of Revelations. They interpret things that way all the time—things that have nothing to do with the book of Revelations. They impose their Rorschach inkblot on the world." He shrugged. "They will deceive themselves."

"They may learn how close the world came to triggering their little apocalypse a few years ago. That particular emanation . . ."

"Yes, I understand that a certain Scouse bastard got in the way of that."

"Who?"

"Oh, John Constantine. The bane of my family, really. Of so many others. A low-class magician, street trash operating out of London last I knew. Still he has his gifts, puzzlingly enough—he seems to have forestalled Lucifer himself. Actually got out of a written contract with him."

"Really! John Constantine, you say . . . I may have seen his dossier." Dyzigi turned to point out a third body—they needed three heads from this site. Then he turned suddenly back to MacCrawley. "Constantine . . . He is not a blond fellow, early middle aged? And ah—in a trench coat?"

"He is. Don't tell me. . . . No! I went to such trouble to keep him distracted from this!"

"I recently received word that an Englishman who witnessed one of our assassinations—of the Blue Sheikh in fact—is believed to be one 'John Constantine.' "

"Oh blazes. And they let him get away?"

"So I am told. Trevino and Morris were behind that little task. They seemed to think the Blue Sheikh might bring the Prophet Muhammad into this, or even Zoroaster himself."

"Idiots! They should know that if the Blue Sheikh allowed them to kill him, the Sheikh *wanted* it to happen!"

"Was he really such an adept?"

"You have no idea! And Constantine was with him—which is something I arranged, to take the Scouse sorcerer out of the picture. I would have killed him, but he had certain people allied with him I did not want to make my enemies, the so-called 'Swamp Thing' amongst others. And now Constantine will have taken an interest!"

"The word has gone out," Dyzigi said, shrugging, "to kill Constantine as soon as possible."

"It isn't enough to kill him! John Constantine is too dangerous. Now that he is against us, Constantine's soul itself must be controlled—or *utterly annihilated!*"

⟶━◉━⟵

Morris was afraid of what the others might do when they found out he had taken the girl to his yacht.

Dyzigi had marked her with the Sign, to contain her psychic powers, but he insisted that she was to die, and soon. He wanted to feed her to his pet in the jar, to increase its powers. The thing that was what remained of Josef Mengele.

What was the point of killing her, really? All evil would soon be eradicated from the world. They were on the verge of the Transfiguration and all evil would be gone, including that thing in the jar. Dyzigi himself would have the evil in his own soul wiped away. Evil was a necessary ingredient in the recipe for the great libation the world would be drinking, and it would be digested soon enough.

Morris looked at the young woman on the bed of his cabin, barely conscious, her eyes slitted, murmuring to herself. She was tied down, she was passive— he could have her, in the gross, purely physical way, anytime he wanted. But he hoped to find some way to make her voluntarily his. He wanted her spirit to open to him, not just her legs. He sensed some great unconscious rapport between them. She could be his consort in Paradise, if she would only convert. Perhaps, a bit later, he might read the Bible to her. Just now, he took a certain satisfaction in gazing at her the way his father had looked at some new piece of art, purchased for his collection. Oh, her tender young breasts . . .

He thought he heard voices, coming from the deck overhead. Had Strucken returned already? He had truly begun to fear Strucken.

There should be only one man there, only Beerfield. He had sent the other guards away, after Strucken had gone off on an errand with MacCrawley—the guards were Dyzigi's men and he did not trust them with the girl here.

He shook his head, wondering what was becoming of the complete commitment he'd felt to Dyzigi and the Servants of Transfiguration. He should trust them implicitly if he was going to work with them, shouldn't he?

Persistent footsteps on the deck overhead. Someone coming to the hatch, thumping down the ladder.

"Beerfield!" he called. "Who is here?" It might well be Coggins, back from Tel Aviv. Hopefully with good news about The Blossom.

There was a clattering of steps in the passage, and then Beerfield stumbled into the cabin, his hands raised. Someone was forcing him in with an assault rifle poked in the big, red-faced guard's back.

"I'm sorry, boss," Beerfield said, "They got the drop on me. Jeez, the guy had a uniform on like he was from the government or something; they said they were just here to get your papers—"

Three men crowded into the stateroom behind Beerfield. One of the men, an Arab in uniform with his mouth slightly open and his eyes unfocused, Morris immediately suspected to be under an enchantment, or possibly hypnotized. The others were a man who looked like he might be Iranian, and a blond fellow in a trench coat, scowling at him as he looked at Mercury on the bunk.

Morris suspected he knew who this was. Someone whose death he had ordered, recently. That assassination didn't seem to be working out.

"Untie her, you vile dirty-fingered wanker," John Constantine said. "And get this floating mansion under way. Where we're going, I don't know. But we're buggering out of bloody Carthaga before anyone else fires a fucking missile my way."

8

A HEART FULLA NAPALM

The Mediterranean Sea, off the coast of North Africa

"What brought you here, to this vessel?" Morris asked, as he eased off the throttle in the bridge of the big motor yacht. "A simple impulse to piracy? You'd make a helluva pirate, Mr. Constantine—you lack only the parrot."

"I had information that she'd be on the biggest yacht in that marina," Constantine said, "and this was it. Right—we've gone far enough for now. Set it to just coast along, say a knot at a time. . . ."

"You don't know what a nautical knot is, do you, Mr. Constantine?" Morris sniffed.

"If it's not some bloody thing to do with tying a rope to the mainbraces then it's some bloody thing about how fast you're going, eh?" Constantine looked out at the blue, sun-sparkled sea. There was land, off to starboard a mile or more: a strip of pale dun, some cumulus clouds on the horizon, and nothing else. They'd just released Abbide on that coastline, Constantine giving him posthypnotic suggestions to come out of his trance after a hundred steps up the beach. "Now—" Constantine gestured with the pistol he'd taken from Beerfield, who was tied up in a supplies hold, and wondered if he was really prepared to use it on this odd little American if pressed. But when he thought about Mercury—the way this bastard had been looking at her, and the state she was in—he could almost shoot him right now. "Let's nip back down the cabin and see about Mercury. . . ."

They found Mercury as they'd left her, wavering on the edge of consciousness in the bunk, her head turning from side to side as if she were in a fever dream. Spoink watched over her, sitting in the deck chair beside the bunk, looking grave; the look made it seem as if the man who'd taken this body over was gone, and the comatose terrorist awakened.

"Spoink?"

"Yeah, dude?"

"Just checking if you were still there. Any change in her?"

"No, man. I tried to, like, talk to her or get some kind of telepathic thing going, but I'm, you know, more about telekinesis, and not very much of that. It's your department, you gotta try it."

"Which devil gives you your power, Constantine?" Morris asked, as if trying to shame Constantine into an admission. "Some pagan god, perhaps?"

Standing over Mercury, touching her forehead to see if she did indeed have a fever, Constantine snorted. "Bacchus, when I can afford a drink, does me a good turn." He looked at Morris. "She's not feverish, but she acts as if she's in a delirium. What did you do to her? Is this drugs? Did you torture her?" With each question his hand tightened on the pistol a little more.

"Eh? No, I did nothing to her. It was . . . another. I don't know how he does it. Magic is not my specialty."

"Oh? And what is?"

"The service of God."

"You had a different kind of service on your mind when I came in here, you bastard!"

"Now I know where I remember this guy from!" Spoink burst out. "When I was alive—he was one of those televangelist assholes! He used to sell prayers on TV! You'd send him money and he'd pray for your kid to get well or something!"

Morris shrugged. "Years ago."

Constantine looked Morris over. He could see him with the well-greased helmet of hair fitting neatly into the television screen. "So you made your fortune exploiting other people's grief and misery, then, did you?"

"I offered them hope. I prayed for them."

"All those people? You prayed for each one?"

"I, ah—some I prayed for, you know, as a group."

Constantine took out a cigarette. "Get a big pile of mail, take out all the money, put your hand over it, say 'Have mercy on them Lord,' and move on to the next pile. That it?"

Morris shrugged sullenly.

Constantine started to light the cigarette, then looked at Mercury and decided to smoke outside. "Who did this to her?" Constantine asked Morris.

"And what's this agenda having to do with God? What's the service of God have to do with kidnapping young women, then?"

Morris scowled. "You wouldn't understand. It's about the greater good."

"Everything from the Inquisition to the fucking Holocaust was some bastard's idea of the greater good! Way I heard it, you're part of some group of circle-wankers planning a big war. . . ." Constantine was largely bluffing. He wasn't at all sure Morris was connected with the world war that Futheringham had nattered on about. But Morris had Mercury in his yacht, and whoever had abducted Mercury was likely to be tangled up in that cryptic agenda. Constantine had picked up that much from the ghost in the pub.

Morris dropped his gaze. "I'm not disposed to say anything more. I took an oath. Were I to betray the oath, they would know it. My death would be quick but awful. You can't scare me with worse than that."

On the word *scare* an image floated telepathically from Morris to Constantine's mind: a spider. A big hairy black one . . . the televangelist's phobia. Could be useful . . .

Constantine stuck the cigarette in his mouth, stuck the gun in his belt, and straight-armed Morris with all his strength so that the thin dark American staggered back through the open cabin door to fetch up against a bulkhead in the corridor. "Can't I scare you with worse? You bloody underestimate me, mate." Constantine stepped through the door and stood over Morris, literally radiating menace. "I can make you, your mum, your old da, your grand-da, your grand-mum, and your fucking family dog all wish they'd never been born! I've got spells that'd pull your soul out of that little cage of bones and stick it in every fly that's about to be eaten by a spider for the next ten years sequentially, you bleeding pustule! Now you pray on that for a while!" Constantine grabbed Morris's arm, spun him around, and shoved him so that he staggered down the hall to the storage hold.

He locked Morris in with Beerfield and returned to Mercury. "Going to try to contact her meself . . . see what I can find out . . ." He noticed a liquor cabinet, made a beeline for it, and was delighted to find two kinds of vodka, single-malt Scotch, Irish whiskey, and gin. He chose the Irish whiskey and poured himself a double in a tumbler he found in a rack under the bottles.

"John . . . listen, I'm feeling kind of . . ." Spoink was looking at his hands—at the terrorist's hands, really—as if there was something crawling on them he couldn't quite see. "Kind of . . . like I can't stick this much longer . . ."

Constantine drank off half his whiskey, shuddered, then looked at Spoink. "Don't feel right, inhabiting someone else's body? Some bloody fanatic who'd peg you for spawn of the Great Satan, if he could see you? What do you expect?"

"See, that's it—I feel like I *am* a spawn of the Great Satan. It's like, when I was young the movie that scared me the most was *The Exorcist*. And what am I doing, dude? I'm *possessing* a guy! I feel like I'm gonna make his head spin around or something, man! I feel like all evil and wrong and shit." He squirmed in his seat, squeezing his shoulders as if trying to feel something inside them that shouldn't be there: him.

Constantine took another sip of "the water of life" and nodded. "It wasn't voluntary, his giving up his body. His soul's still hanging around somewhere, and it resents you. Shouting at you, probably. You're starting to hear it. Can't say he's wrong, either. You are the spawn of the Great Satan—and I'm the spawn of the Little Satan."

Spoink scratched in his beard and goggled at him. "Wha-at?"

"You don't think the First of the Fallen has his hooks in the USA? And the UK? Pulling strings on their governments, their big industries? Getting the people in charge to tell lies, start wars, pollute the air, and tell people it's all good for them? 'Course it's Lucifer, mate. Doing his job, is all. His assignment, really. Can't hold it against him."

"But . . . so we're really doing the Devil's work?"

"Not me, mate. I may be, spawn of Satan but I turned around and bit the old boy in the bollocks, didn't I? Gone rogue on him. Do what I bloody please. Not a big enthusiast for the other side of the fence, either. Got me own rule book, only it's not written down. You've got a conscience, Spoink—but I wouldn't worry about inhabiting this bomb-building bastard. And if he's whisperin' in your ear about being the spawn of the Great Satan, tell him to fuck off. It's not where you're from geographically that matters—it's where you're headed, Spoink. It's who you are, and what you do. Plenty of Arabs—and plenty of so-called Christians—work for Satan on their own terms. But most Muslims do their best to get it done for Allah, meaning nothing but good. And some are like me—make up their minds as they go, choose their path one second to the next. Follow their conscience, like."

"But back there in that battlefield, man—it's like people weren't individuals anymore. It's like they were . . . on strings."

"Yeah. That's the pity of it, innit? *Influences*. They're everywhere. Sometimes they get intense—people lose themselves. Fucking Nazis—how do you explain that, then? Otherwise decent Germans turning goose-stepping zombies. Influences—on a mass scale, like. Psychological—or psychic. In Carthaga it was psychic. 'Course, we're all under some kind of influence, I reckon. Got to pick a good one. Choose it with your eyes open, like. You wanta drink? That oughta drive the fanatic ghost back a step or two. Don't like alcohol, Muslims."

"Yeah, give me something, man. You got any Corona over there?"

"No beer, if you want to call Corona beer. Here, have a scotch and soda and shut your hole now. I've got to concentrate. . . ."

Constantine handed Spoink his drink and then knelt on the deck beside Mercury. He reached out and smoothed her dark, silky hair away from her eyes. Her eyelashes fluttered, but her eyes didn't quite open. "Mercury? It's John—John Constantine!"

No response. "Mercury!" Nothing.

He took a deep breath, laid his right hand on her forehead—and instantly drew it back, as if bitten;

he'd felt something snap psychically at him. "Strewth!"

"What is it, man?" Spoink asked. "She possessed too?"

"No . . . It's not in her. She's too strong for that. . . . It's *on* her."

"I don't see anything. . . ."

"Need the third eye to see the Akishra. Did I not tell you, by the way, to shut your pie hole?"

"Sorry."

Constantine held his hand about six inches from Mercury's forehead. He turned his attention to the present moment, to his sensations, and expanded them to encompass the psychic field that coursed through him and around him. He exerted control over the field and then compressed it, consolidated it, while drawing more power from above, through the top of his head. He shuddered, feeling the fine energies shimmer into him. He directed them down his neck and spine, into his shoulder, his arm, his hand, let them radiate downward from his outspread fingers. There was a faint glimmer of blue light from his palm, shining down as if his hand were cupping a small colored lightbulb. The subtle blue light shone on Mercury's face, illuminating what Constantine had felt a moment before. He drew his hand down her body, not touching it, about six inches over her, shining the etheric light—and a writhing outline came into view. . . .

It was a psychic parasite—an Akishra, as the Hindus called them—looking at first like a transparent feather boa wrapped around her, then like a giant ethereal worm squirming over and under Mercury, twining from her head to her toe, tiny sparkling suckers extruding where it tried to contact her. It was sucking at her, and she had to use all her psychic ability to keep it at bay. She was constantly fighting it off and it left her no opening, no chance to speak, to so much as open her eyes. She was lying on a bunk, yet she was in constant combat.

Constantine sucked air through his teeth in disgust and fury. "The pricks . . . the bloody sick bastards . . ." he muttered.

He studied the enormous psychic worm for a moment, saw an opening in its coils and moved his hand over the opening, pulsing energy through it, along with a telepathic message.

Mercury. It's John. Found you in a dream, kid. Who did this? What can I do? What's going on?

"John?" She kept her eyes closed, but murmured it aloud. "John, don't try to force it off me, not yet. . . . He's put a rune on the back of my neck—if you interfere it'll open a gate for the thing, into my body. It'll eat my soul!"

It's all right, Mercury. I won't do anything yet. But I'm here. I've taken you from them. What's going on?

"I had a vision of a world war. Traced it to Carthaga. To Morris. Dyzigi knew I was probing Morris's mind and he had his men take me. Mengele. They've got him. . . . He's a kind of living demon now. . . . He's still watching me, from afar. Dyzigi put this thing on me to keep me from calling you. . . . Oh, I can't go on talking, it's using my distraction, it's tightening up. . . . John, you have to stay away from me, keep me somewhere dark until—John, it's closing down on me, trying to shut me up. . . . I can't talk. . . ."

But what should I do?

"Go to . . . coast of Syria . . . due east of Cyprus. . . . Church, go to a church on the shore . . . Syriac Church of Saint Thomas . . . Chaldeans . . . wood . . . wooden gate . . . Can't talk, it'll kill me, it's going to . . ."

Then she began to convulse, arching her back—until suddenly the blue energy snapped back at him, like an electrical short, and Constantine was struck by a small shock wave that knocked him away from her, so that he fell flat on his back, groaning. "Oh Christ. Mercury . . ."

He sat up, dizzy, looking at her. She had settled back into flipping her head back and forth, her lips moving soundlessly, lashes fluttering as she struggled to keep the parasite at bay.

"What the fuck was that about, dude?" Spoink asked, staring.

Constantine's reply came dazedly. He was still recovering from the psychic energy feedback. "They've got her trapped, wrapped up in a sort of astral snake. . . ."

Spoink reached out, ran his fingers through the air close to her face. "I don't feel anything."

"You can't feel it physically from here, unless you're attuned to it. Eventually it'll squeeze its way through the field of her life force—and eat her soul. And there's nothing I can do about it right now. Can't even talk to her again without putting her too much at risk."

"So what do we do, just sit here and fucking *watch?*"

Feeling steadier now, Constantine got to his feet

and reached for his tumbler. "No. You heard her. We're heading to Syria, man. Due east of Cyprus."

Southern Carthaga

"Carthaga is allied with the United States and Israel, yes," General Coggins was saying, as the Blackhawk flew across the island to the new place for battle incitement, "but that doesn't mean the USA is going to go to war against the Sudan and the Syrians and Jordan and Iran . . . that whole messy axis."

"It wouldn't be enough under the usual conditions," Trevino said. "But these are magical conditions." He was hunkered down just back of the cockpit, between the pilot, Simpson, and Coggins in the copilot's position, gripping the back of their seats as he watched out the front of the gunship. A village passed below, flat roofs glowing in the sunlight; faces stared apprehensively up at them from the narrow streets, but this was not the village they sought. They passed over it and followed a long, gently looping white road through rocky scrubland. Far below, an old woman in a black veil rode a donkey.

Coggins looked down at her with his binoculars, using her to focus them, and chuckled: the old woman on the donkey was talking on a cellphone as she rode along.

He glanced at his watch. "Get some speed on there, Simpson. It's got to be the right timing. . . . High noon. So they tell me . . ." He glanced at Trevino, eyebrows raised inquiringly.

Trevino nodded. Planetary influences required

the sun directly overhead for this particular rite.

Simpson pulled back on the throttle. The turbine engines roared; the engine cowl rattled, the fuselage shivered.

"Anyway," Trevino added, having to speak loudly now, "Carthaga is just the beginning. It is the first spark in a chain reaction, of sorts. It will be overwhelming. No one with the power to declare war will be able to *think* about it, you see. The fire feeds the fire feeds the fire—and we will throw psychic gasoline on each fire, until at last, He—Ah! There is the village!"

"But the fight's already goin' on!" Simpson pointed out.

Ropes of black smoke twisted up from the village; flame licked from freshly crumpled rooftops. Three sand-colored Carthagan tanks—the Carthagans had all of ten Sherman tanks in their armored cavalry, six in working condition—were advancing on a village square, in the shadow of a mosque. Coggins saw one of the Sherman tanks rock back on its treads as it fired its cannon; a section of mosque blew up. Big fragments of masonry spun through the air, five-hundred-pound chunks of stone and concrete tossed like Styrofoam.

"Whew!" Coggins exclaimed. "Lookee there, Captain! They're blasting a mosque! They got to be totally worked up to fire into a mosque! This country's mostly Muslim!"

"We did nothing here," Trevino mused. "No seeds. The war has a life of its own now. But it seems to me it's the same spell, spreading. . . ."

"A spell can spread?" Coggins asked. Magic was

mostly theoretical to him. He had come to believe, though. He'd seen things, once he'd joined the SOT. And of course he believed in the End Times, and that was something miraculous, a kind of magic.

"This one can—because He has been awakened. . . . Look!"

Trevino pointed, but Coggins couldn't see it. He didn't have the Sight. The Hidden World was still hidden to him. But in time they'd make it visible to everyone. "Is He there?"

"Yes . . ." Trevino could see it: the magnificent head of the god rising up in the smoke; taking definition from screams of pain and fury, a head apelike but reptilian. It opened Its mouth for Its silent roar—silent, yet the roar was heard in the form of guns firing, explosions going off, a hundred men shouting at once. Their mingled shouting was the god's voice.

Then the god looked up from the square—Its head itself high as a four-story building—and looked directly at the gunship. For a moment the god was more than a glassy outline. Trevino could see Its black eyes, the color of space between the stars, looking right at him.

A shudder that went on and on passed through Trevino as he thought: *He sees me. He recognizes me. He knows we are the ones. . . .*

The god seemed to flex Its neck, then, to lift Itself a bit—and Its shoulders showed, filling the village square. The god was decidedly more emerged now—soon It would straddle mountains. . . .

Trevino, gazing into the twin voids of the god's eyes, could bear the sight no more; he had to look away. He felt that in another moment he'd have been drawn by that spiritual vacuum through the air; he would fall into those eyes, fall for all eternity.

"I'm getting a report on the radio here, General," Simpson said. "Strucken. He says Morris has left the harbor. His yacht's gone. He thinks someone has hijacked it and Morris, too. He called SOT for a satellite fix—they're headed for the coast of Syria."

"No shit? The *Noah's Next* was hijacked?"

"That's what he says, sir."

"All right . . . Trevino, we've got to get what, five heads here?"

"Six."

"We should be able to do it on the edge of town. Then we refuel; it's on the way to the sea. We've got to find that ship. Not sure that ship's computer's secure for one thing. Sorry to lose Morris—but it might be better if that ship were sunk. . . ."

9

... BUT THE SPIRIT GIVETH LIFE

The southern coast of Syria

It was an hour after dawn when the *Noah's Next* reached the shore near the Chaldean church. A big, whitewashed structure with a flaking gold minaret and tall, squared spire, the church stood on a bluff overlooking the sea, not far from the Lebanese border. Constantine guessed that it had once been a mosque, then reconsecrated Christian; an ornate crucifix sprouted from its minaret, and gesturing grandly in the windows were stained-glass figures of bearded saints.

"We're in this country without the right papers, dude," Spoink said as they walked up the ancient stony path to the church. "If we're arrested, we're screwed."

"Maybe I can say I captured you, mate—say you're a spy for the Americans. They'll pin a medal on me."

"No way! You wouldn't!"

"If you don't stop fucking whining about the situation I might." Constantine had done too much exploring in the yacht's liquor cabinet the night before, sitting up beside Mercury. He'd been thinking about when he lived with Marj, a sort of stepfather to her daughter Mercury; thinking about the other women he'd loved and lost.

Other people, he thought, *have bad luck with women—me, I'm bad luck to women.*

He grimaced, rubbing his temples. His head felt like the village smithy's anvil this morning.

Spoink, for his part, was clutching at his middle. "I'm not feeling well—"

"*You're* not feeling well! Crikey. Still got the runs, then?"

"No, it's not that—it . . . it feels like he's really starting to wake up on me. The guy I took the body from. Supposed to be in a coma. Feel like I'm pregnant with an angry baby, dude."

"You'd think he'd be off looking for Muslim paradise, all those virgins oiling their bodies, like."

"I guess once I got his body going, he wanted to come back to it. He's wriggling around in there, man. It's fucked up."

"Just deal with it or take yourself out into the countryside somewhere and get out of him."

"I didn't put myself in him, John. I don't know how to get out. The angels sort of poured me in. Not sure how to get in touch with them. Anyway I don't like to get a job here and then just blow it all off, dude."

"Then get a bloody grip."

They were approaching the church from the seaward side; their hijacked vessel was anchored not far offshore, and they'd taken the motorized launch right up to the beach. They had to circle around, passing along the shadowy side of the building, away from the sun, Constantine and his companion dappled by stained-glass colors cast by light from within the church. Singing, punctuated by the *ting* of a triangle and the clash of cymbals, came from within the church. Each clash made Constantine wince.

"Whoa, sounds like a marching band," Spoink said. "What kinda church you say it was?"

"Chaldean. Nestorian roots. Used to be based on a heresy—from the Catholic point of view anyway—believing Jesus was not divine, merely related to a divine Christ some way. Some daft theological contortion like that."

They found the iron-studded wooden doors under the stone archway in the front of the building.

Was this the wooden gate she'd mentioned? Constantine wondered.

The door was open; some parts of the high-ceilinged nave inside glittered with candles, others were in deep shadow. The church exhaled a redolence of incense and antiquity. Swallows had found their way through high cracks in the walls over the windows to dart around the gloomy ceiling. The chipped stone faces of saints looked out from the niches, their faces seemingly carved of benevolent regret; there were no pews and no chairs, but a middling group of parishioners stood near the transept rail under the gawdily gold-painted altar, chanting with the liturgy, as a bearded priest in a cassock intoned in Syriac and waved a censer.

"Dude!" Spoink burst out. "It's like, all—"

"Spoink?" Constantine interrupted.

"What?"

"Shut yer gob." Constantine led the way inside, striding halfway up the nave, past a stone column—and stopped dead. He had to take a step back.

He was in a large, empty part of the room, still sixty feet behind the group of worshippers, but he felt he was jostling his way into a crowd. An invisible crowd.

Light from candles played over incense smoke, and when he looked close he seemed to see eyes taking shape in that smoke, sections of faces forming and dissolving. A crowd of ghosts: children with adults who looked like their parents. Whole families of ghosts. A few odds and sods like that one there—didn't he know that one? That one forming a more and more definite shape . . .

"So you made it, recruit!"

Colonel Futheringham, transparent but as visible as a soap bubble, drifted out of the shadows, nodding in satisfaction and twisting the ends of his ectoplasmic mustache. He shifted to get out of the way of a young man, anomalously Caucasian in a knee-length white Arabic shirt over white pants. He was no ghost, Constantine saw. Futheringham nodded to the young man, who nodded back as he stepped into the shadows, under a statue of Saint Anthony. Who was this, Constantine wondered, who could see ghosts as easily as he could?

"Had some rather dismaying reports about your reliability, Constantine," Futheringham went on. "Glad to be reassured, recruit. Couldn't have been easy, getting here." The colonel was standing in front of a niche with a bust of a saint in it, and since Futheringham was transparent the saint's face showed through his, mingling with it; an unsettling effect. Like someone had drawn a ridiculous mustache on a saint.

"Wasn't easy," Constantine said. "But don't be so reassured—I've still got plenty of time to bollocks it up. And you can bog off with that recruit business; I've still no wish to be a 'peace corpse' or any other kind."

"Whoa, I can *see* that old ghost dude!" Spoink blurted. Then, seeing Constantine's look, he trailed off, "I know—shut up. Jeez."

The colonel stared at Spoink. "Curious dialect for one of his sort."

"Right," Constantine said. "Colonel, I've got Mercury with me. Nearby, anyway. She's out in the boat offshore. She's under a nasty little enchantment—but we've managed to get some soup down her and she's holding steady. . . ."

"A boat offshore? Not a yacht of some kind?"

"Yeah. *Noah's Next,* it's called. Why?" Constantine was aware that the priest and some deacon-looking chaps up by the altar were glaring at him. Hard to miss Constantine, the stranger in their midst, talking to no one. Some drug-addled Westerner who'd wandered into their sacristy, they figured. A human blight.

Constantine noticed the priest sending an altar boy out a side door, probably to fetch the authorities.

"D'ye see that bunch there," Futheringham said, hooking a thumb at a corner, "under the statue of the Holy Virgin?"

Constantine looked and didn't see them at first. He had to focus his attention on his pineal gland, between his eyes—to open his third eye further—and then he saw them, a whole separate set of ghosts: a group of miserable-looking Europeans, possibly French. There were several older people and three others who'd been college age when they'd died, two of them girls in bikinis.

Ghost girls in ghost bikinis, Constantine reflected, were strikingly incongruous in the church. "More ghosts, are they, then? Look a bit startled. The girls still think they're in their little bathing suits."

"I expect they do. Rather fetching, really, if inappropriate attire for a house of worship. They were in a yacht that was blown up by one of those whirlybird things you people drive about now."

"Not me, mate. I don't even drive a car."

"This one fired rockets of some kind at their yacht, shortly before dawn. Whole thing sunk, everyone dead. No reason for it to happen—no one knows why the attack came about. Case of mistaken identity likely. I was wondering why they'd found their way to us. Now I know—fatalistic entanglement, what? Do you smoke it? They're connected to you!"

"Me!" Then it struck him—someone had been looking for the yacht he'd hijacked from Carthaga. They'd blown up that other yacht, somehow mistaking it in the darkness. Chances were they'd found out by now that they'd gotten the wrong target. So they'd be back.

"Oh bloody hell!" Constantine blurted.

"Steady on, old man, you're in a church!" the colonel reproached him.

Constantine strode over to the statue of the Virgin and pretended to gaze reverently up at it while speaking to the ghosts clustered at Mother Mary's feet. "Top of the morning to you, as the Irish never really said. Listen, ah, this helicopter that sank your ship—gunship was it, Blackhawk type? Kind of yellowish, like?"

"Oui," said one of the men. "C'est ça!" He added in English, "It's you, they search for, to kill? You made us dead?"

"Me? Made you dead? No-o-o, not me personally. Listen, ah, sorry about the mix-up. Not my doing. Do be a good fellow and don't haunt me. You want to haunt anyone, haunt the bastards in that chopper. They may well be back soon. We'll see if we can get you sorted out. Give us some time, eh? Send you on your way, right up the tunnel to the light. Next world's better than this, if you've been good. You'll like it. Hot and cold running manna, open wine bar, locusts-and-honey canapés. Patience, that's the watchword, innit? Cheers."

Constantine returned to Futheringham, noting as he went that the service had given up on clashing cymbals, and the priest, giving communion, was glaring daggers at Constantine. "Listen, I'm not sure that ship's safe anymore, Colonel—I've got to get Mercury out of here. They're sure to figure out they hit the wrong one."

"You'll need to go to Paris next. . . ."

"Now look, mate, I'm not at all sure there's anything I *need* to do here except help them I care about—and there's just one of them."

"Then why come here?" the colonel countered. "She sent you here, eh? Helping the world is helping her, John Constantine."

"What? *This* world? Taken a look around it recently? Not at all sure I want to prevent it from wiping the slate clean. Might be better. Lives of quiet desperation ain't in it. Most people are in a bloody existential nightmare, at best. Hobbesian, it is, and worse." Constantine was hung over—and angry that he felt guilt about the ghosts at the Virgin's statue. Yesterday they'd been people having pretty good lives and then they'd gotten accidentally tangled up in Constantine's world and now they were dead. Was it his fault? No—or not exactly. But "not exactly" didn't make him feel much better.

"Look to your childhood, friend, for the roots of that anger," said Futheringham gently. "It's all in your point of view. This world's worth saving."

Constantine snorted. "There's many another world. I don't know how well they briefed you on the other side, but alternate universes ain't a myth. There's a kaleidoscope variation on this full-tilt mess always goin' on. Blue Sheikh told me there's another John Constantine in an alternate universe, has black hair and lives most of his life in Los Angeles. Gets the bloody lung cancer and gets out of it, too, just like me. Black coat instead of a trench coat: he's me but not me. I sure as bleedin' hell don't want to be *him*—point is, with lots of everyone around in some universe somewhere, who needs *this* world?"

The colonel turned and gestured at the congregation near the altar. "They need it, John. The people in it—and of it. People like them need it so they can have the chance to make the right choices—to learn the lessons they need to learn. And so they can celebrate with one another, if only for a few moments, that they were alive."

Constantine shook his head. Personally, he doubted those things were worth it—but there was no time to argue. And next anyway, the colonel would probably come at him with the old "we cannot know the Lord's great design" argument. There was no real way to argue with that particular maddening rhetorical gambit. "Why this church, then, Colonel?"

"That cabinet there, with the gold paint and glass? That's got relics in it. You see that thing, like a mummified hand? Well, *'tis* a mummified hand. Hand of a martyr, struck off when the Romans were torturing him—they were trying to get him to sign on for the old gods. He said he was in his own God's hands, the only God, and whoops, 'Off with his hands!' they said. 'Since you've got God's hands you don't need those.' Bled to death, I expect. But his faith was such that his hand still has great power. Troubled spirits can rest in that hand till God comes for them, what?"

"Can they now? Bully for them."

"The plan is this: you take the saint's hand, and with it you take these spirits gathered in the church. They cannot go on from here, John Constantine. They are already as far from the places of their death as they can bear. Most of them are uncomfortable in this church."

"What's putting all those spirits in a mummified hand got to do with stopping a war?"

"Candidly, recruit—I don't know. I expect all will be made clear in time. The whole plan was assembled rather hastily."

"Assembled rather hastily?" Constantine looked at Spoink. "I can well believe it. Proof is in this one 'ere. But I've got to get Mercury and scarper out of here; they may come back with that fu—" The colonel glared at him warningly. "That gunship."

"I think I can help with that," said the young man in the long white Arabic overshirt, edging close. "I can arrange transportation for us live types . . ."

"And who the bloody hell are you?"

"My name's Gatewood. I guess I'm a deserter. U.S. military. But I can get you to France maybe, for starts. . . . If you want me to do that, you've got to play along with the colonel's plan. Take these spirits out of here. I'm committed to helping them. . . . And you're supposed to go with us. . . ."

"Wait'll I get hold of the bastard entity that got me into this half-baked cock-up. . . . Did you say *Gatewood?*" So that's what Mercury meant. Constantine looked at the cabinet of relics. "And how do I get into that cabinet without getting the Syrian police all over me?"

"I'd suggest the method the looters used in Baghdad," Gatewood said. "You bust the window, you grab the thing—and you run like a son of a bitch."

"How does a son of a bitch run?" Constantine muttered, looking at the cabinet. He could see a brass lock on it. There just wasn't any time to ponder this, to try to explain things to the priest, to do anything but stride across the room, as he did now, take off his

right shoe, and smash the glass out with the heel.
Shards of glass rang on the stone floor.

The room seemed to reverberate with the shock of
the onlookers; it echoed with their gasps as he put
his shoe back on, reached through the broken pane
and plucked out the mummified hand.

"Sorry, all!" Constantine called out to the church-
goers. "Got to borrow this. I'll try to send it back with
some of that bubble wrap—marked fragile." He returned to the ghosts—visible to him and invisible to
the others—clustered around Gatewood. "How do I
use this thing? Quick, before someone brains me with
an incense burner!"

"I don't have a clue, man," Gatewood said with a
shrug.

"Right. Naturally. What else."

"Actually I can be of help, there, I believe," Futheringham said. "Hold it in your right hand and say,
'Here find shelter, in the hand of the servant of God,
until your time of release!' Then with conviction recite
the first two verses of Psalm 91—any translation will
do—"

"I know that Psalm!" Constantine interrupted. He
looked around and saw that the congregation was
muttering, pointing; one of them was pulling out a
cellphone. *Bloody cellphones are everywhere. Probably got them in limbo. Insist on them.* He recited: *"Here
find shelter, in the hand of the servant of God, until
your time of release! 'You who live in the shelter of the
Most High, who abide in the shadow of the Almighty,
my refuge and my fortress, my God in whom I
trust . . .'"* He recited it, and with conviction—one al-

ways did incant with fervor, since nothing else would work.

There was a beat, as if the magical powers-that-be were checking his mystical credit rating, then a whirlwind started up, issuing from the severed hand, an astral wind that distorted the images of the ghosts, making them warp and pull. The ectoplasmic substance of the ghosts tugged like taffy into the spiral, compressing to a downspout that spiraled into the saint's grasp. Futheringham and the other ghosts, all of them, vanished into the whirlwind, condensed and sucked into the palm of the withered hand—and, creaking just a little, the fingers of the mummified hand closed into a loose fist, like a child holding a fragile butterfly and trying not to crush it.

Constantine stuck the mummified hand in an inside pocket of his coat. "Right, I'm off."

That's when the two stocky, turbaned, brown-uniformed Syrian cops came in, carrying Uzis. The priest instantly shouted at them, pointing at Constantine, obviously demanding his arrest for vandalism. The men in the congregation rushed around to join the cops, so that a crowd of hostile men, two of them heavily armed, stood between him and the door.

"This is some fucked-up shit here, John," Spoink remarked.

"Thanks for that penetrating insight, Spoink—now you can try to make yourself more useful than an aqualung on a fish, and tell them in Arabic I'm just borrowing the hand for a DNA test. I've got permission from the, uh—from whoever runs this church."

"You think they'll buy that?" Gatewood asked skeptically.

"No. But, Spoink—try."

"I'll try. . . ." But he'd hardly begun when the cops interrupted with shouts of their own, coming at them, brandishing their weapons.

Constantine reached out to try to take control of the nearest cop's mind, but the ambient mental fields were roiling, all mixed up in their emanations, seething with the anger and outrage of the crowd. It was impossible to pick out one mind or another and it was difficult to concentrate, seeing as he was about to get a bullet in the gizzard.

Then the cops—and everyone in the hostile crowd—stepped back, gasping, as a crucifix on a silver base levitated from its table behind the altar, drifting over to hang in the air between Constantine and, as he saw them, the latest representatives from that perennial demographic: those who'd like to burn him at the stake. The crowd goggled in superstitious awe as the crucifix seemed to warn them not to interfere with the strangers who'd vandalized their church.

"You making that crucifix float there like that, Spoink?" Constantine asked, whispering the question out the side of his mouth.

"Yeah . . ." The reply came out of Spoink in a grunt. A glance showed Spoink was pale, shaking, sweat starting out on his forehead. "Shit, it's heavy. Can't . . . do this much longer . . . not this strong . . . have to hold the Iranian back, too . . . can't do both . . ."

"Right. Just a few more seconds . . ." Constantine took Spoink by the elbow, leading him and Gatewood around the edge of the group, sidling toward the door.

The cops whispered to one another, fingering their

weapons—then one of them spat an Arabic imprecation and aimed his gun at Constantine. He was probably a Muslim after all and not impressed with
Christian magic. But the priest stepped in, stroking
his beard with one hand, his other pressing the gun
down, telling the cop in Syriac—or so Constantine
guessed—to give it a rest.

Constantine, Gatewood, and Spoink made it to the
front steps, Spoink groaning and hissing under his
breath, before the cross clanked to the floor. Spoink's
knees went rubbery and he nearly fainted. Constantine and Gatewood supported him between them,
dragging him around the side of the church. Behind
them, the priest and the cops were arguing.

The priest, Constantine supposed, was claiming
that the levitating crucifix was a sign from God—perhaps in his mind he was already counting out the pro-
ceeds from Christian tourism when the word got out
about the miracle witnessed by dozens in the church.
They'd rename the church, probably: *The Holy Shrine
of the Levitating Cross.*

"You need to be carried, Spoink?" Constantine
asked.

"No . . . no, I feel better now. . . . Let us go. . . ."

"You sure you're okay?"

"Yes, yes, *alhamdolilleh!*"

"Alham what? Never mind, just get into the fucking
boat. Gatewood'll pilot, if he knows how. . . . I need a
cup of tea like an infant needs mother's milk, I do."
But as they tooled the launch toward the big white
motor yacht, Constantine looked at Spoink and
thought he looked deeply, gravely unhappy. Might

crumble under just a little pressure. "Good job back there, saved our bacon, mate," Constantine said. "I'm beginning to be glad you were sent along to help."

Spoink only nodded, gazing into the low waves sliding past the boat. Constantine remembered what Spoink had said, in the church: . . . have to hold the Iranian back too . . .

"Holy shit," Gatewood exclaimed, seeing they were headed for the motor yacht. "That your yacht? *Noah's Next?*"

"Borrowed. I look like a bloody yachtsman to you?"

"No, man. What exactly you look like, I'm not sure. Maybe Sting after he's gone through a few dozen cases of bourbon."

"Gin—or Irish whiskey."

"So we can't take that boat to France?"

"I can't stay on the yacht—they're sinking boats that look like this one around here, according to . . . oh bugger. Look. I don't think I'm going to get my cuppa." He pointed.

They all three saw it then, just before their boat kissed up to the side of the yacht: a wasp-colored gunship on the horizon, coming right for them.

10

PAVED WITH GOOD INTENTIONS

The Syrian coast

"I've got to get on your ship's radio!" Gatewood said. "There's one guy I know will help us...."

They were running across the deck, Constantine for the hatch to the lower decks so he could find Mercury, Gatewood to the bridge. They'd left Spoink in the boat so they'd have a quick getaway. There was no way they could outrun that gunship. Morris's motor yacht, Constantine figured, was about to become a magnet for wreck scavengers off the coast of Syria.

He ducked through the metal doorway and turned and slid down the railing like he'd seen in movies about the Royal Navy—or anyway, he almost managed to do it. After picking himself up off the deck, he raced down the narrow corridor to Morris's cabin. "Mercury!"

But there was no use calling to her. She was locked into her psychic wrestling match with the Akishra. He found her as he'd left her, lying on the bunk, twitching uneasily.

He gathered her in his arms, immediately thinking she was heavier than he expected. He drew his head back a little, sensing the Akishra slithering past his face as he carried her out to the ladder. But it was hard to get her up the "ladder," the steep metal steps to the foredeck. And now he could clearly hear the drone of the approaching gunship.

"Let me have her!" Gatewood yelled. Coming partway down the ladder he grabbed Mercury under the armpits and toted her back up to the top deck. He slung the young woman over his shoulder in a fireman's carry and headed for the gangway that slanted down to the launch, as Constantine went on another, quick errand.

"Not fucking worth it," he told himself. But he ran into the stateroom anyway, grabbed a bottle of Irish whiskey and half a carton of cigarettes he'd found there—*Newports,* but better than nothing—and raced back to the ladder. Then remembered Morris.

"Oh, sod him," Constantine muttered. "Don't be a git, John."

But he couldn't leave Morris and Beerfield to drown. Constantine turned and ran down the corridor to the door of the hold on the port side. He threw the latch with one hand—the other was tenderly cradling the smokes and liquor to him—and jerked the watertight door open.

That's when the first two missiles struck the big motor yacht, direct hits on the flying bridge and the port side near the waterline.

The corridor shook like a baby's rattle, thumping Constantine bruisingly back and forth between the bulkheads. "Ow! Jesus on a—*Ow!*—bike!" The shaking subsided—and he heard screams from the supplies hold. Again the ship wrenched, struck by another air-to-surface missile, reverberating as a fuel line exploded.

But all through the wrenching he managed to cradle the bottle and the cigarettes, keeping them unharmed.

The yacht began to tilt to port, so that Constantine was flung against the corridor bulkhead beside the open door. He braced himself between the two corridor walls and looked through the door to see the room filling up with water, gushing up from a hole in the deck. Beerfield was floating facedown, his hands still tied behind him, unmoving, blood jetting from his crushed forehead. Morris was using his feet to push up against a coil of anchor chain, just keeping his head clear, even as seawater boiled around his chin. His feet were tied together; if he tried to move on his own toward the door, he'd drown. He'd worked one arm free of his ropes and now he stretched it toward Constantine.

"Constantine! Help me!"

Constantine shoved his bottle and cigarettes in his voluminous coat pockets, got a grip on the edge of the door with his left hand and reached toward Morris with his right, even as water began overflowing the hold, gushing into the corridor. The ship creaked and groaned as it shifted; it burbled loudly with the furious influx of water. The air pressure balanced out the gushing water pressure enough so that the hole in the deck below Morris began to suck downward. . . .

Morris threw himself at Constantine's outstretched hand and caught his wrist, but the water still swirled around his neck and the terrible suction from below had caught him. His eyes widened as he felt the strength of the sea dragging him inexorably down, pulling him down Constantine's wrist, his hand, his fingers—he lost his grip and slipped under the waves.

But the water was clear, and Constantine could see him down there, stuck at his hips in the fibrous hole around the fiberglass deck, flailing, frantically signaling for Constantine to pull him free. Constantine knew he could never get him loose—and there was already blood ribboning up from the edges of the gap Morris was stuck in. He was being slashed and drowned at once, and the suction would be too strong to fight. The water was filling the corridor, rising up to Constantine's armpits—but he watched a few moments longer, riveted and helpless. Morris screamed silently, only bubbles pouring from his mouth. In another few seconds his lungs had filled, a great deal of blood had seeped away. . . .

And Constantine—his senses heightened by the emergency, his third eye wide open—saw Morris's soul coming out of his body like champagne from an uncorked bottle, straight up out the top of his head. He saw the ectoplasmic face look around in startlement and then wonder.

Then Constantine saw the demons.

There were three of them. To Constantine the

demons seemed to come from the shadows of the sinking ship, growing from pinpoint size to bigger than a man in a single moment. The three demons came at Morris's soul from three sides.

The First of the Fallen had sent the demons that Morris would most fear—he was an arachnophobe, and these creatures had bristle-furred naked human bodies, with hooks for hands and heads that were entire giant tarantulas attached at the thorax to each demon's neck, each spider big as a terrier; each with extra-large mandibles and clusters of yellow eyes.

Morris's soul wailed; Constantine could hear the cry in his mind.

Please, Lord God, no! I serve Jesus! I am bringing about His Second Coming! No! Noooooooo, Lord Jesus, no!

Since Morris's anatomy existed in his mind it had taken shape astrally; one of the demons pierced Morris's spirit in the eyes with both its mandibles, as if using the soul's eyesockets for convenient carrying. The other demons used their bristly hooks to grip him by the genitals and the wrists. He shrieked telepathic protestations: it was all a misunderstanding, they had it wrong, he wasn't intended for Hell. . . .

But Lucifer knew better—he knew Morris had made millions of dollars deceiving people, he knew about the young women he'd taken advantage of, he knew far worse about him—and his demons dragged Morris's soul down, first into the dark corners of the hold, and then into another plane entirely. The Devil had sent his emissaries to bring another televangelist straight to Hell. Morris's physical body, arms lifted to drift like seaweed, gaped emptily up, as if staring longingly toward Heaven. Not *him*.

Constantine turned and thrashed his way to the ladder, fighting the water as the ship gave another shudder, preparing to go under. He had to grip the handrails hard enough to make his fingers ache, to keep from getting flung back into the water filling the corridor. Feeling like he weighed a thousand pounds he worked his way up the ladder and onto the slanting deck.

He saw immediately that the deck was slanting to port, and they'd left the launch on the starboard side. He tried to clamber up the steepening deck to the starboard rail, but it was like going up a slippery roof that was shifting in an earthquake and he was soon sliding across the foredeck, cursing roundly as he went past the mechanical windlass, fetching up at a stanchion beside the port hawsehole.

He fumbled desperately for a hold but pitched over the side, catching the stanchion at the last moment.

Dangling. Cursing. Wondering if the ship was about to flip over onto him and bear him to the bottom of the sea.

Constantine hung there trying to remember an invocation that would be of use. Hoping his cigarettes hadn't gotten wet and crushed. (After all, he might survive.) Cursing some more . . .

"Constantine! Let go!" came a voice from below him.

"What? Who's that?"

"Gatewood! We came around below you! Hurry! Just drop!"

The ship lurched once more and the decision was made for Constantine; he lost his hold and dropped less than a yard down into the boat, falling on his feet but pitching onto his back. "Ow! Buggerin' shit!"

His head had fallen into Spoink's lap. Dazedly, Constantine looked up at Spoink—at his upside-down face, from this vantage—and past the long hedge of beard, seemed to see another face entirely, a kind of furious ape, almost like the war god he'd seen on Carthaga.

Constantine sat up hastily. "Bony lap you've got there, Spoink." He looked to see that Mercury was safe—she was curled up in the bottom of the launch. "Here, where's that chopper, Gatewood?"

At the tiller, hurrying the motorized launch away from the sinking yacht, Gatewood replied by pointing. Constantine looked and saw that the gunship was headed away from them. Thinking its job done, he hoped.

"Where's Morris and that other guy?" Gatewood asked.

"Dead. Couldn't get them out." Constantine shifted on the seat, trying to get more comfortable in his wet clothes. He could feel sea salt rasping his underwear against his rump. He fished the half-carton of cigarettes from his pocket and found an uncrushed pack. There were only two packs intact, blessedly protected from the water by their cellophane. He tore the pack open, extracted a cigarette, lit it, then found the whiskey bottle in his other pocket and had a pull at it. He wanted to get the image of Morris's soul being dragged down to Hell out of his mind. "Ahhh . . . Christ on a fucking exercycle. Needed that."

Gatewood snorted. "Man, you really think this is the time to get sloshed? We don't even have any water in this thing. Drinking makes you dehydrated."

"Wouldn't dare not drink, now. Be defying God."

"Why?"

"Because it's a bloody miracle this bottle didn't get broken when I was chucked around on that yacht. *Supposed* to drink it, obviously—God's will!" He lifted the bottle to the heavens. "Thank you, Lord." He took another drink.

"Okay, you still got the bottle—what about the saint's hand?"

Constantine felt in the inside pocket of his coat. Funny, unpleasantly funny, to feel a hand there— as if returning his touch. "There it is. . . . No worries . . ."

He watched the yacht's forepeak disappear beneath the waves; it went with a melancholy parting gurgle. There wasn't a great deal of suction from the sinking yacht now; the water here wasn't deep and the yacht ended up only a few feet under the surface. But there were big holes blown in its side.

"There goes a half million prayer donations, down the loo." He turned to look Mercury over more closely. She seemed asleep, breathing regularly—or in a protective trance of some kind.

"What now?" Gatewood asked. "I don't think it'll be safe to hit the shore around here, man. All this action will attract the Syrian military."

"Yeah. Maybe Lebanon, up the shore." Constantine was eyeing Spoink, who seemed uncharacteristically quiet.

"I doubt we've got that much fuel."

"Oh shit," Constantine said, spotting the gunship coming their way again. "Not enough to shoot the yacht out from under us. Seemed sloppy, yeah? Like to be thorough, these bastards."

The gunship had flown in a wide circle and was on a flight path that would take it right over the launch.

"And they're coming right straight for us," Gatewood said.

"Got a knife on you?" Constantine asked.

"What? You're going to fight a helicopter with a knife?"

"Just give me the fucking knife."

"Uhhh—no. Wait, yes, there's a knife in this little boat kit here, for fixing line or something. . . . Here."

He handed over the small pocketknife. Constantine opened it and without hesitation slashed the heel of his left hand. He stretched it out so the blood would drip into the water. He intoned, *"Undina Acqus Deis! Undina Acqus Deis . . . Ave!"* He sent emanations from his psychic field along his arm, into the spreading splash of blood in the water. It was as if the blood were an amplifier for a signal, transmitting his call, both psychic and verbal, into the depths of the sea. *"Undina Acqus Deis! Undina Acqus Deis . . . Ave!"*

The gunship was getting closer. . . . A few hundred yards off . . .

"*Undina Acqus Deis . . . Ave!*" He felt no answer to his call, and he went into the deeper level of the incantation, using words that were known to only a few; they were in the nearly forgotten language of Atlantis:

"*Aq'ye'M'his'zoharzus! Und'neh'immenum! 'Immenum Gi'es'quis!*"

He was aware of Gatewood staring at him; of a peculiar low growling from Spoink. Of Mercury shifting restively in the bottom of the boat. But he kept his focus, concentrating every ounce of psychic strength into the call. And his blood dripped, filtering down into the sea, merging with it like a promise, a promise made with his lifeblood. . . .

"*Undina Acqus Deis! Aq'ye'M'his'zoharzus! Und'neh'immen'm! 'Immenum Gi'es'quis!*"

The chopper was almost upon them.

"*Undina Acqus Deis! Aq'ye'M'his'zoharzus . . .*"

He felt the response, then: a probe from the depths of the sea. It was looking in his mind for his native language, sensing he knew only a few words of its own. Then a voice rang in his head. . . . A voice that seemed female . . .

Who calls upon us?

"It's John Constantine! I've dealt with the Elemental Folk before."

The Green Lord told us. . . . We have heard. . . . We have seen your soul pass through our realm, on its way to a strange destiny. . . . We have known your ancestors. . . . Rather irritating, they were. . . .

And you humans—we are reluctant to do you any favors! You have taken far more than your allotment of fish—and you have poisoned the rest! You have killed large portions of our realm!

"That's not me—I'm against all that! And anyway, ah . . ."

The machine gun projecting from the side of the chopper was tilting down toward them. Constantine could see a big man grinning down at them as he centered the launch in his sights. Constantine turned to Gatewood and made a motion to zigzag the boat, to make a more difficult target. Gatewood nodded and began to weave the boat across the sea, away from the shore.

". . . and I'm sorry about my irritating ancestors," Constantine went on. "Like to make up for it—I'll owe you one big-time, if you can help us out. That machine is about to kill us; it's only about fifty feet over the water."

How will you repay us?

"I don't know—I'll think of something, got no choice and I'm as good as my word!"

But your word does not always mean what it seems, so we have heard. You regard an oath as subject to interpretation.

"Won't be around to repay you if you don't do something—"

The machine gun opened fire and 16 mm bullets stitched down into the surface of the sea, the last rounds of the burst smacking the launch's prow, showering Constantine with splinters. But the strafe missed hitting anyone in the boat. The chopper pulled up short and wheeled about, hovering so the gunner could fire again . . .

Very well, John Constantine—but as you say, you will owe us *big-time*. And one day we will collect. . . .

Constantine had expected the elemental to manifest as a shape of water, the way Mercury had that day, but the she-giant who rose from the water was more a thing of ooze and slime and seaweed, pieces of old shipwrecks, with seawater taking the place of her blood.

And yet the whole came together with harmonious beauty as she rose gigantically from the water. She was made of seaweed and plankton and algae and wood, but her body was translucent—the sun struck through her, making an emerald light that lit the silhouette of her skeleton: a ten-story-high roughly human skeleton made of parts of sunken ships, its ribs the ribs of shipwrecks, its skull sections of hull; her hair was streaming seaweed and her eyes were whirling jellyfish in seafoam; the bones of her hands were spars. And in all she was a breathtakingly magnificent creature, woman shaped and roaring with surging currents. Some elementals were more substantial than others; it seemed to Constantine that this one amounted to a sea goddess.

He felt an unholy thrill looking up at her. She was here of her own accord, of her own free will, but still he, John Constantine, had prepared the way; he alone had summoned and persuaded her. This statuesque, glorious expression of the sea was an expression, also, of John Constantine's will.

Moments like this explained why he was a magician, though it seemed to keep him always with one foot in Hell.

Distantly he made out astonished faces in the gunship staring at the giant elemental. And then she reached out and her fingers closed over the man at the machine gun. He screamed as she plucked at him, trying to pick him like a fruit. But his harness held most of his body in place, so that she was only able to pull his upper half free.

Vermin! Came her voice, reverberating in their minds. **Vermin—infesting my realm!**

Burlington's upper half separated sloppily from his lower half, so that he was gone from the waist up except for his spine, which stuck out from his quivering, blood-spouting lower parts, waggling in the air and dripping spinal fluid.

She flung Burlington's remains into the sea, and sharks came, bid by the sea elemental, to churningly feast.

The gunship began to back away, but she grabbed it by its landing struts with her coursing, solid-but-liquid right hand, her left reaching under the rotors toward the men in the chopper—but she hesitated, seeing the sky suddenly boiling over them then, clouds thickening to black, spitting lightning, and parting for a hideous face.

The gigantic face of the Carthagan battlefield showed itself in the clouds: a thing apish and reptilian at once. It came to Constantine that the face was familiar from some childhood moment of rage. Constantine had seen that face for a flicker when he'd punched Jamie Ellis, the day Jamie had peed on his new shoes. And again, he thought it stirred even deeper memories. Now it reached out taloned paws from the sky, and from the ground, and from the stars, and from the center of the earth all at once. It reached out to slash at her. She let the chopper go and struck back—a force, Constantine saw, not of water and slime and wood, but of psychic presence compacted into the shape of a hand, the power of one colossal soul striking at another. Lightning and water exploded together, a great cloud of steam hissing up to hide the combatants. There was something in the pillar of steam that was like two vaguely human-shaped storms clashing, storm front to storm front. Great waves were lifted up by their clash, threatening to become a tsunami which would smash over the church on the shore and the settlements nearby.

The chopper was making a break for it, heading for the horizon.

And Constantine could see that the tsunami was building strength.

"Oh holy shit, what have you done?" Gatewood shouted.

Constantine shouted, *"Undina Acqus Deis! Great elemental, your task is done—I render you gratitude! Those who would destroy me flee! Now return to the peace of your domain!"*

Your kind have stolen the peace from my domain with your echo machines and your black spills and your poisoned rainfalls. But I go. Only, remember—gratitude is not enough. I will extract a price from you one day. . . .

There was a reverberating finality in these last words, and the elemental suddenly collapsed into the sea with a thunderous surge. Steam dispersed in streamers, and he saw that the brutal god was gone from the sky as well. Instead, a great wave was roaring toward the launch and the shore, carrying barnacled spars and fragments of wooden ships on it, like weapons in a fist.

"Hold on!" Gatewood shouted, turning the boat, trying to outrun the wave.

They raced along for a handful of protracted seconds; then the surge caught them, lifting the boat up and nearly capsizing it. The launch's side was smacked by a fragment of masthead, cracking but not quite stoving in. They spun sickeningly, water cascading over them. . . .

But when the wave subsided they were still afloat.

The wave passed on to crash heavily on the beach, but below the church. Merely a dire hint of what a tsunami could be.

"Shit, man," Gatewood said. "We barely got through that. Hey, Constantine, were you responsible, a couple years ago, for that big tsunami that smashed into Indonesia and India and—"

"No! Christ! Everyone tries to lay it all at my door. You can sod off with that." Constantine groped for another cigarette. He was feeling nearly exhausted by the psychic effort of the invocation and emotional turmoil from so much happening in so short a time. But at least the gunship was gone. . . .

Or was it? There it came again, a chopper on the horizon, bearing down on them. "Oh no," Constantine muttered. "I can't call the elementals again. . . . They won't come a second time today."

Gatewood stared at the oncoming chopper. "Uh-uh. That's not the same helicopter. That's one of ours—should be the one I called from the radio room. My cousin Norm's the pilot. . . . I hope he's not too fucked up. He's scary when he flies loaded."

11

WHERE FLOWERS DEGENERATE . . .

The Mediterranean Sea, in the middle of nowhere

"Y**ou** wanta hit on this?" the helicopter pilot asked, waving a large blunt under Constantine's nose.

"No thanks, mate, I'm confused enough already."

"Ha ha, confused enough . . . !" He paused to suck at the blunt and went on, spewing smoke with the words, giggling, "That's funny!" The chopper wobbled in the air, seeming on the point of spiraling down into the sea. But somehow he kept it more or less on course.

Norm the pilot, a heavyset guy in uniform, with a pointy little beard, small jolly eyes, and stringy brown hair that couldn't have pleased his CO, was piloting a big, double-rotored Chinook belonging to the U.S. Army, a transport chopper with its unmanned guns out front.

Constantine was sitting in the copilot's seat. Spoink was in back strapped into a chair against the inner bulkhead next to Gatewood, Mercury slumped in a harness beside them. All Constantine could see outside the Chinook was ocean, far below them. Way, way below them.

"What's the range on this thing?" he shouted over the engine noise.

Norm blinked at him. " 'What's a raging ding,' you say?"

"How far can you *go?* We've got to get to France!"

"Don't have that kinda range! No clearance there anyway, not for this flight! I already gotta make up a big story about getting lost to get away with this shit! Just doing it for my cuz! I'm gonna have to fucking kick in the direction finder and say it went blooey! Hey, you're not CIA are you? 'Cause if you are I'm gonna have to drop your ass in the Med from here!"

"What? No!" Constantine was taken aback by the sudden change in the conversation's direction. "People are always asking me if I'm in with that lot. Wouldn't go near them."

"Fucking CIA's everywhere—like the bull in the fucking china shop, dude! Those spooky-ass dicks want you to do shit for them without any accounting for it—you know, off the books—but they'll turn your ass in if you're into some shit on your own. Run a little weed into Baghdad for your Gs, and they want to blackmail you or bust you. After all I did for those fucks."

"What'd you do for 'em, then?"

"Oh, brought in a bunch of 'detainees' from a secret base in fucking Kuwait, is all—they put 'em in a special wing at Abu Ghraib, same system as Gitmo. This wing, the 'detainees' got no designation, no offi-

cial status, see, nobody knows they're there. Red
Cross don't know. So the CIA's assholes can interrogate 'em any way they want. I took a few dead ones
out of there since then. . . ."

Constantine glanced at Norm. He might've been
talking about boosting stereos instead of smuggling
hooded human beings for the CIA.

"But I do a lot of 'extracurricular' shit, of course;
my cuz back there, he knew that. I owed him a favor.
He got me some other backdoorsmen. Pays good.
See, those guys wanta get out bad."

"Backdoorsmen?"

"Deserters. They go out the back door, like. More
of those than the Pentagon wants you to know. Too
much freaky shit going on in Iraq—backdoorsmen
can't deal." He turned in his seat to Gatewood, held
out the blunt. "Hey cuz, you wanta hit this?" Gatewood shook his head and yawned. Spoink only
glared. Norm turned back to Constantine. "What's
with that Haji guy? He an Ali Baba?"

"He's not what he seems, mate. Nothing to worry
about."

But Constantine did worry about Spoink—if he still
was Spoink. He had seemed reluctant to board the
Chinook, hesitating halfway up the rope ladder. He
hadn't said a word since the yacht—and that was un-
natural for Spoink. Constantine suspected that the
Iranian terrorist who'd originally belonged to the
body had returned to it and shoved Spoink out somehow. Or perhaps he was in there, too, but repressed.

Constantine wasn't clear on what to do about it. If
he assumed that a terrorist had taken over the body,

he had to turn the guy in somewhere—didn't he? But it went against Constantine's nature to turn anyone in. Snitching was antithetical to him. And even though Spoink had said the guy was a terrorism big shot, Spoink might've misunderstood something. Maybe he was just a radical Muslim fundamentalist. That didn't make him a terrorist. And if Constantine did turn him in somewhere, he risked Spoink's spirit life. Could be a problem in the afterlife if you think you're in a body all cozy, and then, bam, somebody puts you up against a wall and shoots you. Trauma makes ghosts.

Spoink wasn't easy to like, but Constantine liked him anyway. And Spoink had come through for him. Ought to try to stand by him.

All Constantine could do right now though was keep an eye on the bearded git. *And hope I know what the bloody hell to do when the time comes. . . .*

Trouble with that plan was said bearded git might just kill him, first chance he got. Best not turn his back.

"Gotta let you guys out right here!" Norm shouted over the booming of the rotors.

Constantine leaned in his seat to look out the window of the chopper. "But—there's nothing out there, mate! We're in the middle of the bloody sea! You going to dump us in the ocean?"

"Look over that way! Down at five o'clock!"

"At five o'clock? Oh, right—twelve o'clock high and all that . . . looks like a tanker of some kind."

"Of some kind is right, man. The sinking kind if you, like, kick a bulkhead or something. A real rust pot called *Medusa's Revenge*. Greek guy named 'Papa' Papandreis is captain. That's where you're going next. Don't sleep facedown on his ship or he'll, like, sneak in and sodomize you."

"Here! I'll not sleep at all on the fucking ship. He expecting us is he?"

"Yeah, I radioed him before I picked you up. You got to pay him something to drop you on the coast of France. Get you there tomorrow I expect. I got a regular thing with him: I drop him deserters and money, pick up dope. He gets me the pretty good shit. Deserters pay him to move them across the Med."

Fifteen minutes later, Constantine was dropping from the rope ladder to the deck of the creaking old supertanker. He moved to stand protectively by Mercury—Gatewood had stretched her out on the deck, between him and Spoink—and he handed Papa a bundle of cash that'd come from Norm.

"Includes our fare to France," Constantine said, lying cheerfully. Norm couldn't hear him over the racket of the chopper.

Papa was a potbellied man in a T-shirt and a pea jacket, a hand-rolled cigarette poking from his beard; its smoke made him squint. He scratched at his groin, then shrugged and stuck the money in his coat. He attached a plastic shopping bag full of pot and hashish to the ladder's lowest rung and watched as Norm cranked it up into the hovering Chinook.

"See you on the avenue, Cuz!" Norm shouted, before piloting the chopper toward Iraq.

In another minute, Constantine and Gatewood,

along with the bearded figure who'd once called himself Spoink, were standing over Mercury on the vast rusty deck, slightly dizzy with oil fumes, looking at the crew gathered to look them over and wondering if they'd get off this tanker alive.

Paris, France

"Oh my Lord," Coggins said, "I feel strange. . . ."

"What did you expect, sir?" Strucken asked. Although supposedly subordinate to him, Strucken always seemed condescending, Coggins noticed. He vaguely remembered Morris remarking on the same thing. "You have had an unsettling experience in that helicopter. . . . There is always a time of adjustment, ja?"

The two men sat at a glass table on the gardened roof of an elegant apartment building owned, indirectly, by the SOT. Strucken sipped a pale German wine; Coggins nursed a beer. It was an overcast afternoon, with lowering clouds like muscles rippling under dinosaurian skin, and those dark, restless clouds made Coggins nervous. They were like the ones that the War Lord had come out of to fight the water giant that'd killed Burlington.

Coggins had seen many men die, but they'd died in a way that made sense. Until Burlington. He'd been killed by a thing that shouldn't exist. And the War Lord—Coggins had never seen it that way before. He'd thought it was just a state of mind that people shared, the kind of archetypal symbol that Professor Peierson had talked about at Yale. He'd thought it was a shared symbol—though a powerful symbol that you could actually see sometimes—that would push people into accelerating God's agenda. But he had seen it interacting with the elemental and he knew it was a real, independent being, it had physical form in its own world, and it had come partway into their own.

And then Dyzigi had told him that Morris had gotten away from the British asshole, and it was okay to sink that yacht—only, Coggins doubted Morris had really escaped with his life. He hadn't come back or been in contact, and after they'd sunk the yacht, Dyzigi had muttered, "If Morris didn't make it, well—sacrifices are necessary, on many levels."

"You're sure their boat sank, sir?" Strucken asked now. "The smaller boat, I mean."

"I . . . yeah. We strafed it. Anyway as we were leaving we saw a big damn tsunami wave bearing down on . . . on what was left of them."

Why am I lying to Strucken? he wondered. *I've got no confirmed kill on that mission.*

Strucken nodded, but without conviction.

Coggins had been bothered when he'd taken out that first yacht and it turned out to be the wrong one. He'd thought he was indifferent to civilian casualties—hell, there'd been plenty of them on the bombing runs he'd directed in Kosovo and Afghanistan—but somehow when you do it yourself, personally, it was harder to look away. There would be billions of deaths, of course, after the War Lord was unleashed; that's the way it was supposed to be.

Even so, he was surprised by how taking out those yachts had affected him. Then there was Burlington's death. . . .

Am I getting soft?

General Coggins looked at the sky and shuddered. "Burlington was a . . . well, maybe 'good man' ain't the right term. He was a reliable man—he could get a job done. He was loyal. Qualities hard to find."

"You let your pilot fly too close to the manifestation." Strucken shrugged dismissively.

"Look, what the hell *was* that thing? The water giant . . . thing. Do you know? I mean, sure, I was told water elemental. Okay, there are nature spirits. But that thing was . . . if that was up against us, what *else* is? You know what I mean? Any other fucking giants I ought to know about?"

"You ask me? I am but an assistant."

Coggins snorted, but said nothing more. He wanted to talk to Trevino. But he was sure about one thing—the way the world was now just couldn't stand. The Muslims were reproducing like rabbits. The Chinese and Hindus were reproducing like rabbits getting fertility treatments. The sword of God would have to come down and soon and cut them all away, and the world would start over again. He couldn't turn his back on this project just because it freaked him out a bit. Hell, he got used to cooking people with napalm in Vietnam.

He'd get used to the War Lord.

Coggins's cellphone chimed. He flipped it open. "Coggins. Yeah. So The Blossom has been cut?" He exchanged a significant look with Strucken. "Right." He closed the cellphone. "They're close," he told Strucken. "But there's still prep to do: the seed heads, and you know, what we have to do at the second target. Getting the altar in place—. They want to coordinate everything."

"Naturally," Strucken said, nodding to himself. Just as if he understood exactly what would be entailed.

Who the fuck am I in bed with? Coggins wondered. Morris had had his own doubts toward the end, Coggins knew. Could it be that Morris's doubts had marked him for death? That the SOT had *let* things get out of hand so they could dispose of him, without any unrest in the ranks?

Had they used Coggins to get rid of Morris—so that Coggins would get the message himself?

Coggins gazed up at the lowering clouds and thought, for a moment, he saw a face in them. A brutish face, gigantic, glowering down at him, its eyes like holes in reality . . .

But only for a moment. Then it was gone.

"I think," Coggins said, "I'm going to have a shot of bourbon in my beer."

Off the coast of France, near Marseilles

Constantine didn't want to sleep on the *Medusa's Revenge*. They were within sight of the French coast, but Papa claimed it wasn't safe to let them disembark until about an hour before first light. So Constantine had sat up into the night, watching over Mercury and keeping an eye on Spoink, who dozed on a bunk across from his own in the rank, mildewy little cabin they shared with Gatewood; and he kept an eye on the cabin's door, too. Mostly for Gatewood and Mercury's sake—the captain had been ogling Gatewood and the crew had been ogling Mercury.

"Ya'll dope her, huh, chief?" the guy with the tattoos on his shaved head had asked, when they'd first moved Mercury into the cabin. He had an accent from the American south and his left eye, probably glass, stared off to left field no matter where his other eye looked. It had mostly looked at Mercury's ass.

"No, I didn't bloody dope her. She's ill, is all. I'm taking her to a doctor."

" 'Cause you know, we get 'em sometimes, through here—women being, you know, shipped, to them sex factories over to Marseilles, and on to the Balkans. Asian chicks, 'specially Filipino broads thought they were going to get a cushy housekeeper job, and whuh-oh, lookie here, they get chained up to a bed in some dump. I mean, you know, whatever, I just want mine, chief. I mean I figure if she's doped up and gonna get screwed anyway and since I'm the second mate on the ship I ought to get some goddamned pussy."

"What's your name, mate—or should I say second mate?"

"My name? Harl."

"Right. Harl, if you touch that girl, if you come within ten feet of her, if you even turn either of those barmy eyes of yours her way, they're gonna say, 'Hullo, where's Harl? Is that 'im, a-bobbin' in the wake back there? Someone pitch 'is useless arse overboard, did they? What's for lunch, then?' I doubt they'd go back for you. You understand me, Harl?"

"You threatening me, you Brit fag?"

"He might be, but he doesn't have to," Gatewood had said. "I'll fucking kill you myself." He'd reached into his waistband, behind, and pulled out a small .45 automatic pistol. Just to give it a little more juice, he added a lie: "That girl's my goddamned sister."

"Oh, oh well shit, nobody told me she was your sister, criminy, forget it; I can just wait for the next shipment."

Gatewood, now, was sitting up in his bunk playing solitaire with a greasy deck of cards he'd found under the bunk.

"That a complete set of cards, is it, Gatewood?" Constantine asked, lifting up his whiskey bottle to see what was left in it. Just over half.

"More than complete. It's got six aces in it."

"Really! I see now why it was hidden under a bunk. Fancy a drink?"

"I'll have a shot, yeah, thanks."

"Here you go, this old coffee mug'll have to do. Might taste ever so slightly of shaving cream. Thanks for stepping in with that Harl oaf." He lifted the bottle in a toast. "Cheers."

"*Skol* and all that shit, man."

"Me name's John, you know."

"I'm Paul. And I don't know what I know. Not any more, John."

"You seemed to take it rather well, when that elemental put in an appearance. Some would've screamed bloody hell."

"It did sort of fuck with my head, as the guys in my outfit would say. And I did think of what Mirabeau said about the word 'impossible.' *Never let me hear that foolish word again."*

Constantine smiled. It seemed Gatewood was a more educated man than he'd let on. "But of course you'd already walked in the Hidden World . . . with a mob of ghosts."

Gatewood nodded. "I walked and drove . . . and walked some more, to that church, with dozens of dead people. I came across Iraq and Syria with ghosts—they led me there through places where there just wasn't anyone around. Walked me right across the border. So yeah. And then I saw a crucifix levitate." He looked at Spoink, lying on his bunk turned away from them. "You did that, right, Spoink?"

Spoink didn't reply. He just squeezed further over into the corner of his bunk.

"Spoink's going through something," Constantine said. "Best just let him be."

Gatewood looked at Constantine's coat, hanging over the back of the cabin's only metal chair. "I can see where that mummified hand is, in your coat. You see? A hand-shaped outline, kind of."

"Felt it twitching a couple of times, too."

"Fuck! I couldn't deal with that. Ghosts is one thing. . . . Hey, are they really all *in* that hand?"

"I wouldn't think so, in any literal sort of way. It's more like a gateway to a dimensional pocket, like. Hyperspherical pocket. Read your Rudy Rucker. The hand's in the pocket and there's a pocket in the hand." Constantine got up and checked on Mercury, touching her forehead. She seemed unchanged.

"You going to be able to help her?" Gatewood asked.

"I don't know, mate. I hope so. Another drink?" Gatewood stuck out his cup and Constantine poured. "What'd you mean, you don't know what you know? I mean, I've had that feeling myself, of course. Not sure if you mean the same thing."

Gatewood looked at Constantine narrowly. "John, I saw you call a fucking giant out of the water. I don't see you feeling confused about things. You know some damn secrets, for sure."

Constantine shrugged. "When you're a mortal, there's always more to know. A man lives all his life in, say, a little place like Fiji; some ways he's not sophisticated, is he? Now I'm like a man who left the island of Fiji and saw some of the USA and China and Japan and maybe Holland. And I know how to use a tram schedule in Holland and the folks back home don't. . . . Doesn't mean I quaff my pints with the prime ministers of the world. Doesn't mean I know anything about why we're all here in this life. I just know a little more than the other chaps in Fiji, is all. If you take my meaning."

Gatewood looked at him blankly. "You're from Fiji? I thought you were from England?"

"No, shite, it was a metaphor—"

Gatewood burst out laughing. "I was just fucking with you, John. I get it. You see more, but it's still a small part of the big picture. But you must've had a *glimpse* of why we're here, what the Big Picture is."

"You've walked with ghosts, mate. Didn't pick up anything about the Big Picture yourself, doing that?"

Gatewood swished his drink in his cup and then nodded, slowly. "Maybe some. Tension between . . .

between how transient everything is, and the eternal. Everything dies—but something essential's always there. Sense of . . . people trapped by states of mind. It's only more obvious in ghosts. But it's *everyone*. Still, some states of mind set you free. Things contradict, but they . . . they come together some way it's hard to understand. . . ."

Constantine nodded. "That's the right track. Universe runs on paradox, mate. It's the framework for the big engine, is paradox. Everything's temporary, everything's eternal at once. Kind of how you plug into it. Quantum uncertainty."

"You know, I walked with ghosts. I got like images of the next world, sort of, but I didn't really understand it. I mean, if there are ghosts here, what's there? Do they go to Heaven sometime? Hell? Do they reincarnate? Do they just . . . dissolve?"

"Yes," Constantine said.

"Yes which?"

"Yes all of it." Constantine took a deep breath. "Here's a short version, and it won't be right, but it's as close to right as I can come through the bourbon and how tired I am just now: you die, and if you're clinging to this world, you become a ghost. But most let go, sooner or later. When you do, you come to the 'River of Forgetfulness'—some call it that. It's a kind of barrier between our world and the Hidden World. Beyond it, the higher dimensions all coalesce at a certain point and become the Sea of Consciousness. It's the raw consciousness, like, that we all arise from. We're like waves on the surface of it, when we rise up into mortal life. Then we sink back

down into it, like a wave does, when we die. Then
the wave rises again—only it's shaped differently
now, yeah? That's like a different life. Your next incarnation. So it's not like people think, soul going
from body to body like pouring wine from one bottle
to the next. It's like there's a relationship between
the waves, but they're not the same wave. Mostly
when people die they sink into the big sea—where
something is kind of, like, recorded of them, what little thin 'soul' they have. It has some experiences,
then, that may seem to take eternity, based on what
their relationship is to the light—they're drawn to
the light in the sea of consciousness or to the dark
places. They eventually reincarnate. People *are*,
after death—and they *aren't*. Except some people
are more than others."

"Some 'are' . . . more?"

"Some 'are' more if they build up their spirit in life,
keep their individuality afterwards. They evolve. The
little thin spirits can do it more and more over many
of those 'waves' . . . till they can eventually remember
themselves. Remember who they are, see themselves
as they are. When they build up a bit, they may take
talents with them, one life to the next, like our Spoink
has. You understand?"

"Sort of yes, sort of no."

"Best you can hope for. Have another drink." He
considered Paul Gatewood, and wondered what he'd
done with his uniform. Gatewood had told him that
he'd been with the U.S. military in Iraq. "Have another drink and tell me, how'd a sharp bloke like you
get to be a private under that bunch of confused bas-

tards? You know, the same outfit that let Osama slip
away in Toro Boro . . ."

"Nine-eleven, John. And a desire, I guess, to get at
the nub of life. Things just felt too . . . too much like
you were in a fucking *mall* all the time, where I was
from. No matter where you were, it was always a
shopping mall somehow. Nothing seemed real
enough. Being an officer was too far from the reality. I
wanted to meet life and death, both of them, head-
on. . . . Test myself against them, you know?"

"I reckon. Never had the slightest inclination to
sign up m'self. Have another drink, that's my fighting
motto. It's on my bloody coat of arms. . . ."

✦✦◈✦✦

But about four-fifty in the morning, Constantine was
regretting the last tumbler or two of whiskey. His
head spun, and when the launch he was in started
lowering into the darkness, dangling and swaying on
the cables, it seemed to pick up the wallowing of the
sea, and he felt himself close to heaving his guts out.
He was out of practice at drinking, after his time in
the monastery.

Always a mistake to let your liver get healthy.

The launch slipped jerkily down the ropes, the mechanical crane creaking as if it might snap at any moment. Constantine was greatly relieved when the boat
settled into the water.

The *Medusa's Revenge* was still in deep water,
within a half mile of shore. Harl started the outboard
and tooled them through the dark sea. under cloud-

muted stars and a declining half-moon, over to a spit of land stretching out from a remote beach about halfway between Marseilles and Toulon. The boat touched land; Harl watched irritably, twitching, his glass eye slipping so its fake iris looked back into his socket, as Spoink got out, splashing up onto the rocky ground, and then Constantine and Gatewood carried Mercury up onto shore.

Harl let the boat drift away from them, glaring like a white-trash Cyclops, before shouting, "Next time ya'll come around, yew better show me some gawd-damn respect!"

"I respect you so much," Gatewood said, putting Mercury's feet on the ground and drawing his pistol, "I'm gonna shoot some holes in that boat, 'cause I know you're tough enough to swim back to the ship!"

"Fuck you, asshole!" But Harl hastily put the little boat's outboard in reverse, swung it about, and headed for the ship with all possible speed.

Constantine and Gatewood carried Mercury along the finger of land to the beach, picking their way carefully across the rocky ground. Constantine kept a cigarette clamped in his mouth, so he had to squint against its smoke the whole way.

At last they stretched her out on a soft patch of sand in the lee of a charred driftwood log.

"Someone's had a fire here," Gatewood said, kicking at the cold ashes and hugging himself. "You think we should risk one? Mercury's shivering. Me, too."

"Like to—can't. We're in this country illegally. Got to get to Marseilles. If the Old Balkan's still there, he'll hook us up." Constantine was rather proud of using this Americanism, "hook us up." "The Balkan owes me. I yanked an evil spirit—or so he thought—out of his daughter some years back. He's the man for forged papers. Might be in jail by now though . . ." He looked around and noticed a moving light, about five hundred yards up the beach, spearing along the shoreline road. "You see that? Looks like cars up there on a highway. I ought to be able to get someone to stop. . . ."

"But how do we get her there without attracting too much attention? We're a strange group anyway. I mean, with your friend with the beard and the . . . oh crap, where'd he go?"

They looked around and couldn't find Spoink. "Uh-oh . . ." Constantine looked around. The eastern horizon was redefining itself in gray, but the sun hadn't truly risen yet. He cast his psychic net out and picked up a confused signal from down the beach: a fearful, muted word or two from Spoink, soon locked down under another presence, darker and cryptic.

John. He . . . it's . . . crush . . . pressure . . .

"Just stay here and watch over Mercury, Paul, will you?"

Constantine started off after Spoink, not at all sure how he was going to deal with him. But Constantine didn't want to abandon him to a living hell in another man's out-of-control body.

He had gotten only about fifty paces when his foot struck something soft and warm. He crouched and in the dim light made out the shape of a large dead sea-gull. He could smell blood. A little more light leaked

into the sky and as he kept looking at the dark shape
he perceived that its throat had been cut. Some Muslims still performed animal sacrifices at Mecca—and
this freshly killed seagull's body was turned so its
head pointed southeast, toward the Holy City.

Constantine stood, and saw the dim outline of the
man Spoink had inhabited, standing near a boulder at
the foot of a hillside overlooking the beach.

"Oi—Spoink!" he called. There was no response.

Constantine sighed and trudged toward him, thinking he might be able to take control of the man's
mind long enough to let Spoink reestablish himself.
"Oi, Spoink, you in there? You got to take control
again, mate!"

John . . . help me . . . he's too . . . And then the contact faded.

But the man was turning his way. He stared, for the
space of several panting breaths, and then started toward him.

Too late, Constantine remembered the Blue
Sheikh's prophecy, his warning about a man slashing
the throat of a bird. . . .

The man Spoink inhabited was picking up speed,
running full tilt, teeth bared, a dark shape with only his
teeth showing in the midst of the silhouette of his head.

He shouted something about Allah, as he came—
it was the same word in Farsi as Arabic—and something more about *daevas,* and *Iblis.* Probably calling
on God to help him in his fight with the Devil. In that
split second, Constantine picked up a loose mental
image flickering from the Iranian: he'd seen Spoink's
memory of him and Constantine chucking a couple

of the Imam's friends overboard in the Caspian. He was sure Constantine was an agent for the Little Satan.

Face contorted, the Iranian knocked him flat on his back, roaring obscurely in Farsi—face close, breath hot, his beard in Constantine's mouth, left hand on his throat, his knees pinioning Constantine's arms. Metal gleamed in the thin light: the knife in his right hand, poised to stab. The very knife Constantine had used to cut the heel of his palm.

Constantine reached out with his mind, managed to focus his mental field on the Iranian's brain stem enough to interfere with its signals. The man became momentarily paralyzed, body going rigid. . . .

And the knife blade stopped a quarter inch from Constantine's throat. It hovered there.

But Constantine knew he couldn't hold it long. The Iranian began to shake, to struggle against Constantine's control, making a gurgling sound deep in his throat.

There came the sound of feet chuffing rapidly through sand, then a crunching thump—and the Iranian groaned and let go of Constantine, slumping to the sand beside him.

Constantine sat up to see Gatewood standing over them, one side of his face limned in the increasing dawn light, the pistol in his hand. "Didn't mean to hit him quite so hard."

"Glad you thumped him good," Constantine said, turning to examine the bearded Iranian. "Another second and he'd have cut my throat."

Gatewood crouched beside them. "How is he?"

"Um . . ." Constantine could feel no pulse in the man's neck. "He was in touchy health right along. He was in a coma when Spoink took him over. My guess is . . ." He bent close and pressed his ear to the man's chest. "Yeah. He's dead."

"Dead!" Gatewood tried pumping the man's chest, attempting to restart his heart. The body shook limply in the sand with his efforts, but the heart refused to start beating. Gatewood stood up, shaking his head. "Shit. I was just trying to get him off you!"

"He was barely alive, in a way. Probably some blood clot in the brain, keeping him in the coma. You knocked it loose and it closed his accounts. It's for the best, you know."

"What? Your friend was in there."

"He was *trapped* in there. This has set him free. He's probably glad of it. He was disillusioned with being embodied again anyway. Getting that nasty meat-puppet feeling." Constantine stuck out his hand. "Bloody weeping Christ, I'm tired. Here, help me up."

Gatewood pulled Constantine to his feet. "We'd better get back to Mercury, John."

Grunting, Constantine picked up the body Spoink had been using in a fireman's carry, and trudged back to Mercury. Blood dripped from the back of the dead man's head, leaving a spotty trail behind them.

They found Mercury still apparently dozing in the shelter of the log; the wind reached around the log sometimes and made her hair ripple past her closed eyes; her lips moved silently.

Constantine put the body down and sat on the log

beside the two supine figures—a bearded stranger and Mercury, one growing cold in death and the other twitching in an uneasy trance.

"I'm shagged out with lugging limp bodies around. . . ."

Constantine sat a good while, just to make sure the man was dead.

The sun edged into view, the clouds around it salmon colored; the wind died out, but the Mediterranean's surf rolled in, drew back, and rolled in again, rumbling and whispering, repeating the same cryptic message it had repeated since before the time of Ulysses: *A movement . . . and a rest. A movement . . . and a rest. A movement . . .*

Was Spoink really gone? Constantine wondered. Was he truly set free?

He closed his eyes, widened his mental receptivity, and called out.

Spoink? Oi, Spoink!

Was there a response? A faint echo of an echo? Maybe. And something brushed at his ankle.

He opened his eyes and looked down at the sand. The wind had died down, but the sand near his feet was lifting up as if blown by a breeze, only it was moving in precise directions, handfuls of sand slipping this way and that, as if guided by a sculptor. Beach sand and bits of shell drifted and feathered and traced, until a picture formed in the sand, drawn by an unseen hand.

It was a man's face—a young man with long, unruly hair, a wide, grinning mouth. . . .

Constantine intuitively felt this was an image of

Spoink as he'd been in life out in California. As if in response to his recognition, the face in the sand rearranged itself so that one of its eyes winked.

Then the wind skirled up from nowhere and erased the image—but Constantine had gotten the message. "Okay, mate. See you at the local. . . ."

"The local what?" Gatewood asked.

"Forget it."

"Were you talking to that Spoink, dude? I could tell he was still around somewhere."

"I expect he'll head across the River of Forgetfulness soon enough." Constantine looked closely at Gatewood. "You could 'tell he was still around'? Some ghosts are pretty easy to see, but if they're spirits, really independent, more than a lost and lonesome ghost, like, they're harder to see. Can you see him?"

"No, I can feel him."

"Can you, then?" Constantine lit a cigarette, drew deeply on it, squinting at Gatewood knowingly. "You can *feel* him. . . ."

"Um, what about it?"

"The ghosts in Baghdad didn't choose you because you're a kindly personality, though that probably helped. You've got a deeper connection to the dead than I do. You're a medium, Paul. That a specialty in the U.S. Army, is it? 'Spiritualism Specialist Gatewood'? "

"A medium? You mean like . . ." He snorted, and shook his head firmly. "No way! They're all frauds!"

"They are. You're right. Except for a very few. If

some oik says he's a medium, that's a sterling indication that he's not a medium. None of the famous ones are the real thing. But the talent does exist, it's just quite rare. It's been sort of hidden away in you, I expect. That's the real reason you've come along on this daft expedition. To guide them to me, and to stay in touch with them."

"Hey, I don't *want* to be a medium."

Constantine shrugged. "I don't want to be a fuckup, but I am."

"Great to know I'm in good hands with you." He bent over the dead man and touched his throat. "He's not coming back, unless it's as a ghost. But I don't sense the Iranian guy around. Hey, this being a medium, is it going to get . . . worse? I mean, won't they start, like, coming around and waking me up at night and scaring my girlfriends off, that sort of thing?"

"No doubt they'll make you spit up white ecto-goo, and you'll be trying to chat up a pretty girl and some old lady'll take over your mouth so she can tell her husband what a bastard he was. Get used to it."

"Oh . . . crap."

Constantine went to hunker down by Mercury, taking her pulse. Still steady, but he'd need to get some food into her, first chance.

"So what now, John?" Gatewood asked.

"Now we bury this bearded git as best we can and say a few words to wish him onto Allah. Wish I had my Iranian friends with me—got a couple of good mates, Persian Muslims in London. Top of the line blokes, they are. They'd give him a pass to the Prophet, all right. Best we can do is consign him to whatever crustacean burrows in this sand, and then we'll head for that road up there. I'll have a go at getting someone to stop."

Constantine took the little figure of Zoroaster out of his pocket and held it up to glimmer in the morning sun. "With any luck I can . . . *persuade* them to give us a lift."

12

PROBLEM CHILDREN: REALITY AND UNREALITY

*A village near Jalalabad, Afghanistan,
close to the border with Pakistan*

Abdur and his brother Halil were playing army in the dusty, empty lot next to their house, mostly staying in the shade cast by the houses on either side. It was a hot day. They were on the edge of town, and in the distance angular blue hills rose from the haze. They liked to imagine they were patrolling those hills with the Afghani army and the American army. They had visited their Aunt Noesh in Gandahar, near a U.S. military base, and she had said the Americans had arrested the Taliban men who had been threatening her for not wearing her burqa. Abdur and Halil's father hated the Taliban: they had killed his brother for selling some American DVDs. He had merely been trying to survive, selling these movies which he got on a trip to Egypt—mostly early Adam Sandler films and one starring Annette Bening—and they had killed him for "spreading the dirt of the Great Satan." The

American soldiers had befriended the two boys, had taken them on rides on their motorcycle, and let them climb up into a parked Chinook helicopter; they had given them candy and showed them how to use a baseball mitt. They liked Americans and they often played American soldier. Lately Abdur, the oldest at eleven, had been playing President Karzai, pretending that the president was leading the army against the Taliban in the hills. Halil got to be the general in the game. "You are only nine. So you cannot be president yet," Abdur said.

They were throwing rocks, standing in for grenades, at a stack of old tires on the other side of the vacant lot just now, and smelling the delicious scent of meat and flatbread cooking inside the house. Their mother was cooking; their father was home for lunch from his job as a taxi driver. Halil was suggesting they go look to see if there was anything ready to eat yet when they heard the rumble in the sky, and looked up to see the American plane.

It was an F-16, equipped with missiles; higher up, they could see one of the big strange airplanes, with the mushroomlike hump on its back, that sometimes, Abdur had heard, directed the other planes.

But they were not frightened of the American planes. They were their friends, after all. They might know where some Taliban were hiding. They were going to "give them hell"—that was an expression Abdur was proud of knowing; he had heard it used at the base.

"Ooh, where do you think they are going to shoot?" Halil asked.

Abdur said nothing. He had seen the F-16 tilt and come around their way, and he was seeing the air-to-surface missiles launching, and he couldn't speak, he was too awestruck by the sight. He knew they couldn't be aiming at his house—it must be someone nearby, it must be—

When their house exploded, Abdur and Halil, though not indoors, were close enough that they were killed immediately because the exterior walls of the house were propelled outward with terrific force, smashing them flat.

Abdur and Halil hardly felt it, they were both dead so quickly. Their father, however, had been protected by having stepped out for a moment to get something from his taxi, and the car had sheltered him from much of the explosion's force. Blinded in one eye by glass from his overturned cab, he staggered back to the smoking crater where his house had been and stood on the edge of the wreckage, looking past the crust of walls, seeing parts of his wife sticking out of the rubble here; more parts twenty feet away.

Abdur and Halil watched him from above the house. They seemed tethered to it, like balloons. They did not understand, and they could barely remember who they were, or who this man was. He was important to them, close to them, and they must stay here and determine who he was and what had happened, they must stay and stay in this broken place, they must not go anywhere, they were closely connected to this weeping man with the face of blood, they must not go. . . .

Paris, France

"General Coggins, sir?" Captain Simpson's voice, gently prompting, calling him from a troubled sleep.

. . . this weeping man with the face of blood . . . like a painting of Jesus he'd once seen. Like . . .

"Oh Lord Jesus!" Coggins sat up abruptly on the sofa in the suite's main room where he'd fallen asleep; a midmorning nap, really, after a long sleepless night.

The image of the man staggering through the wrecked house, the ghosts of two children hovering over him . . .

It stayed in his mind. . . .

Just a dream, though. That was all.

"General? I'm sorry, sir—you told me to get you this report, no matter what, when it came in, but if you want to finish your nap—"

"No, Simpson, give it to me. . . . I just . . . Lord, what a dream . . ." He smoothed his rumpled hair, flipped the folder open. "Remind me what this is?"

"That raid you directed in Iraq, right before we went on the 'special assignment.' You got some guys you thought were Al Qaeda. They gave us that safe-house location in Afghanistan? Jalalabad?"

"Oh right. That was my raid; I wanted to know if it'd borne any fruit, yes. . . . I need some coffee. . . ."

"Shall I—"

"No, dammit, you're a captain, not a corporal. I'll buzz for it. This report . . ." He flipped through the pages. "Seems like . . . shit . . . they hit the wrong place?"

"Yes and no sir. It's been confirmed as the location that the prisoners gave us. But they—either they were wrong or they were lying. Seems to've been a family sympathetic to the Karzai regime, anti-Taliban. Looks like in fact the guy was a cab driver doing a little spying for the CIA on the side. One of our own people. Chances are the Taliban found out. They make up lists, disinformation lists, try to get us to target innocent people, even our allies. . . ."

Coggins felt sick. "And the pricks score a two for one—a propaganda victory and—" He broke off, realizing. "Was this place on the edge of town? Vacant lot next door?"

"Yes sir, you can see on the surveillance photos . . ."

"Holy shit." The house from his dream.

"Sir?"

"General!" It was Strucken, carrying something into the suite. Whatever he was carrying was hidden under a gray cloth. Strucken looked coldly at Simpson. "This one will have to leave. I have something important. . . . Vital. It must not wait. . . . We must discuss. No one must be here with us, General."

"Whatever, fine, Simpson, thank you. Go ahead on downstairs. Oh, before you go, they, uh—they're still regarding me as on 'special assignment,' are they?"

"Yes sir. That's the designation on the communiqué."

"Good. How long the chief of staff will go for that smokescreen I don't know. . . . Okay, I'll see you downstairs in about an hour."

When Simpson had gone, Strucken set the object

in his arms—something glassy, about as big as a gallon jar—on the ornate coffee table beside the sofa.

"What's this?" Coggins reached to pull the cloth away.

"No sir—no!" Strucken stopped Coggins with a firm grip around his wrist. Seeing the cold anger this impertinence elicited, Strucken drew his hand back and bowed slightly. "I'm sorry, General. Best not to . . . expose this. I have certain instructions."

They both looked at the object as a faint sloshing sound, conveying contained agitation, came from under the gray cloth.

Coggins rubbed his throbbing head. "What the devil?"

Strucken shrugged. "Not precisely. Now, sir, I must inform you that you have been under psychic attack today. Our friend, Herr Dyzigi, informed me of this. He was quite clearly informed himself. You were sleeping just now. Did you have any strange dreams?"

"I . . . well, yeah. Seemed like . . . it was about something real. Apparently. Couple of kids and their folks caught in a bad intelligence strike. Surgical strike on the wrong damn house. Sad as a son of a bitch, too. 'Course it won't matter soon. You know—after."

It wouldn't matter after it all started—would it?

"Ah yes," Strucken was saying, thoughtfully. "I see. I see their tactic. Empathy, guilt. Cunning of them."

"What? Whose tactic?"

"Ah—" Strucken looked at the window, made his face neutral. "As to that, I cannot say. That is, I do not know. But no doubt—Lucifer and his minions."

Coggins was a bit startled to realize, without the shred of a doubt, that Strucken was lying. Whoever had sent the dream at him like some kind of supernatural "psy-ops" ploy, it wasn't Lucifer. So who was it? Maybe that Constantine bird. Maybe some other hostile magician type. The question was, why was Strucken so nonplussed by the question? Why was he lying about it?

He looked at the object under the cloth on the coffee table. He figured he knew what that was. He'd glimpsed it before. He didn't like to think about it.

"What'd you bring that fucking thing in here for?"

"It is very sensitive. It will sense if there is a . . . an influence over you now. Dyzigi sensed the enemy influence sending powerful images to you and trying to establish control. We need to know if—"

"Oh really? And if you find this so-called influence, what then?"

"Why, we . . . we shall remove it."

"And how'll you do that?"

"Dyzigi will know."

Coggins snorted. "How do we do this little test of yours?"

"Kneel down with your head close to it, and it will respond in a certain way if their influence is upon you."

"Oh really. Strucken—*Herr* Strucken—fuck that."

The German hoisted an eyebrow. "I don't understand."

Coggins turned, reached into the coat he'd left folded on the arm of the sofa, and removed a small .25 caliber back-up pistol. He flicked the safety off. He didn't point it at Strucken yet, but he didn't need to. "Now you tell me who is it attacking me. Who's doing this 'psychic attack' stuff?"

"I have told you."

"The hell you have. That was bullshit. Who is it? There's a good deal here I thought I understood, and I'm beginning to realize I don't. Maybe Morris found out. . . . Is that it?"

"I do not understand."

"You said that before and you were full of shit then, too. I'm not disputing someone's fucking with me—that report there, that Simpson brought me, it confirms something that happened an hour and a half ago. I just had that dream. Implies it isn't any accidental connection. Some kind of black psy-ops program, maybe, or maybe it's supernatural bullshit, like you're telling me. Now who did it? Who did it really? Who's trying to influence me?"

"I do not know who—we merely wish to confirm that the influence is still there—I must insist—"

As Strucken spoke he was reaching smoothly behind him.

Coggins felt a red fury rising in him then. He felt as if the War Lord were rising up in him, urging him on. He stuck his pistol up under Strucken's chin and grabbed the elbow of the hand reaching behind him.

"You will not draw a gun on me, you Nazi son of a cocksucker!"

"I do not—!" Strucken struggled, jerking his hand free. Coggins saw the dark shape of a gun in Strucken's hand and he fired, the bullet passing through the soft flesh under Strucken's jaw, up through his palate, through his sinuses and his brain, blowing off the top of the German's head. Bits of skull stuck to the ceiling.

Strucken slumped and Coggins let him fall, staring at the body. "Well Lord, that did a lot of damage for a .25. . . ." He broke off, looking at Strucken's hand.

There was no gun in the dead man's hand—it was a cellphone: a dark object about the size of a small gun.

He looked at the .25 in his hand. It was an unregistered gun—a good precaution he took, having a weapon that couldn't be traced to him. He took the cellphone and put the pistol in Strucken's hand.

Simpson came in then. "Thought I heard a noise. . . . Kinda funny noise . . ."

He stopped, seeing Strucken's body. Stepped back as bits of tissue fell from the ceiling.

"A pitiful suicide," Coggins said, winking. "He couldn't deal with carrying that fucking thing around." He pointed at the jar under the cloth.

Captain Simpson nodded slowly, taking it all in and asking no questions. It just wasn't in him to question the general, which was one reason the general kept him around.

Simpson went to stare at the thing on the coffee table—reached to pull away the cloth . . .

"I wouldn't, if I were you," Coggins said.

Simpson drew his hand back. He swallowed. "What'll we do with it?"

"I'd like to chuck it in the Seine. But it's part of the Big Picture. So we leave it here and Dyzigi'll deal with it . . . and this asshole's body. And Dyzigi'll have to accept I don't submit to any 'tests.' I'm putting you on notice now: you're watching my back close from here on out, and I mean close, pard. But they got to know, I'm not their little lap dog."

No sir, I'm not, Coggins thought. *I'm the hand of God or I'm nothing—just nothing at all.*

Paris, France, seven hours later

Dyzigi had unpacked the black velvet curtains he had brought with him from Israel—the curtains that had been such a puzzlement to the French customs agents—and now he hung them over the hotel room's windows, tucking them at the edges to thoroughly block the fading daylight. When he finished, the only appreciable illumination in the room was from the small lamp beside his bed. Yet he could see another glow: the curtains were textured with shapes, images, cuneiform writing; invisible to the naked eye, but outlined in black light now, projecting the figures, barely visible, across the room; across Dyzigi himself. The room muttered to itself, chattering *sub voce* about these symbols.

He then took a greasy yellow candle from a canvas bag—a candle made partly from the bone ash and fat of children—and set it up in a hotel cup, on the center of the floor. He lit the candle, muttering certain ancient names and switched off the electric light. A sickly glow encircled the candle; a rancid smell pervaded the room. Perfect.

He had no need of magic circles for protection. All such were irrelevant to Dyzigi. . . .

He drew a chair from the desk, and sat on it, staring at the candle. He said the name only three times—and each time the Guiding Entity emerged a little more.

Then Dyzigi—the true Dyzigi—found himself hovering in an upper corner of the room, near the ceiling, where a cobweb fluttered in the air-conditioning.

His living point of view was up here, looking down on himself, his body, sitting in the chair in front of the candle. He felt quite distant and lonely and paralyzed, up here. Like a helium balloon, released by a child at a party, trapped against the ceiling. Bobbing up there till the one who toyed with the balloon should grab the string and pull it along behind him again.

But Dyzigi's body, in the chair down below him, was speaking. It was speaking to the figure whose shadowy outline formed in the attenuated heat waves from the candle.

"You were right, he has been drawn into the fray, after all. . . ."

Yes. MacCrawley tried to prevent it. But what the one called the Blue Sheikh supposes is his will, what the Seraphim suppose to be their will, is actually my will. Let MacCrawley imagine he controls things; let our enemies suppose they guide Constantine. It is I who summon the British Magus. It is I who will consume him in the end. He does not realize that his soul is already anchored in N'Hept. . . .

"I am concerned, Master, about General Coggins—there is a radiance sending visions to him. They are trying to show him he serves *our* Lord when he supposes he is serving his own. . . ."

You are concerned that this Coggins is being influenced by the Enemy? That he is beginning to suspect the truth? It is nothing. He will have his place, before the end. Another will take his place in the ritual: we will not want for errant warriors.

"Still—you are trapped, my Master," said the thing in Dyzigi's body. "It wounds me to see you without your former glory. I ache to be the instrument of your revenge on Constantine. He has thrown down your throne; he has trampled your raiment."

Dyzigi's soul, a pale, insubstantial thing not much larger than an infant, emaciated for want of light and sustenance and hope, pressed back against the ceiling, wishing it did not have to hear this conversation; wishing it had the strength to break the etheric bond that held it to the body, to get free once and for all. It was well that the face on the body inhabited by the dark spirit was invisible to Dyzigi's detached soul. He knew that face would now be hideously contorted—a gargoyle's face. Over time, since the fatal moment when he'd made the mistake of inviting the demon in—believing its lies of great freedom, greater power—his appearance had by degrees become warped by the possessor. The true form of the demon G'Broag'Fram was beginning to show, even in ordinary times, in Dyzigi's mortal face. . . . He was glad, was Dyzigi's soul, that most of the time he slumbered, fitfully and alone, within the possessed body. He was very much afraid of looking out of his own eyes, for fear he would encounter a mirror somewhere; he might see how the face had changed since the possession. . . .

He barely remembered the young Dyzigi, a student of abnormal psychology who'd slowly become convinced that some of the patients who claimed to be possessed really were. The young Dyzigi became too drawn, too intrigued by the Hidden World. How long ago now? Thirty years?

Oh God, when would it end . . . ?

Yes, G'Broag—John Constantine has thrown me down from the posting awarded by Lucifer himself; Constantine has displaced me from the hierarchy of Hell. But still, I have you, my faithful servant. . . .

"My Master, may I not destroy the soul with which I cohabit this body? May I not propel it into the outer darkness, so that it may feed you? Its presence troubles me. It is sometimes aware that I have taken over its body. . . . It squirms. . . ."

So they all do, as Constantine has learned—he was nearly killed by one such displacement. But you are stronger by far. You will keep the true Dyzigi subdued. Without him, you would not be able to sustain an appearance of humanity for long—your true form would burst through. This is a testament to the superb purity of your malignance. It is a compliment. But it is a problem, too—we need to sustain the disguise, to deceive Trevino and Coggins and those Servants of Transfiguration highly placed in British and American government, awaiting word. You will need that mask. I must go— Lucifer wishes to chastise me once again. He plans to feed me to something particularly vile today. Oh, to have Constantine here! He must be seduced! In-

duce in him at the first opportunity a remember-
ance of Konz—and the dark thread that binds
him. . . .

"I will, my Master. Your time of liberation will
come. . . ."

Then the candle fluttered, its flame spiraled and
hissed. . . .

And the dark entity, that Baron of Hell, was gone
again to the backwaters of Satan's realm.

Dyzigi's soul wailed within itself. Feeling drawn,
pulled inexorably, back into his body, into close proximity with living darkness, so that he was coiled
around the spine of evil, so that he was clasping the
kundalini of predation.

He was dragged back into the body sitting on the
chair in the hotel room—and in despair, sought black
unconsciousness.

The body, however, was quite alert. It stood up,
guided by its possessor, who fetched away the candle, took down the curtains, and went about Hell's
business.

Marseilles, France

Constantine picked one of the grubbier casinos at the
gaming end of the boulevard. It wouldn't do to go to
the ones looking like they'd been designed by Frank
Lloyd Wright, with swooping roofs and circular windows and expansive drives, uniformed doormen
opening limo doors; they might not let him in, seeing
as he'd only patchily shaved with the rusting razor
he'd found in the ship's cabin and seeing as he was

getting a bit ripe, his clothes overlong for laundering. And they'd have the brighter casino security operatives at the posh ones. He didn't cheat at cards in any *detectable* way—but he did cheat and though they didn't know how it was done, if they were reasonably alert they could tell it was happening someway. They'd figure he had an inside man, or he'd palmed cards. They mostly didn't believe in psychics. And that was mostly wise, until you met a real one.

This place was smaller on the inside than it looked on the outside, as they all were; it was painfully lit, garishly decorated, noisy, and crowded. There were men who looked like a central casting call for "gangster types" in distinctly ungangsterish suits, strolling around.

Constantine glanced at his watch—it was a wristwatch with a broken band so he had to take it out of his coat pocket to look at it. It was 4:00 P.M. This was a twenty-four-hour casino. But mostly there were gambling addicts and pros here at this hour, he supposed. He didn't want to make Gatewood wait long; Gatewood was waiting with Mercury at the Balkan's place while their traveling papers were coming together.

Constantine was looking for poker; he'd found it more reliable, with his talents, than blackjack and baccarat. "Evening, squire," he told the floor manager. "Got an open poker game, have you?"

"Pok-air, monsieur?" A long-nosed specimen with dark eyes, too close together, and a bad toupee, the floor manager looked Constantine up and down. "We have zuh Texas Hold Zem and zuh Stud, monsieur."

"What, in France—? That Hold 'Em thing?"

"It is *a la mode,* monsieur," the manager sniffed contemptuously, "mais c'est pas a'mon gout."

"Not my taste either, squire, but it looks to me they have a higher buy-in on the stud games. I'll need two hundred Euro in chips."

Constantine was soon at an oblong green felt table with seven other players. He had to win soon to stay in the game because this was no-limit and he only had two hundred Euro, cobbled together between him and Gatewood.

He hadn't played Hold 'Em before, but he knew how to do it, more or less; he'd seen it on telly just when the new poker rage was spreading. They dealt you two cards, facedown. When everyone had bet or folded based on their cards, they dealt "the flop," three more face up in the center of the table. More betting, then they dealt two more cards, the turn card and the river card, betting on each. The five cards face up in the center were your cards, too—community cards anyone could use, with the cards in their hand, to make the best five-card hand they could from them.

Constantine needed time to expand his psychic awareness to the others at the table, and he was determined to take no chances with his meager betting money. He folded the first two hands. At the third deal he got two eights. "Pocket eights." Constantine called the one-hundred-Euro bet. It was a risk, but he was tired, it was late, and he had an edge. A tanned guy with receding blond hair, looked Swedish but sounded American, whistled when he looked at his own cards and muttered, just as if he didn't intend the others to hear, "My Sweet Lord. Sometimes you get the cards. . . ."

He did it pretty well, and two people folded right there, but Constantine knew it was "table talk" and the guy was just acting stupidly open about his cards as a bluff. He didn't even need to read his mind to know he didn't have a good hand.

The flop came: a queen of hearts, a jack of spades—and an eight. That gave Constantine three of a kind. He could still be beaten, though.

He extended his psychic field, focused it on first one, then another of the three players remaining beside him and read their minds, picking up their hands. A pair of aces for the French lady wearing the crokies on her glasses, a pair of sevens for the fat guy—and the smug table-talking blond guy had a three and a six off suit. Nobody had the makings of a straight or a flush. Even so the balding blond guy chuckled to himself with satisfaction and raised everyone three hundred Euro. The guy with the sevens folded. Constantine had the best hand with three of a kind. But that could change when the next two cards came. . . . The pair of aces folded. . . . And the blond guy looked at Constantine expectantly, counting his chips out so it looked like he was going to make a big bet. He was trying to frighten Constantine into folding.

Constantine couldn't see what cards were coming up—he didn't have X-ray eyes and his precognition had its own timing. He couldn't see into the future at will. The other players would have to see their own cards first, before he could read their minds and know what they were.

So he was still gambling, despite knowing what the others had in their hands, when he went "all in," betting everything.

"Ohhh-kay," the balding guy said, swallowing. He couldn't win even if the next two cards gave him three of a kind—his cards were of a lower value than Constantine's. Two deuces came up, giving Constantine a full house.

Moments later he was scooping in the chips. He folded the next hand, but the following one gave him an ace-high diamond flush. The bald guy had a straight and this time he was acting as if he had nothing. Constantine had read his mind and knew he had a straight, and again, when it came down to the end, he went all in. The blond guy's triumphant smile faded when he saw that Constantine had an ace-high diamond flush.

Having cleaned the table talker out, Constantine spent another forty minutes winning every hand he bet on. There was a sense, he liked to think, in which he wasn't cheating; he only played the cards he was dealt; he didn't palm cards, didn't use sleight of hand to make good hands. But of course knowing what someone else has in poker is critical, and if you do it any way but guessing, you're cheating.

Constantine noticed the floor manager watching him, consulting with a chunky, greasy-looking man in a tuxedo with a coffee stain down the front. The "kingfish" maybe. He made sure to lose a hand, coolly, while these guys were watching. They wandered off.

He still had four thousand Euro and decided it was

enough to get a serviceable car. They couldn't keep the Balkan's car and they needed one to transport Mercury—she couldn't go on a train in her state. They had to pay for a nurse for Mercury, to come with them to Paris. They'd also need plane fare later, he suspected. He got up and went toward the door, and found himself stopping at the crap table. The money was piled up, the dice were rolling; you'd win the casino's money. Unfortunately he was not significantly telekinetic. Not enough for this. He shrugged and turned away.

And the mummified hand in his coat made a fierce clutching in his pocket. He shuddered, jumping a little. The floor manager stared at him, scowling. Constantine waggled his fingers at the guy. He started to turn away again; again the hand twitched. He felt an overpowering urge to bet his money on the dice.

"Don't be daft," he muttered at himself

But he hadn't gotten to be *the* John Constantine—with all the good and bad that went with that—by ignoring powerful intuitions.

He went to the craps table and put four thousand Euro on sevens.

Everyone at the table looked at him in astonishment. He didn't look like a high roller. He looked like he'd gotten high, and then gotten rolled. But he put four thousand down on a bet that the dice would come up two sevens.

"Daft," he muttered.

The dice rolled . . . and almost stopped. Then they gave a strange twitch and rolled sevens.

He didn't even count the money they paid out to

him. It was a great deal. He thought he ought to give that another try. . . .

But two large thugs in suits were coming his way. They sensed he was up to something. He blew them a kiss and went to the cashier's window to exchange his chips for cash.

Best leave while I'm still quids-in.

The spiffy thugs watched as Constantine stuffed his pockets, debating as to whether they should stop him. But Constantine projected a feeling at them, though his back was turned and he seemed to be ignoring them, a feeling that whispered, *Don't interfere with him. It might be dangerous. Just let him go.*

It was just enough to make them hesitate till Constantine could dart out the door.

As he went he thought, *Spoink, I don't know how you did that, from wherever you are, but it had to be you. Thanks, mate.*

Paris, France

Tchalai didn't seem terribly surprised to see John Constantine at the door of her Paris flat after a six-year absence. She had a gift for divination; she had probably "seen" his arrival days ago.

"Hello, 'Star-eyes,' " he said, winking.

"Hello, John. So now you're here."

She was a Gypsy in her midforties; with her long softly curling black hair and dark eyes she was a Mediterranean beauty who might've been a consort to a Phoenician king—a Gypsy, but a sophisticated Parisian before all else. She stood barely over five feet tall, small but proportionately womanly. She was barefoot, in a low-cut purple shift clasped at the waist by a belt of gold medallions.

"You look just the same," he said.

"As do you, six years later—or perhaps there are more lines in your face. I believe that's the same awful trench coat, no?" She had a slight accent, difficult to identify: she was from Hungary but had been raised chiefly in Paris. He was one of the few people who knew she had a degree in quantum physics; she'd written her paper on the intellectual tension between Niels Bohr and Einstein. But she made her living mostly doing Tarot for French movie stars. She was also, quite discreetly, a sorceress, which is one reason Constantine had come to see her.

The other reason was, he hadn't been laid since that milkmaid. He was hoping to get lucky.

"So you are hoping to 'get lucky,' is that why you've come here?" she said, either reading his mind or his eyes.

"What? Me? Who hasn't come around for years? Here, I've no illusions. Just wanted to use your library, darling, that's all."

Her full lips—almost too full for her face—twisted with amusement. "Don't darling me. But come in, and introduce your friend."

"First, got to tell you that my goddaughter—you remember Mercury—she's out in the car. Hired a nurse to look after her, but we need to bring her up. Thought you could help her, I'll explain, once she's inside."

"Little Mercury! I remember, I met her once! Of course, bring her in!"

They got the nurse—a dour woman with a cap of brown hair and a fuzz mustache—to help bring Mercury upstairs in the gurney they'd stowed in the back of the SUV. "But, monsieur, we need to take her to a doctor, no?"

"Le docteur arrivera bientot," Tchalai said smoothly, helping them with the gurney. They stowed Mercury in Tchalai's guest room, paid the nurse, and sent her on her way.

Gatewood seemed self-conscious as Tchalai returned to the living room; he was embarrassed at his ragged, dirty state. He'd stopped and bought a pair of jeans and a blue workshirt, but he was unshaven, his hair dirty, there was still sand from the beach in his shoes, and he hadn't brushed his teeth since the *Medusa's Revenge.*

"This is Paul, Paul Gatewood. Talented boy, he is."

"Oh? He sings, he dances?"

"He dances with the dead when he wants to."

Tchalai sensed Gatewood's discomfort and smiled, putting a hand on his arm as if she were a lady with a fine gentleman at a nineteenth-century ball. "Spitlove and I are very honored to have you here." She indicated an enormous, evil-eyed red and green parrot in an opened cage near the sunny bay windows looking out on the boulevard.

Constantine snorted, noticing the parrot. "Oh God, he's still alive. . . ." He remembered Morris's remark: *You lack only the parrot.* Odd. "I'd have thought someone would've strangled that flamboyant buzzard by now."

"*John Constantine, John Constantine, eat my shit, merci!*" the bird chanted, bobbing its head. Then it made a spitting sound, with which it punctuated most of its comments; hence its name.

Gatewood laughed. "He's served you, John!"

"I'd like to serve him with barbecue sauce."

"Don't listen to him," Tchalai said. "He and Spitlove are old friends."

Constantine looked around and found the flat largely unchanged, just a little more cluttered. There were houseplants dripping from most of the shelves, figurines of goddesses stood on the floor, adorned paintings in frames—goddesses from every culture. There were a few Gypsy good luck charms on the walls, some hanging from the cobwebby chandelier.

"Come," Tchalai was saying, guiding them toward the kitchen. "I'll make you some tea, and perhaps a salad, and you tell me what has transpired. Nothing normal with you, John, I'm sure, except the normally abnormal, yes?"

"You're too bloody right, Tchalai." He was glad she seemed to have no grudge against him for leaving—and for staying so spottily in touch. He'd sent her the odd postcard now and then, and a few minor gifts. A book, a charm, a pressed flower. But he hadn't been back to her bedroom in years. She always had been a forgiving sort, unless you really got her ire up.

If she was well and truly mad at you, she just might enter your bedroom, quiet as a shadow, and slit your throat as you slept.

But, fair is fair; she'd have a good reason.

✦═◎═✦

Tchalai's library was comfortingly redolent of incense and the peculiar perfume of old book paper. Most of the volumes crowded on the shelves of the little room were at least a hundred years old, though she had a special section with the most up-to-date works on quantum theory. Constantine was seated at a low Japanese table, on floor pillows, feeling his legs cramping badly after two hours, as he went through half a dozen relevant *grimoires* and mythologues. The declining sun was streaking through the window, making ballet dancers of dust motes as he pored through the brittle old pages.

"Ah Hulneb, Alaisiagaie, Anat . . ." he muttered. The names of gods of war. "Anhur . . . Banbha . . . Begtse . . ." He scanned descriptions of the gods, based mostly on statuary and fragmentary tales. "Six arms . . . three eyes . . . not my chap . . . Honos . . . Ogoun . . ." There was good old Mars, there was Wotan, there was Tyr—that one almost felt right, so old was Tyr. The entity he'd encountered on Carthaga was something very ancient, he was sure of that. It was Tyr but not Tyr, somehow.

He selected another volume, *Warlords,* by a fellow named Jameswood. He'd never seen the book before. Early nineteenth century by the look of it. Who the devil was Sir Churchill Jameswood?

Constantine felt himself drawn to this volume, and he pushed the others aside, closed his eyes, raised his hands over the pages, and murmured certain words of power. Then he closed the book, held it balanced on its spine, and removed his hands so it fell open. It had opened to a page near the end, a description of "Donar."

Teutonic, was Donar. . . . Corresponding to the Norse God Thor . . . some relate him to Nergal. . . .

Constantine sat up straight. "Nergal!"

. . . A very ancient Sumero-Babylonian deity: the overseer of the Netherworld. Sometimes he is the evil aspect of the sun god Shamash. He rules a certain particularly bleak and charnel level of Hell with his consort Ereshkigal. Nergal is an evil god who delights in war, pestilence, fever, and devastation. It is difficult to imagine any devotee actually worshipping Nergal although a temple was built to him in the sinister city of Kuthu. Likely he was simply conciliated—or called down on one's enemies. . . . His attributes are the club and the sickle. . . . There are of course more ancient versions: his supposed father (some texts say "sire"), N'Hept is perhaps just another manifestation of Nergal, or he may have been a separate deity. A purer god of war, N'Hept was known to men of the age of stone, and earlier, to those beetle-browed Others who still roam the mountain fastnesses. N'Hept is the primal wargod from whom all others descend. He is

the original image of whom the others are distorted reflections. His face is brutal, animalistic, both crocodilian and baboon. It is he whom the handsomer gods of war mask: behind Mars is N'Hept....

❖═◉═❖

" 'Men of the age of stone,' " Constantine said, as Tchalai came in, bringing cookies and a cup of coffee on a small lacquered-wood tray. Was he, Constantine wondered, referring to Neolithic men? Even earlier men? He glanced up at Tchalai. "How's Mercury?"

"I have removed the psychic parasite. She sleeps now. She was exhausted. But there is still some kind of enchantment on her."

"I'm just glad you got the Akishra off her. I knew you were the one to do it."

Tchalai shrugged. "I often work with addicts, helping them get free of their sickness, and the Akishra normally swarm around addicts, feeding off the energy they lose to their addictions. The Akishra speak to the deep wiring of their brains, keeping them in their addiction." She glanced at the book Constantine had open, and his notes. "So you have found N'Hept. When you described what you saw on Carthaga, I thought it might be him. The primitivity of the features argues as much. I may have an unpublished transcript by Jung on him, somewhere. The archetype of all wargod archetypes. Some call him 'the War Lord.' " She knelt beside him, looking at the book.

"Never heard a word about him."

"Because until recently, he was buried, gone, forgotten, except perhaps as some strange echo in our genes."

"What's our Gatewood lad up to?"

"He took a shower, I gave him some clean clothes—some old things of yours, actually, here for years, I should have burned them—and he was having a nap on a chair outside Mercury's room, standing watch."

"Good. Haven't got any liquor to put in this coffee, have you?"

"I already put cognac in it, because you are a disgusting, hopeless drunk."

"Here! I'll have you know I was weeks at a time without a drink at the Blue Sheikh's place."

"The Blue Sheikh! How is he?"

"Dead, I'm afraid. Much as anyone can kill him."

"Is he. Then he is set free. I once saw their monastery, but the brothers would not let me in. Did they take you to the top of the mountain?"

"Not likely. I was never initiated that far. Not sure what they do there. . . ."

"I have heard that they go to mountaintops, the Magi, and they read the stars, and they offer themselves to the powers of nature there. They contemplate nature as another monk would contemplate his own soul."

"The Sheikh was an impressive bugger. Sees everything intertwined, he does. But he says we only see one or the other of the twinings, like, till we grow past that. Maybe it's easier to see them from a mountaintop." He took out a cigarette, and she calmly plucked it from between his fingers, crumbled it up, and piled the loose tobacco on the table. He sighed. No use arguing; it was her place.

She smiled teasingly. "And did you meet 'Ahura Mazda'?"

"Blue Sheikh says we meet him every day. Says the Supreme-o Bigshot, Ahura Mazda, made the 'twins' who create reality and unreality. Only later do they become 'good' and 'evil.' Reality is, like, *objective meaning*. Unreality is subjectivity. Seeing things, you know, in our identified, 'stuck' kind of way . . . You need the subjectivity though or you can't function as a mortal, but we mistake it for reality, yeah?"

She nodded. "This all has some . . . some particular *piquancy* for you now, yes?"

"Just wondering, at times, if I only think the end of the world should be stopped because . . . because I'm subjective. Objectively, some kind of cleansing might be part of the big plan."

He expected her to demur, but she only tilted her head to one side thoughtfully and murmured, "I do know what you mean." She winced, adjusting her position. "I am at least sometimes weary of this life. I am only forty-five, but I am beginning to get arthritis. Already I'm looking forward to being freed from this body, to the freedom of the astral body. . . ."

He leaned toward her and put a hand on her knee. "I rather like that body of yours, creaky as it might be. . . ."

"Ah no, *pardonne-moi, monsieur!* Just keep your hands to yourself! My heart will not be vulnerable to Mr. John Constantine again, *mais non!*"

"Right. This is good coffee—good cognac. I'll tell you what disturbs me about all this . . . this god of war business I'm encountering. Well, it's hard to say what disturbs me most. Levels on levels of disturbing implications, there are, in this bloody business. But . . ."

"Nergal?"

"There he is, bold as brass."

"He is defeated, gone—no?"

"Are they ever really? They're immortals. They just change shape and go to ground for a while. He may be behind this—he could be a link to his old pop, N'Hept here. Some kind of family relationship, it seems."

"If you're right, and these cultists are starting a world war, then I must help you, John. I cannot continue my researches in an incinerated Paris." She brushed hair from her eyes and looked at him gravely. "All the people who pay my bills will be dead."

Constantine laughed. "Shall we do a summoning then, see what we can find out?"

She pretended to pout. "That would seem to be why you have come here, to use me for libraries and summonings."

"What! All I do is dream about coming here to see you, but every day it gets longer since I last saw you, so I figure it's a little less likely you'll want to, you know, open your doors to me, so to speak. So I lose me nerve, don't I?"

"Oh yes? Or perhaps the women you have been with would not have understood, eh?"

"Women? What women?"

"Oh, John!" She gasped in apparent outrage. "You

are the worst actor in the world when you are not trying to con someone from their money! You rogue! You bastard! Oh!"

Her mouth shouting *oh!* was a very kissable circle, and he could not resist. She let him kiss her, only pretending a little to fight him off. Then she melted against him. He ran his hands down her shoulders and arms with experienced artfulness, snagging the straps of her dress and dragging the cloth down, exposing her breasts. She let him kiss his way down her jawline to her throat, her shoulders, her breasts, her brown nipples—one of them had a single curly hair growing out of it, and that turned him on—she moaned—

And then she pushed him away, panting as she did it. "You cannot make love until after the summoning! You will need the energy of that chakra for the rite!"

"I've got plenty of chakra energy, more than enough to go 'round, I'll show you—just put your hand right here—"

"No! Just drink your cognac and do your reading— and think about the Queen Mother in a bikini!"

"Brilliant, now you've gone and turned my chakras inside out."

⊷≡⊙⊜⊶

Mercury woke in a modest curtained room, a bit dusty, with much dark velvet in folds hanging on the walls around the old, carven four-poster bed.

She stretched on the down-filled mattress, seeing she was wearing only someone's borrowed purple silk nightgown. The bed and the gown must belong to the dark woman she'd seen with John earlier. Mercury had caught just a glimpse of them as they'd brought her here. She'd only been semiconscious, but she had a vague, comforting memory of the woman chanting words over her, sending pulses of cleansing energy from her fingers, clinking little bells, driving the Akishra off.

Mercury sat up, looking around. There were figures of Pan and naiads and grape clusters carved into the headboard; the posts were shaped like twisted tree trunks. A candle burned on a low table nearby, giving off a soothing lavender scent.

She felt comfortable for the first time in days, though weak and a bit hungry. The astral worm was gone, and it was an enormous relief. It would take time before she would stop seeing its inhuman face licking at her. . . .

"John!" she called. "Anyone?"

No reply. Yet she knew he was somewhere nearby. He and the sorceress were off doing something important, she was sure.

Still, it'd be a comfort to talk to him. So Mercury closed her eyes, lay back, relaxed, extended her sensations to her psychic field, and reached out with her mind, to probe the texture of reality; to try to find John. . . .

And she recoiled. She saw the crookedly aligned eyes, staring at her from the shadows of her mind.

The thing in the jar.

It was not here—and yet it was here.

It was still watching her. And if she directed her mind out into the world, if she put out her feelers, it would cut them off. Like a child slashing the antenna of a snail with a razor, it would slice off her psychic feelings. It promised her that.

I have you. I am connected to you. I will watch you. I will wait. They can protect you only when you keep to yourself. Reach out, reach out . . .

It said something else in another language she didn't understand—it sounded like German. . . .

She wasn't sure what it was saying now. Mercury only knew that she never wanted to see or hear that thing again, not in her mind and not in person.

She withdrew her psychic senses and curled up in bed, like a fetus, whimpering.

13

NINE EYES, CIRCLING

Paris, France

"Are you sure about this, Tchalai?"

"What do you mean, John?"

"It's only . . ." How could he explain?

They were on the roof of her building; she was its landlord as well as occupying the best apartment. Constantine and Tchalai stood in the center of an old octagonal greenhouse she used for her invocations. She'd replaced the original tinted glass on the roof with panes of transparent crystal, which made the stars seem to project downward at them on a clear night. It was such a night tonight, but for a few clouds tinged to the color of brass by the smog-yellowed moon. The interior of the greenhouse was tropically warm, and the plants were tropical, too: there were dwarf palms wound about with purple orchids, huge waxy orange bird-of-paradise plants looming over them, and enormous light green fiddlehead ferns, all of them arranged like some exotic shaman's grove around the magic circle on the floor. Tchalai had created the big magic circle with its pentagram and encompassing names of power from ash-tree withes pressed into the flooring, of consecrated copper and psychically infused crystal; she had fixed her intent in her mind, chanting the names of power, as she'd prepared it, moving in the right direction around the circle; she had made the candles herself, one burning at each point of the pentagram, out of ingredients Constantine preferred not to know about.

The circle was a beautiful magical artifact, using methodology set out by Eliphas Levi, yet they both knew Constantine scarcely needed it. He had the gift of seeing magical symbols in his mind so sharply that it was as if he had spent days drawing them out in dragon's blood on the skin of a lamb. Constantine's connection with the Hidden World was implicit, intrinsic to him; an expression, he suspected, of his genetics and perhaps something built up in his soul over the course of many past lives.

They had taken their places on either side of the magic circle, about to step into it and begin, and then Constantine asked if she were sure.

"It's only, Tchalai, that it'll tie you into this thing, I'm afraid. Just now the bastards who tried to kill me might figure me for dead, drowned in the Med. That's what I hope. But this may expose me to them again. It's like . . . if the Chinese set off a nuclear bomb for a test, NATO *knows*—its tech types pick up the radiation of it, yeah? These guys are going to pick up the 'radiation' of this summoning. They may trace it to me, and those with me. Dangerous for you, 'Stareyes,' innit? I reckon I can . . ."

She put her hands on her hips, pretending pique. "And what? You are saying you don't need me for this?"

"I need all the help I can bloody get, love. But I can *manage* this, anyway—and I just . . ."

He hesitated, knowing he had no time to tell her his reasons; he'd have to recount a series of tragedies. He thought about old bandmate Gary Lester, killed in New York in a ritual; he thought about his girlfriend Emma, killed by the Invunche; about the love of his life, Kit Ryan, driven away by his adventuring; about Agent Frank Turro, a man he'd liked, killed on Constantine's watch; about his niece Gemma, seduced into magic and caught up in an agenda that she didn't understand . . . perhaps destroyed herself by now, for all he knew.

He shook his head. "I just think you'd be wiser not to get involved in any of my doings, any more than you have to. You've done enough. I shouldn't have involved you as much as I have already."

"You told me you weren't sure you're doing the right thing in fighting this, John," she said. Her dark eyes glittered in the candlelight. She had clustered her fingers with special rings, and her jewelry flashed as she gestured. "But you were—you are. I am on your side, so I help you. *We have to choose sides.*"

"Do we? I'm not so sure that's wise. One side or the other loses. If you don't choose sides, you don't lose."

She shrugged out of her gown and stood naked on the other side of the magic circle, her skin golden in the candlelight. Like many sorceresses, she did her best magic nude. Though Constantine had taken off his shoes and socks, he wore his clothes, even his trench coat, which had soaked up a good deal of magical pungency over the years.

"I think it's almost the opposite, John," Tchalai said, kicking her dress aside. "Those who don't choose sides are simply caught in the chaos of the struggle. Look at what is happening in Iraq. There is no escape from the war, whatever form it takes. And you know, I think there is a right side. There is, for us. I think you know that."

He *tended* that way—certainly the Blue Sheikh had encouraged that idea, that Constantine ultimately belonged to the forces of Light—but he resented it, and he always had. He didn't like being assigned a rank in an army he'd never signed on for. He didn't like being drafted. At heart, perhaps, he was an instinctive Nietzschean. He wanted to find his own way in the universe. But still he found himself taking sides. And he knew there was no way around the cosmic laws. If you weren't part of one thing, you were part of another. Swim out of a current in the ocean and you'll soon find yourself in another. The thing might be to take part in the whole, while still crystallized into individuality. It was one of the great functional paradoxes. But you had to work your way to that resplendent state.

And he'd rather have a drink down the local, most of the time.

"Just one thing more," he said. "This entity we're contacting, it may incinerate us both, if we say the wrong thing. If the bloody great supernatural toff gets in a mood . . ."

She nodded, and gestured at the circle as if to say,
Let's begin. He let out a long slow breath, perceiving
that Tchalai had made up her mind, and nodded back
to her as he stepped into the circle.

He took up his place at the top point of the pentagram; she stood at its foot. Neither of them chose to
use a magic wand, but Tchalai's jewelry was not
picked at random; each ring of a different metal, each
metal with a different magical significance, each figured with a different rune. She held her hands out
and began to intone, going into her summoning state
with a kind of inner dexterity, extending her psychic
field out from her spine to her arms, to her hands. It
was intensified by the bands of power on her fingers,
then sent in widening spirals from the rings to encompass the magic circle. She let her supernatural
energies interact with John's the way the yin flowed
with yang, 'round and 'round, each partaking of the
other.

She came to the end of the priestess's litany,
broke off chanting, and Constantine took up the incantation, establishing his priesthood in this circle;
calling names that resonated out through the ether
because, as he spoke them, he made them into three-
dimensional forms in his mind, each one a cabalistic
exactitude that emanated a specific signal. . . .

Tchalai was shaking a little as she stood there, rein-
forcing his summoning with her mind, taking the
names of power he spoke into her brain and womb,
sending them out again with feminine energy; male and
female energy circling within one another, alternating
the way waves do on an oscilloscope, up and down, an

inversion and yet each a version of the other.

Over and over again they incanted, using every erg of psychic energy to call out across the Hidden World. The air thrummed around them as the force of their demand built; the plants around them rustled and leaned closer, like animals sniffing a scent; the stars overhead grew more intense and hummed to them, as if channels from the stars had opened up through the atmosphere directly to the supplicants; lines appeared in the steam on the glass of the greenhouse's walls, a cryptic orthography marking out the symbols Constantine envisioned appearing there, vanishing, appearing again, pulsing in and out of appearance with the pulsing of the power they channeled to the Hidden World.

Something approached....

Constantine felt its approach with a chill, then a thumping in his head like the booming of a bass drum—and then a cascade of agreeable and oddly disturbing smells filled the room, a perfume that kept changing its scent from one flower to another sort entirely, to the smell of earth just after it rains, to the smell of a tree freshly blasted by lightning. Music soared from the air itself, like a great church organ playing a song that constantly altered its own composition without dropping a beat. The symbols on the magic circle, in Hebrew and Greek, lit up to project their configurations over the pentagram as if lasers were writing the letters over and over in the air; the light shifted from red to green to white; it played over Tchalai's limbs, writing words in ancient script on her hips, her arms, her breasts.

Tchalai still had her hands extended, and she was shaking, ecstatic, her arms trembling like the limbs of that lightning-blasted tree.

Dark apparitions seemed to congeal into form outside the magic circle, but none of them was the being Constantine and Tchalai had summoned. These spirits of nightmare had been drawn here by "the action," almost as idle men on the street are drawn to look at a house fire or the arrival of police. Constantine caught melting glimpses of froglike men; of living gargoyles with three snarling faces on three sides of their craggy heads; of evil infants with wings made from the severed limbs of cats; of jackal-headed men; of giant flies in Armani suits; of beings with the bodies of angels and the heads of drooling, skew-eyed hydrocephalics. . . .

They were spiritual predators—called Nightmare Makers in some quarters—kept at bay only by the magic circle. . . . They shuffled hungrily just outside the invisible barrier. . . .

All at once the five candles blew out, and then relit, of themselves, with a surge of flame that licked up toward the ceiling as a voice cut through the air.

Who calls upon us?

To Constantine it seemed a male voice, young and old at once, speaking in English; Tchalai would hear it as female, and in her native language.

"It is you I call, and no other," Constantine responded, speaking aloud in English. The seraphim they had summoned—more precisely, the seraphim who had chosen to visit—comprehended all languages. "I call you in the singular, and I beseech you to appear before me, that I may serve the higher." There was none of the arrogant, even condescending tone that Constantine often used with other beings of the Hidden World; those were lower beings who served better if you put them in their place. Even if you didn't control them it was best to act as if you could. But this being, above mere angels, could not be jeered at or condescended to. It'd be like taunting a supernova.

Whose higher would you serve? Which eminence? the voice demanded. **The true eminence of the Absolute or the sub-eminence of the Archons? The mountain under the ice-locked sea or the mountain against the sky?**

Constantine responded: "It was said, Heos ho phos echete pisteuete eis ho phos hina huioi photos genesphe . . ." While you have light believe in the light so that you can be its children.

Well said. I see into your hearts, priest and priestess. Confusion I see, especially in the priest. You are not fully committed to service, John Constantine. But as evanescent as you are, yet the pearl beyond price resides in your heart, in the nest of your confusion. In honor of this pearl, the reason for your creation, made in the course of suffering many lives, I will show you one face, and to this you will speak your request.

The seraphim manifested itself then, so they could see it with the eyes in their heads. Their inner eyes saw this lord of angels extending into infinity like pi working itself out in a corridor of mirrors.

On a nearby rooftop, a potbellied old man named Louis Malheur was feeding his homing pigeons. He was caught up in the swishing and whir of their wings, their gray iridescence, when a flash of light caught his eye and he turned to see the strange octagonal structure of glass on the opposite roof glowing from within, limning the silhouettes of exotic plants which split beams of light to oscillate like dancers in a slow ballet.

The light grew in intensity till to Louis it looked like a lighthouse beacon, shining so blindingly that the glass enclosure seemed to vanish for a moment.

Once before he had called the gendarmes and told them that that crazy witch Madame Dermitzel was playing with fire on her roof. The gendarmes had investigated the greenhouse, finding only a puzzled woman in her bathrobe, watering her flowers, and no trace of fire or bright lights. Louis had almost gone to jail for filing a false report. He was not going to call them again. But he was not going to stay on this roof either, though his pigeons were fluttering madly now, disturbed by the subsonic pulsing from Madame's rooftop and by a drone that was like organ music, but then again was like the sound of a jetplane approaching. . . .

No matter, only a few of his birds would die, he supposed, this time, in their terror. His wife thought he had too many pigeons anyway. He was not going to call the gendarmes. Madame Dermitzel would only cloak her witchery again. No, Louis had quite another plan.

He was going to go to the brasserie to have a smoke and a very large glass of brandy. . . .

—⊷═◉═⊶—

The seraphim appeared to Constantine and Tchalai in congruence with their Judao-Christian culture. It appeared like a figure from Isaiah, like something glimpsed by Ezekiel. Were they Hindus, it would have appeared as a Hindu deity; were they Africans, it would have seemed a loa; were they Muslim it would have been an enormous djinn.

Hovering over the magic circle within a translucent sphere of light was a being with nine wings; three on each side, three more along its spine. They were of a restless whiteness that flashed inwardly with other colors; the being was a nude human figure, its skin the color of the blobs of color one sees if one looks too closely at the sun; it was both male and female, but somehow was no mere hermaphrodite. Its male organs emerged from within its female organs which somehow then changed places with its male which emerged from its female organs which . . .

Its iconic face, to Constantine's eye, was like that of Michelangelo's *David,* except for the eyes. There were no eyes in the head, its eye sockets were blank skin: instead there was a ring of nine eyes floating around about four inches away from the head, as if slowly orbiting its skull at eye level. They were like emeralds set into balls of ivory.

Its perfect lips opened; its eyes looked at Constantine, one after the next, as they circled around its head. It was a beautiful creature, really, the very definition of proportion and elegance, as much a perfect iconic symbol as a being—yet somehow it was harder for Constantine to look at than the most hideous demons had been.

Now speak, and I will consider if your furtherance, within the current of time, is justified; or if the pearl in you is better served by the fiery reduction of its husk.

Constantine knew this meant that if he said the wrong thing, his mortal form would be incinerated. It was an instantaneous incineration, he knew, and wouldn't hurt. Not physically.

But he wasn't ready to be incinerated. That would be a bit of an inconvenience.

Well, here goes . . . hopefully not here goes nothing . . .

"Right. Great Seraphim, a little more than a year ago, in our time, the Red Sepulchre opened a way, and the day of Armageddon nearly chanced—"

Yet it did not come about. It is of no great moment: a mere change of venue, a shift of governing agencies, a relocation, when that comes about—if that way is chosen. . . .

Constantine filed that knowledge away: the apocalypse that in his culture was called Armageddon is not an inevitability, only a possibility. Scriptures didn't always get it right.

He went on, "Great Seraphim, was there a door I failed to shut? There are those who bring about another transfiguration—is it the Armageddon of prophecy?"

It is not. Deceptions disguise the working you speak of. Yet if this working is completed, only one-eighth of those now living will survive. It is the making of a great war amongst mortals, which will lay low many so that a few may be elevated. But all are cast into the wind, ashes when time feeds the furnace. . . .

"How can we put a stop to this war, Great Seraphim?"

Your question is asked without sincerity. You are full of anger, and you are not concerned in your heart to stop it. Your anger would consume all the world, John Constantine. . . .

"Great Seraphim—"

You speak out of turn. . . . I have here a fire that already knows your bones. . . .

It lifted one of its immaculate hands, palm upward, and a flame with a hungry face appeared there and looked at Constantine as if eager to devour him.

"I stand corrected, O Seraphim." Hating to be threatened, he wanted to say other things to it—earlier in life he would have—but in memory of the Blue Sheikh he held himself back. There would be time yet to denounce God and his servants if it came to that, if it felt right. . . .

"A glimpse is all I ask, of the way to end this working. Then I will choose my course. I admit my uncertainty now."

I can show you only one doorway; there are many to go through. I show your priestess. And this time . . .

It closed its fist, smothering the eager flame.

I will not let your flesh be consumed. There is another coat of Being, within this vestment, to add to the pearl that grows within you.

Then its body folded up, falling inward into itself, so that it sucked away into its own vagina and mouth, its upper parts going into the head, its lower into the groin, till the two came together, merged into a sphere, which spun and exploded joyously—and was gone.

Tchalai collapsed, moaning, slumping across three candles, snuffing them out, her arm falling across the magic circle, breaking its integrity.

Triumphant cackling came from the shadowy demonic forms flitting about the fractured circle and the drooling idiot-headed angel extended five boneless rubbery arms into the circle to snatch at Tchalai. It tore at her hair and scratched at her shoulders even as another demon, in the form of an enormous snake that'd had its scales shaved away, slithered bloodily over its shoulder and the fly-thing buzzed above them both—

"Get *BACK!*" Constantine shouted, sending a furious burst of negative psychic energy at them—and they recoiled. "You heard me, you louts! The seraphim couldn't be troubled to notice you, so low are you hodgepodge beasties compared to him—and he put his wisdom into her heart! The seraphim selected *her* to convey a truth to me and if you touch her he'll take a vengeance on you that'll make you wish you were snug in Satan's jaws! Now *FUCK OFF* or I'll fucking *kick your foul little abscessed souls* right up to the seraphim for disposal! I swear I will, you reeking little goits!"

They drew back, hissing foulness, and Constantine lifted Tchalai in his arms, restoring the sanctity of the circle. He spoke the words that would disperse the Nightmare Makers and the rubbernecking evil spirits fled.

◆—◎—◆

"Hi, uh . . . how you feeling?" Gatewood asked.

The girl in the bed was hugging herself, frowning, but her eyes were wide open and she seemed conscious.

She glanced over at him. Suspicion was like a fly crawling on her face. "You might not be who you seem to be. . . ."

She had a British accent—Gatewood wasn't sure which one, London or another sort—and she had dark tousled hair and a rather ordinary face, but there was a depth in her eyes that drew him.

"I'm just . . . Paul," he said. "Gatewood. I'm a friend of John Constantine's. At least I hope he's my friend. Wouldn't like to have him for an enemy. Can I bring you anything?"

She sat up, pulling up a drooping shoulder strap of her nightgown. "I guess you're not . . . I don't know . . . I remember you."

"You do? You weren't really awake . . . for days."

"I was and I wasn't. I was sort of in between. I saw things sometimes. You were carrying me once over a metal floor. . . ."

"The deck of a yacht. They sank it but we were picked up by a guy I know. You're in France now. With a friend of John's. Tchalai something. Gypsy lady I guess."

"I know who that is. I've heard of her." She seemed to relax, somewhat. "I'm hungry. . . . Can I have a salad? I feel too weak to get it myself, and I feel safe in here."

He smiled and went to the kitchen, found the makings of a salad, decided Tchalai wouldn't mind, put it together, and brought it back to her.

"This is a queer sort of salad, Mr. Gatewood."

"Sorry, I improvised. Call me Paul."

"Sliced apples and cheese and spinach and broken up pieces of stale baguette and sliced raw turnip, and—what are these, green olives? But it's good. . . . Everything tastes so good to me right now. Sit down, on the edge of the bed, it's okay. Long as you keep your hands to yourself. Did you feel something strange, a little while ago, from upstairs, maybe the roof—something . . . like electricity, but talking electricity? I must sound crazy to you."

"Naw, not after what I've been through. John told me you're a psychic. He said 'Don't believe in psychics, it's a load of rubbish—except for her and a few others.' "

She laughed. "That sounds like John. Is this a carrot? No, it's more like a rutabaga."

"And in fact, I've got some of that myself, only just, I guess, for dead people. I mean—well, just a few minutes ago I had a talk with an old lady in the hallway outside your door. Madame Duval, she said her name was. Only, she was a ghost. She lived here about seventy years ago. Didn't speak much English. She asked me when were we going to finish working on the house so she could move back in—at least I think that's what she said. Poor thing's kinda confused."

"I wish I could help her. Once I could. But I've lost most of my ability, or anyway I can only pick up things that sort of come *to* me. I can't reach out anymore. I used to be able to leave my body, all kinds of things. . . . It's nice to be able to talk to somebody about it. I mean, the other young blokes, where I'm from, they tend to think I'm a freak. There was one guy but . . ."

Mercury shrugged and looked away, absentmindedly chewing on a piece of apple.

After she ate, he brought her tea, and they spoke quite easily, comfortably, as if they'd always known one another, about their lives, and as she listened to him talk about the war, her eyes filled with tears. She saw his regret when he talked about leaving his outfit; about going "AWOL." She didn't need her psychic abilities to see his sorrow at the desertion. "Those guys didn't like me—but they were still the guys in my outfit, and that's that. I just . . . something snapped in me when I saw the guy in that room upstairs shot dead. He was just a harmless nut, as anybody could see if they opened their eyes and *looked*. And then his brother, that kid's father, downstairs . . . a tense situation, he makes a wrong move, and the dumbasses kill him. And the boy runs out of there, into fucking nowhere . . . and it just seemed like some kind of sick spiral, going on and on and on, and I had to get out of it, somehow. Do something about it. But I didn't know how. Then the ghosts came to me. It was like this ability I'd always had just sort of . . . woke up. There they were. Felt natural to me. And I knew what to do. Doesn't change anything, though. I'm still a deserter."

She stopped him when he used the word *deserter*.

"You didn't desert them. You walked away from it. You went to help some people who had no other way to be helped. That's what you did. Like Marla Ruzicka, who was helping people caught in the crossfire. You did it for those people after they'd died. . . . They were living their deaths over and over again."

"I don't know. . . . It's kind of fundamental, where I come from—you stand with the guys in your outfit. I failed the most basic thing."

Mercury reached out and took his hand. "No! You didn't. You did the right thing . . . Paul."

"When you're there, at a summoning, it all happens so quickly, so powerfully," Tchalai said, her voice betraying awe. "You have such a gift, John, to successfully call one of those. I would never have dared to try . . . and if I had I'd have worked at it for many hours, perhaps days. But you!" She was wearing a kimono, lying on her bed with one arm thrown over her eyes, still shaking a little.

"Here, don't try to talk, love, just drink your brandy and rest," Constantine said, sitting on the old, ornate chair beside her. It was a Louis XIV era piece, he judged. The summoning had filled him with sexual energy, as usual, and he was looking around to keep himself distracted. He was remembering the title of a White Stripes song he fancied: "I'm Finding It Harder to Be a Gentleman."

Just concentrate on the furnishings, old cock, he told himself. The room had gotten more lavish since he'd been here last.

This was a much larger bedroom than the one Mercury was in; a similarly carved bed frame, but twice the size. The room was lit by violet lanterns, casting purple shadows from the clutter of fertility artifacts, sculptures, and fetishes from a hundred cultures; from the South Seas, from Africa, from Asia, from South America. There was a painting on the wall Tchalai had done herself—her signature was gaudily large in the corner of the canvas—depicting a kind of ray of energy that descended a stepladder of worlds, stratified from the top to the bottom of the painting; from cosmic egg to a continuum of galaxies, down to star systems, down to planets, to a dead moon, and at the bottom the same cosmic egg starting it all over. It was not a very well crafted painting, the technique was just a little better than amateur and the colors were garish, but it seemed to speak of some wisdom that he almost remembered, that hung in the back of his mind, throbbing with significance and yet perpetually forgotten.

He turned to ask her about the painting when her expression made him break off. She had propped herself up on her elbows, letting her wavy black hair droop to hide half her face; her lips were slightly parted, and she'd let the robe fall open, her breasts rising and falling with the eagerness of her breathing. "John . . . ?"

"Present and accounted for."

Her voice was suddenly quite husky. "You know what happens to me when I engage in a successful summoning. The electricity of life charges the air—and it gets inside me and curls up between my legs. So afterwards I am very . . . very . . ."

Constantine licked his lips. "Ah, me too. But . . . we do need to, ah, investigate the . . . I mean to say . . . what did old boy with the excessive wing structure say to you about, what I . . ."

She had drawn her knees up, and now she crept toward him catlike on the bed. He was sitting within reach and it was all he could not to leap onto the bedclothes. The very air seemed charged with sexual energy; the bedposts seemed to strain and creak with it. The statuette figures on the shelves, seen from the corners of his eyes, seemed to pump their hips.

"What did he say to me? He . . . she . . . said that I should speak to the bones at Denfert-Rochereau. . . ."

"And . . ." He could smell her perfume—something herbal, he didn't quite recognize, but with hemp in it—and, mildly, her sweat. The combination was maddening.

" 'Ow about this Denfert-what'sitsthingie?"

"He must have meant the Catacombs of Paris; they are at that station, John. I will speak to the bone here first, I think. . . ." She reached out and put her hand on his thigh, ran it up to his crotch—he hadn't had an erection before she'd touched him, though he knew he wasn't far from one. But in the moment it

took for her to run her small, electrically lively hands
from his knee to his thigh to his crotch, he stiff-
ened—that rapidly.

He knew they ought to follow up on the tip—the
fate of the world, diminishing time to act, and all that
sort of thing—but in a moment she'd crawled onto
the chair with him, was straddling him, and he gave
in completely. They kissed deeply; she unzipped him
with consummate skill and for a time they made use
of the chair.

But after a while she dragged him by his engorged
member to the bed, and he felt himself devoured. . . .

⊷⊙⊷

At that moment, in the next room, Paul Gatewood
was pouring Mercury some more tea. He was trying
not to be too obvious about admiring the rosy pale
complexion of her shoulders; he found a sexiness in
the stolid simplicity of her features.

That's when they both heard the groaning, the out-
raged recurrent shriek of bedsprings from the room
next door.

As one, they turned to look at the wall separating
this bedroom from Tchalai's, just as the cry pierced it
almost as if the wall hadn't been there: *"Oh oui, John,
tres forte, plus forte, oui oui c'est ça, c'est superbe, oh,
John, oh mon amour tres forte, don't hold back—oui!"*

"Whoa," Gatewood muttered. "Take 'er easy
there. . . ."

The wall shook rhythmically; a picture fell crashing to the floor.

"I don't think they plan to 'whoa' anytime soon," Mercury said, swallowing.

She pulled up the bedclothes to cover herself to the neck and whistled softly between her teeth.

Gatewood smiled at her reassuringly. "Want some sugar? I mean—want some sugar with your tea?"

"Oh—please, yes."

The wall shivered, the phantom bedsprings groaned. Constantine seemed to be growling like a bear. Tchalai continued, *"Oh oui, John, entre, entre encore, and now here, here, do it here!"* This was followed by an ambiguous shriek.

Mercury drew back a bit more from Gatewood. But he felt that she was drawing back from herself, really; from her own inclination, her attraction to him. He was just glad she could feel that way.

"So," he said. "You want . . ." He cleared his throat. "Some music? I see a radio there. . . ."

"Oh yeah—thanks!"

He grinned and went to the radio.

"Oh, John—plus forte! Ouiiiiiiiii!"

Mercury grimaced. "And Paul?"

"Yeah?"

"Turn it up loud."

The big parrot flapped up and down the hallway, shrieking, *"Eat shit and die, John Constantine!"*

14

THE DEAD CAN DANCE

Paris, the Catacombs

The door to the Catacombs was locked, and not just because it was three in the morning. The gold-painted sign over the door said

Entree des Catacombes

But underneath it was another, temporary, cardboard sign, in French and English both:

Catacombs closed for structural repairs.
We apologize for the inconvenience.

And there was a big, brand-new stainless-steel padlock on a heavy-gauge chain wound around the door handles.

"I don't have those kinds of spells, to open locks, in my répertoire," Tchalai said.

She looked at Constantine then in a way that annoyed him a little; of course, he was quite knackered after the relentless shagging she'd put him through, and fatigue made him irritable. But it seemed to him that Tchalai was hinting that someone like him would have "magical burglary skills." It was as if she was assuming he was some kind of semireformed criminal.

The really irritating thing was, it was more or less true.

It was just the three of them, Constantine, Tchalai, and Gatewood; Mercury had been sleeping peacefully when they'd left. Gatewood was shaved and dressed in black pants, a white shirt, a tie—Constantine's old clothes. They looked like they were wearing the same uniform. "The fucking Blues Brothers," Constantine had said on seeing him.

Tchalai wore a purple jumpsuit, which she evidently thought was suitable for investigations under the streets, and red Converse sneakers, which made her small feet look surprisingly large.

"Can you do some magic to open this lock, John?" Gatewood asked.

"Certainment, mon ami," Constantine said, doing an old Frenchman's voice. He reached into his coat and drew out something he'd hooked to his inside pocket so the taxi driver wouldn't see it. He'd brought it along just for this purpose: a crowbar he'd found in Tchalai's utility closet.

He slammed the lock hard several times with the crowbar, the clang echoing with frightening gusto up and down the narrow, curving Parisian street. The fourth time, the lock snapped open. "There you are— Scouse magic!"

He and Gatewood had to work together prying the doors open to get past their built-in lock, and then they hurried in, bringing the chain and lock in with them and closing the doors as quietly as possible.

"Bloody flics'll be swarming 'round with all that noise," Constantine muttered, making almost as much noise again as he tossed the chain, lock, and crowbar aside.

They looked around in the light of the electric torch that Tchalai had brought. Beyond a cash register counter and gate—for the Catacombs were a famous tourist attraction—they found a twisting narrow stone stairway, winding downward. A good dark distance downward . . .

As they descended, Gatewood seemed increasingly nervous. "Um, Tchalai, you know what's going to happen in the future? I mean, you do divination, right?"

"In some circumstances, yes."

"So did you, like, do a reading for this? About what we might find down here?"

"No. It is not the sort of thing I do—anyway, it's sometimes better not to know. One might lose one's resolve to meet destiny. I felt that might be the case tonight."

"Thanks. That's so reassuring."

Constantine glanced at Gatewood as they reached the bottom of the stairs. "You're the one talks to the dead, mate. The ones you brought to Syria told you anything about what we might find down here?"

"What? Me? I haven't heard a word from that bunch since you put them in that saint's hand. Hey, you talk to them, man, you're carrying them around in your pocket."

"Haven't got the gift. I can see them if they're in the mood to be seen, easier than other people can see them, but . . ."

But in fact Constantine was sensing something in the air here. And he sensed it was aware of him, too. They were looking at one another, third eye to third eye. . . .

A stranger. But someone he almost knew.

A name floated to him. *Dyzigi.* Was it a man's name or a condition—some kind of esoteric status? A man's name, he decided. And a face went with it: *Zigzags cut into his close-cropped hair . . . eyes glistening black, unblinking in deep sockets; clownish black eyebrows, red lips, a small sharp nose like the tip of a knife blade . . . so very pale, that face, that the dead-dark eyes and red lips seemed to project out, separate, independent. And the pale man was aware of Constantine—was looking back at him across the telepathic gulf. . . .*

Constantine drew his psychic senses back, like a soldier not wanting to give away his position.

He thought about the strange face he'd seen. Was this a mortal human being? Constantine had met demons who closely resembled men, but whose demonic nature seemed to leak through around the edges of their human semblance.

But there was no one to be seen in person, not so far, as they walked through a damp stone gallery, shored up in places with walls of mortared stones. Still, the presence of something malevolent tingled the air.

"Do you feel that, John?" Tchalai asked, looking around.

"Yeah . . . let's keep on." He led the way down a narrow arch-roofed tunnel of stone; the air was charged with the smell of wet minerals, and just faintly, the moldering, chalky scent of human bones.

"What the hell *is* this place?" Gatewood asked.

"You have truly never heard of it?" Tchalai asked. "Now it is a tourist attraction. Once it was a stone quarry; the Romans began it. A mine, of sorts. Then it was expanded by the Franks, and finally abandoned. But the cemeteries in Paris began to fall apart, to sink, to flood, you see, and they had to move the bones, thousands and then millions of bones. So almost at the end of the eighteenth century they decided to put them together down here . . . the bones without a home. They were nicely arranged, you will see; it seemed more respectful than a big pile and mess, no? So, up ahead, that is the 'ossuary' . . . the place for bones. . . ."

The tunnel widened into a gallery in which stood a sort of gateway, rectangular pillars on either side of the entrance to the ossuary. They opened the gate and saw lights in the distance, playing along the tunnel roof; voices drifted to them, unintelligible. They might have been the voices of the abandoned dead; the moving lights might have been their restless spirits.

"Switch off the torch," Constantine muttered, noticing that the voices they'd heard had ceased.

"You sure you want to do that, bro?" Gatewood asked in an undertone. He was breathing kind of hard.

"You're supposed to be a medium. Better get over being scared of the dead, mate."

"I don't know anything about being a medium. Those ghosts in Baghdad just seemed like people to me. But this—there's such a lost, displaced sort of vibe here. Makes me want to hide."

Constantine shrugged. "Too late to hide from something when you're in the bleedin' thick of it."

Tchalai turned the electric torch off and they followed the curving tunnel back, along the twisting ossuary passage, into deep dark dampness, into the cool final outbreath of death's peace. Their tentative steps and their breathing seemed quite loud in the silence.

They moved along slowly, unsure of their steps with only a little light from far ahead, until suddenly the string of overhead lights were switched on.

Gatewood gasped, seeing now that they were surrounded by skeletal human remains. At first it was as if the walls were made of human bones. Then they saw that the yellow bones were stacked floor to ceiling, with femurs and other long bones nearer the bottom in layers, then a layer of skulls, then more femurs, then another layer of skulls, staring at them sightlessly. They were missing their lower jaws, but they seemed to grin nonetheless . . .

"Bonjour, medames et messieurs," Tchalai breathed.

C'est toujours "Bonne soirée" pour nous, came the wistful response, whispering soft as a gentle midnight breeze. Perhaps only in Constantine's imagination. Perhaps not.

Then they heard footsteps, a repeating creaking

sound, and the murmur of male voices. Live human beings.

They moved past a dark side passage up to a switchback corner, and Constantine looked around it to see four men pushing a big multicolored metal cylinder on a rubber-wheeled cart. It was too large for the cart and angled up in it, its tip almost brushing the ceiling. They were guiding it down the passage with exquisite care. One of them seemed in some way familiar—he wore the uniform of an American general, but that wasn't it. More like he'd been somewhere nearby, at some time, and Constantine had gotten a "psychic background" impression of him. Perhaps in that helicopter that sank *Noah's Next?*

Behind them, as part of a strange procession, walked the man Constantine had glimpsed telepathically: Dyzigi, carrying a footlocker-sized wooden chest in his arms. And beside him walked a man in spectacles, hair slicked back, who flickered in and out of existence: a ghost. His face looked vaguely familiar. Some German scientist?

The three men with the general looked like hired thugs of some kind. Big red-faced, blue-eyed men in cheaply cut suits, with AK-47s on straps over their shoulders. Russian maybe, or Ukrainian. Men used to lethal brutality the way a gardener is used to weeding.

What was the cylinder on the cart? Constantine looked closer, taking in the tapered snout, the fins. . . .

It was a missile, about twenty feet long. A cruise missile, Constantine thought, casting his mind back to photos he'd seen in the newspaper during the Gulf

War. The warhead looked like it wasn't the same make as the rest of it though; the body of the missile was red and white, but the nose cone was mostly dark green, fitted without being quite flush. He'd heard that smaller nuclear warheads, the modern micronuke with Hiroshima-sized blasts, could be attached to a cruise missile. *What will they use to launch it?* he wondered.

At his elbow Tchalai sucked in her breath, looking at the cruise missile. He was distantly aware of her backing away. But he kept watching, fascinated, especially when he saw the cruise missile moving against the backdrop of rows and rows of skulls, like some conceptual art project. . . .

"That general," Gatewood whispered. "That's Coggins. I've seen him in Baghdad. He was a big deal and then he got, like, disgraced and they sort of put him on some kind of sabbatical or something."

Constantine was still looking at the missile. It took him a few moments to make out the runes drawn on the nose cone; the silvery paint only showed when the four men pushed it directly under the overhead light. A combination of magic and high technology?

The runes seemed post-Neolithic, an era he associated with Atlantis, primordial days a long time "BC." The runes seemed to declare submission to a god of some kind. He thought he made out one that meant, "To Your Glory." But not much was known about the period and most translation of runes that old was guesswork, unless these bastards had some kind of a key to ancient writing the scholars didn't have. It was possible—black magicians were secretive.

Constantine thought of MacCrawley . . . a man he'd never met, but had heard much about. He'd been involved in the recent conspiracy to bring about the Christian apocalypse—the fiasco he and Gemma had been involved in—but Constantine hadn't found out about MacCrawley's involvement till afterwards. It seemed he was related to Aleister Crowley in some way. And Constantine had heard he was an expert on ancient runes, possessing scrolls and vellum the paleographers hadn't seen.

"John, where's Tchalai?" Gatewood whispered.

Constantine turned and saw she was gone. "Oh Christ on a motorized skateboard."

Then a tall, lean American with gray eyes and an icy smile stepped out of the side passage behind them. He wore a pilot's green jumpsuit, and he was pointing a .45 automatic at Constantine. "Dyzigi was right—there you are. You're that John Constantine shithead, aren't you?"

"Got the name right and the modifier wrong, you stupid tit," Constantine said. "I reckon you lot got this place closed down, bribed somebody, did you, so you could hide your toy down here?" He heard footsteps behind, and turned to see the general come at him with his lip curled in fury, raising an assault rifle.

"You the prick that's been sniffing around us all this time?" Coggins demanded. "Constantine is it?"

"You the disgraced general?" Constantine replied breezily. "The one betraying his country, is it?"

The general snarled, stepped up and smacked Constantine on the side of the head with his gun.

Constantine fell through scattering blobs of disintegrating light and never felt himself hit the floor. But he woke a few moments later, to stare up blearily through waves of pain; it was literally as if he could see the pain rippling through his eyesight, warping the scene as it went. He saw a distorted image of Coggins driving the butt of his gun into Gatewood's gut, knocking him gasping to his knees.

"Now who the fuck are *you,* boy?" he shouted at Gatewood. "Huh? You answer me or I'll blow your testicles all over this floor."

Constantine was trying to get control of what power he had. But the pain in his head drove all cogent thought away. He felt sickened and weak. Maybe had a concussion. He could feel blood tracing his face from a wound in his scalp.

And where was Tchalai?

"What are you doing with these two?" Dyzigi's voice. An Eastern European accent. Not quite Russian. Rumanian?

"We have no time for this," Dyzigi went on. "Kill them, hide the bodies behind the bones. Not that it will matter shortly. Hurry it up!"

"Captain Simpson?" Coggins said, nodding to him. "Will you do the honors?"

Was there a curious rattling amongst the bones?

Constantine managed to get painfully to one knee, only to see Simpson step up to him with the .45. "You first, smartmouth."

The ossuary bones began to rattle furiously then, all around them. . . .

"What the fuck?" Simpson muttered, looking around.

The bones were visibly jittering in place, clattering against one another—and suddenly scores of them *leapt into the air* so that Coggins and Simpson yelped, covered their eyes. But the bones didn't fly right at them, instead they began to organize themselves into the rough semblance of intact skeletons, standing on the stone floors. Most of them were missing part; they were without ribs here and vertebrae there and all of them were missing their lower jaws, but the partly intact skeletons began to dance in place, to music they made themselves with the clacking of bone on bone, of femur ends and pieces of skeletal feet on the floor, making their own percussion the way tap dancers did. The percussion went *click, clack, a click-clack-clack; click, clack, a click-clack-clack;* and *click, clack, a click-clack-clack . . . clickety-click-clack!* And then it started over again. *Click, clack, a click-clack-clack . . .*

The skeletons danced together like a chorus line, working their way between Constantine and Gatewood and the other men, only there was something absurd and distinctive in the motions the chorus line of skeletons made, ducking their yellow skulls and jerking their cracked shoulder blades. As Gatewood helped him to his feet, Constantine realized where he'd seen it: *The fucking skeletons are doing the thizzle dance. They're "getting dumb!" It's Spoink!*

Dyzigi and the others seemed momentarily baffled; the very ludicrousness of the dance confused them.

"Come on!" Constantine hissed, pulling Gatewood after him, angling toward that side passage.

Shedding bits of themselves, the skeletons followed him, wedging several chorus lines in rows between Constantine and the gunmen. Dyzigi was shouting to stop them. Guns fired, but the bullets were dispersed by layer on layer of bone, not stopped but deflected enough to miss, so that some of the bones shattered into handfuls of calciated specks and dust, and the ossuary echoed with gunfire and choked with gunsmoke, and still more skeletons rose up, dancing, clattering to the thizzle dance. . . .

The gunmen with the missile started toward them, shoving at the barrier of dancing bones, but Coggins yelled, "No, go back, stay with The Blossom! On no account leave it!"

Constantine and Gatewood reached the side passage, Constantine feeling sick, his knees weak, but able to propel himself forward through the rippling mist of pain. He heard Dyzigi shouting something that sounded like names of power, a dispersal spell, but it was having no effect, probably because the magus was directing the spell at spirits he supposed were animating the bones. Only they weren't—Spoink was, telekinetically, and he was somewhere invisibly close to Constantine.

More gunfire—more bones flew apart, bullets crashed into the stone floor near Constantine.

He looked back in time to see the skeletons flying apart, the disconnected bones pitched upward, flung in a last anarchic gesture at Dyzigi and Coggins and Simpson exactly like the card men flying at Alice in the climax of *Alice in Wonderland*.

Constantine would've laughed, were it not so painful to laugh, and then he stumbled into another side passage after Gatewood.

And where *was* Tchalai?

—————•⊙•—————

Coggins picked himself up off the floor, brushing off ancient bones; they clattered to the floor, seeming as inert as they'd ever been, as if they hadn't been leaping about moments before. He picked up a femur in his hand and stared at it, then tossed it aside in disgust. "I thought you were some kind of magician, Dyzigi, goddamnit. If that wasn't supernatural bullshit I don't know what was. You're not doing your part of the job. I got you The Blossom; it was me that got in touch with those old boys in Russia with the right warhead, not you!"

Dyzigi was brushing himself off, too. "Yes, I mistook the situation. I thought it was the ghosts belonging to the bones . . . but it was another . . . someone with a telekinetic speciality, I should imagine. Quite talented. We really should get control of him."

"So let's get after those sneaky sons of bitches."

"We don't have time," Dyzigi said, consulting a pocket watch. "We are late. For a very important date, ha ha. We must go, yes? Come . . . it doesn't matter—they will soon be dead. Trevino has everything set up. We will be away in the helicopter. All will be well."

"No, uh-uh, they could still screw with us," Coggins

insisted. "I'm gonna send one of these Ukrainians back to find them and kill them dead."

⊷━◉━⊷

Constantine was feeling a little more human, though his head still throbbed. He muttered softly to Gatewood as they followed Coggins's procession down a passageway. "Tired of being done over by goits with guns, knocking me in the gut, knocking me in the head, shooting at me, blowing whole ships out from under me . . . goits with guns and missiles pushing us all around . . . and they love it, the pricks; when we pick up guns to shoot back, gives them all stiffies, it does. . . ."

"There's a place for guns," Gatewood whispered. "Wish I had a sixteen-millimeter machine gun about now . . . maybe an RPG. . . ."

"I fucking hate guns, always have."

"John—I feel odd. . . . Do you hear something, like, buzzing in the air? And someone laughing? A voice . . ." Gatewood had stopped, looking dizzy, one hand to his forehead.

"No. I don't hear anything like that. You okay?"

"I always . . . whoaaaa, this feels weird, what's up, dude!"

"What?" Constantine looked at Gatewood—and saw an expression on his face that would normally never be there: unmitigated delight, and a kind of pleased bafflement.

"This place looks so different now, inside a—oh man, I can't remember why it looks different. . . . John—your name is John, right?"

They stopped in the corridor. Constantine stared. "Spoink?"

"Yeah! You do know me!"

"You've taken over Gatewood. . . . Spoink, is there a reason you're doing this, mate?"

"Doing what, man? I've gotta get back home . . . my old lady's gonna be looking for me. She's such a bitch if I'm home late."

"Home. You're going home—to where?"

"Where? Oakland, man."

"Oakland, California? Spoink, you're forgetting what's happening. . . . Think what happened to you. Don't you remember, making the skeletons dance, everything else we've been through? You and me?"

Gatewood blinked at him, his mouth slack, trembling. "Yes . . ." The voice sounded distant, filtered now. Changing its pitch and timbre word by word. "Yes John . . . I'm sorry I was forgetting all about . . . I died, didn't I. Then I wanted to do something good, make up for wasting my life and they said I had a gift, and I'd always had this weird talent with dice and they said it was more than I knew and they sent me here. . . ."

"Look, there's a reason you're in this guy's body. You're losing yourself—it happened to me, too, when I was out floating about too bloody long. You went for the nearest anchor, like. I reckon you were knackered from controlling all those skeletons. That was inspired; it was brilliant, but you wore yourself out, mate."

"You really liked it? They did the thizzle dance. . . ." He seemed almost stoned.

"I know they did. You've got to let go of Gatewood. Go into this . . ." He took the saint's mummified hand out of his coat. ". . . and don't come out again, you've reached the end of your strength. When it's over, they'll find you a new life—probably a reincarnation."

"Go in . . . yes . . . it's open to me . . . they're waiting . . . I can't help you anymore, John, . . . I'm sorry, John . . . I'm so tired . . . John . . . they don't know what they're doing. . . . They think it's for Christ and it's for the Big Asshole, bro, you know?"

"I suspected that. Some of them think as much, maybe. Go into the hand, the way is open for you, go there and rest with the others. You've done brilliant for me, mate. Ta, Spoink . . ."

"Yeah . . . later, dude . . . I'm so . . . tired."

Gatewood shuddered. The hand twitched open wider . . . and then closed. Spoink was safely tucked away.

Gatewood slumped back against the wall. "Oh fuck . . . my head . . ." Gatewood was himself again.

"Your head? Try getting a rifle butt in the head. But take it easy. You were channeling a spirit, Paul."

"Was I? I sort of followed some of it, like I could hear voices in the next room. But it was my voice."

"He was using your voice. It was Spoink. He's in here now." He put the saint's hand in his coat.

"This what I've got to look forward to—I'm walking along and boom, somebody burgles my brain?"

"You'll get more control over it. Learn to keep them from getting in. Ignore them most of the time. I know a chap in London, he could give you some instruction. Only other real one I ever met. Now hark, old cock, we've got to get along. There's a room up ahead. Come on."

Another fifty feet, then the corridor opened out into a high-ceilinged bell-shaped quarry chamber. Their footsteps echoed in it, and on the far side was a wooden door, standing ajar; the door was one few people knew about. Someone was stalking down the corridor beyond the door, coming their way. Constantine hurried up to the door and listened—then bent down and untied a shoelace, tugged it quickly off his shoe.

Gatewood stared. "What the fuck are you—?"

"Shhh!"

He reached into an inner pocket and shuddered as he came into contact with the mummified human hand. Thought he felt it twitch against his fingers. He reached past the clawlike hand, found the tiny statuette of Zoroaster, pulled it out—

The footsteps were very close now—

And tied the string around the statuette's neck, hung it from a stone knob so it dangled in the doorway at about eye level, swinging back and forth . . .

Hope to God this sodding bastard speaks English. They seemed to understand Coggins. . . .

Three seconds more, as Constantine and Gatewood pressed themselves to the shadowed stone on either side of the door, and then a man somewhere in the vicinity of six foot eight inches tall, bending to get through the door, came to a bewildered stop, staring at the pendulous figurine as it swung back and forth on a shoestring before his eyes, glowing from within.

Constantine was transmitting the power that made the figurine work by pointing his hand at it from the shadows. He wasn't very good at transmitting power from a distance. Only a few adepts could do it well in any sustained way.

The man said something in a cryptic Slavic dialect, his voice like rocks grinding together. Constantine caught a few flickers from the thug's rather dim mind. His name was Zalvich. He stared at the figurine, transfixed . . . and receptive.

"The bastards are devils, who sent you here," Constantine said. He probed Zalvich's will, expecting to find it crudely powerful, but it wasn't; he was the kind of bloke with a powerful physical will who could make himself do three hundred push-ups and run on a hot day till he puked and then run some more, but with a mental will like congealed borscht. It buckled under Constantine's mind with surprising ease. *"They have brought you into a hell, deep underground and filled with dancing demons! Skeletons dance before you! Now they send you back here to fight with demons while they escape! You must find them and stop them. They will explode the device and you will be trapped here!"*

"Go after them! Stop them, interfere, and save yourself!" Constantine said urgently.

Zalvich grunted, turned, and walked, with just a trace of zombie stiffness, back the way he had come.

Constantine retrieved his figurine, retied his shoes—he wanted to give Zalvich a chance to get a little ahead anyway—and gestured to Gatewood. The two of them followed the Ukrainian.

The passage was low and narrow, dripping with water in places; it smelled faintly of sewage and the floor was slippery with mud. It wended back and forth, traveling a surprising distance. Under the occasional, flickering lightbulb they made out muddy tracks from the cart's tires.

At last the passage came to a seeming dead end, dimly illuminated from above, but then they saw the hoist and boom to one side, a rope dangling down beside a metal ladder. Under the hoist, empty of its cargo, was the rubber-wheeled cart.

A blue white beam of moonlight angled down the shaft to them. Zalvich was just climbing the metal ladder, his head turning dull silver like a robot's as he ascended into the moonlight. Constantine and Gatewood waited till he'd gone from sight over the top, looked at one another doubtfully, and then Constantine shrugged and started to climb.

They emerged from an opening usually covered by locked-down metal doors, flush into the stone dock. But they had been flung open, and now Gatewood and Constantine clambered up to stand at the edge of the River Seine, broad and green brown and lazily shouldering through the city of Paris.

Here the bank was reinforced concrete, a long flight of flagstone stairs down from the street; above the river old gray apartment buildings crowded together, brooding down at them, with only a few lights showing. The river slid by syrup-slow, rank but alive.

To one side a group of men worked at a stone dock where a forty-foot hydrofoil was tied up. Affixed to the rear deck of the hydrofoil was a kind of gantry, wired and tilted upward. So that was how they were going to fire the missile.

The missile was being fitted into the small gantry; Dyzigi was opening the casket near its tail fins. A distant helicopter, a smaller one than Constantine had seen before, perhaps an Apache adapted for civilian use, was approaching over the skyline. Zalvich was . . . where?

And then gunfire erupted, and Constantine saw him, lit up by the muzzle flashes, standing in the deep shadow of the wall; he'd simply opened fire at the men working on the boat. Two of the Ukrainians, caught directly in the line of fire, went down immediately.

"Oh Christ on a Jet Ski—if he hits that bomb . . ."

Gatewood shook his head. "I don't think it'd set it off. They don't work like that. But it could spread radiation around. Like—bad."

Bullets were shooting sparks off the side of the cruise missile. . . . *Just a cloud of radiation, that's all . . .*

"Me and my genius ideas. Typical. Fuck!" Constantine started toward Zalvich, opening his mouth to shout, but the surviving gunman had returned fire and Zalvich staggered, his gun spitting fire into the dock. Bullets ricocheted past Constantine's ears with a reek of burning metal, and then Zalvich collapsed, shaking in death.

Dyzigi was walking toward Constantine, carrying the chest he'd had earlier. He was smiling.

Another boat was coming down the Seine. Sirens

were ululating in other parts of the city as the police moved in, attracted by the gunfire.

"We'll never get this thing off," Simpson shouted. "The wiring's all shot through here—"

"Constantine!" Coggins roared. "He did this!"

"Yes. Admirable isn't it?" Dyzigi said softly, walking up to Constantine. "I have misjudged Mr. Constantine. A few minutes ago I took counsel with Mr. Trevino, who has been informed by Dr. Mengele that Mr. Constantine could be of great use to us. His resourcefulness is truly admirable."

Admirable? For once Constantine was at a loss for words.

Dyzigi reached around in front of the box and opened it. Constantine looked down to see three skulls, side by side in soft wrappings, with eyes in them and carved with runes. All the eyes swiveled to look right at him.

"You will remember who you are," said Dyzigi. "They will remind you. Because they remember *you.*"

And all at once, Constantine remembered. . . .

15

TO WAKE THE FURIES

Somewhere in the British Isles, the early Bronze Age

Konz had decided to wait till his mother died before going to the Grotto of the People of the Sea. There was still time for vengeance. He waited with her, close to the low fire in their hut of mud and sticks and fir fronds, at what remained of the settlement.

His mother, Selem, an old woman of nearly thirty-four summers, one of the longest lived of the Tin Mound community, was lying on her side on a bearskin, under the sheep's fur blanket. She was trembling with the King of Death's footsteps; they came like the heavy hooves of the great horned beasts, and Konz could almost see the King of Death in the shadows outside the hut. But the King of Death was not coming the way another man came from a far place, walking on the surface of the land; he was coming from the world that cannot be seen with the first looking, but only with the second looking.

"Cold, Konz, I am cold," Selem hissed. Her right

eye was abscessed, but it had been that way for a long time, though it no longer had maggots squirming in it, and her left seemed heavy lidded and dull. She was almost bald with the sickness; her hair was wispy and gray.

He threw another stick onto the fire so that she would feel a little warmer, and drew his knees up close, putting one hand on the leather-bound hilt of the bronze knife stuck in the ground beside him.

"Will you not kill the men of the blue paint?" his mother asked him yet again, barely able to speak for her panting, her struggle for breath. She had asked him this many times that day, too many times. He always answered the same way.

"I will kill the men of the blue paint for you, Mother."

He looked at the way the firelight glimmered in the blade of his knife, and it soothed him as always. The power of fire was entering into it. . . . Always he sought ways to make the great powers of the world his power. He had meditated atop a crag during a thunderstorm, calling to Skygod to ask for instruction on how to make lightning spears like Skygod's. He thought he'd heard a reply at times, a mockery of his pretensions. But also a hint: *Some portion of this sky fire can be yours; some portion of it circles round within your bones even now. . . .*

So much he had heard from Skygod, and nothing more.

He had gone to Bregg, the god-speaker, and endured the foul smells of his speaking—his teeth were rotting out of his head—to hear him describe the marks of the People of the Sea; to hear him speak of which marks bore the greatest power. He had used them to summon the Snakegod from the tarn; Snakegod had risen up before Konz, speaking in his mind: *Some portion of my power can be yours; some portion of it swims up and down your spine even now.*

So much had he heard from Snakegod and nothing more, before it slipped back into the tarn.

At Bregg's urging, Konz had spent ten days neither eating nor sleeping, in the deepest forest of the coast lands. On the tenth day he had eaten the red mushrooms and said the Names, over and over, and Greengod had appeared to him, demanding sacrifices and mocking him—but Greengod had told him this much: *The sap of the highest trees rises in you, too; it rises in your groin even now. . . .*

So much had Greengod said and nothing more.

His mother had been fourteen summers when he'd been born to her. Now she was withered and dying because the men of blue paint had killed his father, and they had attacked her and taken her till something broke within her womb, so that she bled unceasingly from between her legs. The men of blue paint had left her for dead; they had killed most of his people. The few survivors had scattered.

There was still a smear of blue paint on his mother's neck; the print of marauding fingers. He had wished to wash it away, but she would not let him put the water on her for fear it would steal the heat of her body.

He had let them do this to her; he had let them kill his father and the others.

He, Konz, the strongest and fastest young warrior of the settlement, had been away from the Tin Mound settlement, had been wandering in search of the gods of the sea people, those who had come by sea from the Fallen Land, from the land that had crumbled into the sea.

Bregg had told him about them; about their great boats, each as big as twenty of the boats of his own people; beautiful boats shaped like ax heads, with scarlet sails; they wore brightly colored cloth so soft it was like the skin of infants; their metals were harder than any bronze. Some of their magic, too, Bregg had learned as a boy when he was a slave to one of their god speakers; he had only learned a little before the colony from the Fallen Land had been wiped out by disease and the depredation of the men of blue paint. He had learned many of the marks and many of their god summonings; he had learned the names of their principal gods. They had been trying to call on their war god, N'Hept, when the raiders had come. They had called him too late.

"They were reluctant to call N'Hept," Bregg had said. "They had tried to leave the memory of N'Hept behind. They blamed him for the sinking of their land into the sea. But they knew his power would give them strength to destroy their enemies. They put their reluctance aside, but it was too late. The blue paints came before N'Hept could be summoned. The sea people were weakened from disease—they had no strength against the foreign sicknesses of this new land—and so they were easily killed."

Now Konz sat by the fire, brooding, blaming himself again for the death of his father and the shaming of his mother. "Will you not kill the men of the blue paint?" his mother asked again, her voice rasping.

"I will kill them, Selem my mother. I know a way."

This was not wholly true. He merely knew a way that he might try. He could go to the old warrens of the sea people. The remains of their colony still stood. Their altars still stood, and some of their wall markings and magical tools remained. . . . He remembered the way there that Bregg had shown him. Bregg was dead himself now. The pain in his mouth and fever in his body had maddened him so, he had finally thrown himself off a cliff.

Konz's mother had stopped panting and shaking. She lay with the inertness of clay and stone.

The great footsteps had ceased their approach. King of Death had come and gone. Konz's mind had been distant, in the colony of the sea people, when it had happened.

"Good traveling, my mother," he said.

He waited a while, singing a song to help her to the far land, and then picked up her body and carried it in his arms, to the barrows.

⊷═◉═⊷

Konz led Barasa and Pel into the Grotto of the People of the Sea, at the base of the high forested hill almost within sight of the western ocean. A low stone cliff stood to their left; its brow was mossy, overgrown with drooping ferns. The ferns thrived from the stream that became a sparse waterfall off the cliff; the falling water sparkled in the late-afternoon sun. The cliff jutted over a damp, lichen-spotted undercut riddled with caves.

"I see no colony," Pel said. He was a short, angry, heavy-browed figure, his face ritually scarred, his nose split by an enemy's ax so that now his breathing was rough. He and Barasa had been away hunting when the men of the blue paint devastated the settlement. It was a warm afternoon and like Konz and Barasa, a lean man with a twisted right foot from an accident that Barasa had never explained, Pel wore only a girdle of woven sheep's fur; all three men bore symmetrical scars on their chests, and their hands and arms were painted red, up to the elbows, to signify preparation for battle. All three of them carried wooden spears with bronze points. Barasa had a long straggly beard; Pel and Konz had carved their beards away.

"They did not use huts," Konz said. "They were building houses of stone, away to the south, and in the meantime they lived here, in these caves. They were here only a hot season when the end came. But—" He pointed. "You see the marks of their fires; and there, the remains of a boat, unfinished. . . ."

"You come here because of their knowledge," Barasa said, "but their knowledge did not save them. How strong could it have been?"

"Bregg showed me things . . . they were true. Bregg knew."

"Bregg is dead." Barasa was always skeptical. If you said there was a herd of the great horned beasts to the south, he would say that perhaps by now they've moved to the east.

"Come on, let us look anyway," Konz said.

"You have not been selected to be our leader," Pel said grumpily.

"Then stay here," Konz said. "Or come, as you choose."

Konz strode into what remained of the colony, immediately seeing the white flash of man bones amongst the plants growing along the edges of the clearing, and green and blue cloth flapping in the thin breeze close by them. The remains of some of the dead sea people, he supposed. He walked along the edge of the stream that ran from the waterfall's pool, and climbed the gravelly path up beside the falls to the caves.

N'Hept! He called the name in his mind, as Bregg had taught him. *N'Hept! Where are you? I've come to sacrifice! N'Hept!*

There was no reply in words, but he felt a kind of tugging sensation from one of the caves. . . .

The stone over the entrance to the cave was inscribed with a magical sigil: the incisings of the sea people. Konz entered the cave, and after a few steps in darkness, he saw, with surprise, that there was light at the back. Had one of the sea people survived? Was someone else camped back there? There could be men of the blue paint here. He drew his knife from his girdle in his left hand, hefted his spear, and stalked forward.

But the light came from a natural hole in the ceiling of the cave, a rugged shaft, a vertical crack really, that rose crookedly up to the hilltop, showing a little sky, diffuse sunlight.

At the base of the shaft were the remains of a stone altar. On the altar was a broken skull, incised with markings familiar to Konz: the invocation to N'Hept.

But the skull was mostly smashed; an intact skull was needed. . . .

"What have you found?" Barasa asked, coming into the shaft behind Konz.

"I have found the place of power I sought," Konz said. "Where is Pel?"

"He is watching for the men of blue paint."

"He is afraid!" Konz jeered. A certain giddy energy was working its way up in him. He thumped the butt of his spear on the stone floor and walked back and forth, calling in his mind: *N'Hept! N'Hept!*

He looked at the images painted on the walls here: the faces of N'Hept and other gods; he looked at the wooden debris, smashed by the men of blue paint; he looked at the shaft of light overhead. . . .

N'Hept!

"What is it you do, here? It is foolishness! Their gods have no power," Barasa said peevishly. "Let us go hunting instead. . . . I am hungry. . . ."

"N'Hept!" He called the name aloud and in his mind at once. He visualized the face of N'Hept. *"I offer you glory and blood!"*

"I am going," Barasa said, turning his back.

Konz shouted, *"N'HEPT!"* and spun about, swinging the butt of the spear, clouting Barasa hard across the back of the head with it. Deliberately not hitting him hard enough to knock him unconscious.

Barasa staggered and turned, snarling, raising his spear, as Konz had hoped; he could not offer a sacrifice of Barasa if he did not fall in real battle. Murder was not enough for N'Hept.

"Barasa is not fully a man!" Konz taunted. "His feet are twisted and his penis, too! Barasa is an infant to leave outside in the cold!"

That was too much for Barasa, who charged him, teeth bared. Konz sidestepped and drove his spear into Barasa's throat with all his strength, shouting, "For N'Hept!" The bronze spear point drove deep into the soft flesh of Barasa's neck and severed his spine; the spear head thrust out on the other side, accompanied by a spurt of bright blood. Barasa quivered, his knees shaking, and then collapsed.

Konz felt weak himself and sick to his stomach, but he did not want Barasa's death to be wasted, so he made himself pull the spear free and then he used his knife to finish removing Barasa's head from his shoulders. As he did so, he said, "Barasa, you died so that we can take revenge for our people. . . . Do not trouble me with your spirit, but give me your blessing in the battle to come." He carried the head to the blocky altar and placed it in the center, so it gushed blood into the runnel marks on the side. And he gazed at the painted image of N'Hept, a face like two animals and one of the Old Ones, and he called out, "N'Hept! This man was my friend! I have given him to you in battle! Come to me and give me the strength of ten! I have heard of the strength of ten from Bregg, whom you know!"

There was no reply, but he sensed that N'Hept was waiting for something more. It was not yet done. . . .

Konz took his bronze knife and—gritting his teeth

so that he could bear the work—he scraped away the
skin from Barasa's staring, startled face; he scraped
away his scalp, and wiped the bloody bone with
Barasa's loin cloths, till it was clear enough to begin
the carving. Then he incised the runes. He knew
them by heart; they were carved, as well, on the surface of his mind.

His hands were covered in blood when he was
done; his nose was full of the stench of drying blood
in the first stages of decay.

He put his right hand on the skull and stretched
out his other, palm upward, toward the image of
N'Hept on the wall. "I have given you blood in battle! I
have carved my intention on him as I was bidden!
Now will you not give me the strength of ten men that
I may kill my enemies?" And he called out the incantation in the language of the People of the Sea, that
he had learned from Bregg.

A voice came into his mind . . .

**Carve away his eyelids, so that he may look un-
flinchingly on the task before him, in the Hidden
World.**

Konz was shaken by this voice, ringing in his head
like the bronze gong rung in the barrows before the
call to the Greengod. But he did as he was bid so that
the skull's eyes stared without eyelids, unflinchingly
looking at death and the Hidden World.

And again Konz called out, *"N'Hept! N'Hept!
N'Hept!"*

"Konz!" came Pel's voice, echoing down the tunnel.
"Konz, why did you bring us here? The men of the
blue paint are nearby, that was their fire you saw!

They have taken this place as a hunting camp! They are coming! Konz, we must run!"

Konz had known the men of blue paint were nearby; he had assumed he and the others would be found here. He had planned for it that way, and now he continued to chant, at the top of his lungs:

"N'Hept! N'Hept! N'Hept!"

"Konz!"

"N'HEPT!"

Then he heard the voice in his head again.

Here is my power, because you have come to me: the one who lives within you and is so easily forgotten. Because you have remembered the god inside you, who taught you and your kind to kill, now remember killing . . . now remember the true joy of killing. . . .

Then Konz saw N'Hept himself, his face glowing before his mind's eye, N'Hept's mouth opening as if to roar—but out of it came no sound, only a feeling, a feeling that rippled from N'Hept into Konz.

It was like the strength that came into him when he had coupled with Venn, his only mate, who had died two years before.

He still remembered the power he'd felt when driving himself into her, as if he were a god himself.

It was like the strength that had come into him when he'd killed his first man, the man with the braided beard, from the northern tribe. . . . The power and the joy of it, roaring through him . . .

But so much more strength than that—ten men more!

"Konz! They're coming!"

Konz picked up his knife and spear and ran back through the cave. He could see Pel silhouetted against the mouth of the cave, jabbing his spear at something, backing toward him.

"Pel! Feel the power of the War Lord!" Konz shouted. "Feel it, from me! Come with me and kill them, in memory of our people!"

And Konz rushed past Pel and out of the cave, into the group of close to twenty blue-painted men. They were naked, clothed only in blue paint, with red rings around their eyes, shells on sinew string around their ankles and wrists, their hair caked in dung; their spears, mostly of flint, were short but lethal close in.

"Pel!" Konz shouted, as he stabbed with spear and knife, "Call to N'Hept! Feel his power!"

"N'Hept!" Pel shouted, rushing into the fight.

Pel was feeling it then, flowing from Konz to him, and he shouted, "N'Hept! The Tin Mound!" and thrust his spear close in at the men of blue paint, shrieking like a hill cat, and red blood spurted to make blue paint run.

At first the men of blue paint backed away, frightened by their fury, stunned by six quick deaths in seven breaths; many had fallen under Konz and Pel's onslaught, twitching in their dying, as Konz rushed the others, shrieking.

But then the leader of the men of blue paint shouted in their outlandish language and rallied them and in moments Pel and Konz were surrounded by a ring of jabbing spears. Konz left his knife stuck in a man's breast and took hold of his spear with both hands and began to thrust, and thrust again. His spear was longer than theirs and it kept them back a few moments more. He felt the power of lightning, snake, and tree in him; he felt the rage of N'Hept. He stabbed and he stabbed and he laughed and he stabbed. . . .

Konz turned to see Pel howling with kill fury, and his face, Konz saw, was the face of N'Hept. The face of Pel had been quite replaced by the face of N'Hept.

If the men of blue paint saw this god face they did not react to it, but only pushed in closer, knocking Pel's spear haft aside, jabbering kill words and stabbing him with their spears, again and again, piercing his stomach and side and neck and eye. Pel went down, shrieking rage as he went.

Konz was stabbing the leader of the men of blue paint with his spear in the soft place under the arch of ribs in front, but he felt their spears slam into him at the same moment. He felt no pain, no weakness then, just the sensation of impact. He twisted his own spear in the guts of his enemy and howled for vengeance. "For Selem! For Zal! For the Tin Mound! N'Hept, N'Hept!"

He drew his spear out and smashed it into another raging blue face, shouting in glee: "You cannot kill me! I have the power of ten warriors in N'Hept!"

But he felt something then that he'd never felt before, a heaviness in his limbs, a sudden draining of strength, and he looked down to see that a spear was driven between his ribs and into his heart. His blood ran thickly out of the wound, to twine along the shaft of the spear.

He looked up to see the blue-painted face of the

man who'd driven the spear through his heart. The
man grinned with his yellow, filed teeth. And for a moment, the man's face became the face of N'Hept. . . .

And that was the last thing that Konz . . .

. . . that Constantine saw. . . .

Before the red clouds filled all the world and the
sun set forever.

Paris, France

Tchalai was on the cellphone, talking to her contact
at the French secret service, when Mercury opened
the front door of the apartment, expecting the man
delivering groceries, and finding instead four heavily
armed men in black ski masks.

One of the men backed Mercury into the room
with a silenced pistol against her forehead. He lifted a
free hand to his mouth, one finger pressed to his lips,
as he looked at Tchalai, standing in the midst of the
living room with the phone at her ear. . . .

He looked at Mercury, he looked at his gun, he
looked at Tchalai—and pressed his finger again to his
lips.

Tchalai nodded miserably—and hung up, tossing
the phone aside.

Two of the big men went silently to Tchalai, one of
them taking a syringe from his coat pocket. He took
the cap off the syringe's needle, and squirted a little
fluid into the air as he approached her, smiling. The
mask hid everything but his cold black eyes and his
cold bright smile. Tchalai's parrot, Spitlove, began to
squawk, to flutter. . . .

"Tchalai . . ." Mercury began, stammering, lips trembling. "I see something—they plan to . . . they're going to . . . I think we should run. . . ."

"C'est trop tarde," Tchalai replied huskily as the man stabbed the needle into her shoulder. "It's too late. . . . They . . ."

Then she collapsed.

Mercury did try to run for the hall door—and one of the men struck her down with the barrel of his pistol.

She lay there on the rug, stunned, unable to think, her mind seeming truncated—looking up to see Spitlove the parrot flapping furiously around the room, shrilly squawking, *"Burn in hell, bastards! John Constantine, John Constantine, John Constant—"*

Until the man with the silenced pistol shot the bird, in midflight, so that Spitlove smacked bloodily into a wall and tumbled down, shedding green feathers.

London, England, the twenty-first century

The first thing Constantine became aware of as he came back to himself, was Gatewood's saying, in a voice of despondent amazement, "She was right there, John, and I couldn't say anything. I was looking at Tchalai through the window of the car, but it was a tinted window and something wouldn't let me talk and—"

"You're talking my bloody ear off right now," Constantine growled, rubbing his head.

Constantine was sitting up on a cot, next to the one Gatewood was chained to. He looked around, at first thinking himself back in the Catacombs. He was underground, in a tunnel, wasn't he? Wrong underground.

He needed to make up his mind which way to move, what to do—but he felt almost numbed by what he'd seen. Lost. He was sickeningly disoriented, being back here in the twenty-first century again. He could still taste blood in his mouth; could still feel the spear through his heart; could still feel Barasa's skin peeling away under his bronze knife. . . .

Get oriented. Get involved in this life again. Take stock.

There were lights on overhead; there was a familiar multifarious smell in the air. Wet concrete, rodents, dirty socks, and very distantly, curry.

"London!" he burst out. He was in the London Underground—a tube station. An abandoned one, by the look of it. The train tunnel was walled up on one side; the other mostly blocked by debris.

"Yeah, John . . ." Gatewood and the cot he lay on were shackled to a guard rail at the end of the tube platform. "We're in Britain. . . ."

A group of men stood about thirty feet away, looking into a television monitor. Dyzigi, Coggins, Simpson, and two men he didn't know. One of them was MacCrawley, maybe—he was rumored to be related to Crowley and this man looked much like the Great Beast. As Constantine watched him, the man turned and smiled almost charmingly at him, nodding in acknowledgment. He knew Constantine, surely.

"It's London, yeah," Gatewood went on. "You've been out of it for like twenty-four hours. In a coma or something."

Gatewood was shackled lying on his back; Constantine was only chained up by his wrists. He wondered vaguely why. But it was hard to think, just then; he felt distant from everything. Here and not here. Some part of him still clung to Konz. . . .

"What happened to you?" Gatewood asked.

"I was someplace else," Constantine muttered. "Just . . . someplace else. And some time . . . else." *N'Hept*. It had been nothing planted in his mind, no illusion. The memory of Konz had been his own genuine memory. He did have a strong connection to N'Hept . . . perhaps he'd always known—but tried not to know.

He was sitting on a cot, on a dirty gray, cracked platform near the train tracks. The place was coated with dust, clearly not maintained. Not far away was the chest that Dyzigi had opened to reveal the staring skulls. Constantine was glad it was shut. It was sitting on an altar of stone, brought to the platform just for a ritual, he supposed; there were runes on the altar and a circle on the floor around it, in which images and names of power were written. They were not the names of power he himself used—not anymore.

He looked at Gatewood and realized why he was so thoroughly shackled: it was so he couldn't remove the pendant that had been strung around his neck. The pendant showed a leering face—Ba'al, probably—carved in onyx. It was capable of blocking contact with the spirits. It neutralized Gatewood's mediumistic power.

"What were you saying about Tchalai?" Constantine asked.

"She was . . . oh God I'm thirsty, they haven't given me anything to drink for a full day. . . . They took us out of there, you they carried, me they forced at gunpoint. They brought us up to the street, loaded us into a limo. I guess they blew off the chopper because the authorities were coming. Tchalai came in another car with these two guys, and a bunch of French special forces types arrived with 'em—they just ignored us. Diplomatic plates, Dyzigi said, like he thought it was funny. 'We are someone special.' They didn't see us through the tinted window of the limo we were in. I couldn't seem to speak. We drove off and went to a helicopter and another limo and . . . here."

"These blokes she was with, what sort did they seem?"

"Like—spooks. Not my kind of spooks—secret agent types."

"Yes," Dyzigi said, walking up. "Your friend Tchalai Dermitzel is an agent for the Direction Centrale Police Judiciaire. A branch of the French secret service. Indeed, one of the men with your friend that night was a certain Monsieur Vallee, part of their 'esoteric investigations' branch. A branch which does not exist in the French government's budget meetings."

Constantine shrugged. "I always suspected she was tied in with the French secret service. When she saw the missile, she had her priorities. I don't blame her."

"It was too late to fire the Tomahawk, thanks to that lunatic Ukrainian," Coggins said, coming up to look Constantine over. "But it doesn't matter, we didn't need it, really. Just wanted to prime the pump."

"I heard 'em talking about it, John," Gatewood said, his voice raspy. "It's not a nuclear weapon, not really. It's kind of a dummy."

Dyzigi smiled, watching Constantine as he spoke. "It *would* have exploded with a certain amount of radioactive material in it. Something like a dirty bomb. Not so much to create damage—more to spread suspicion. It would have been blamed on Iranians. We saw to that . . . but its deeper purpose was to spread a certain yellow compound—the bones of ancient warriors, consecrated to N'Hept."

N'Hept. Constantine shuddered, remembering N'Hept staring at him from the face of the man who'd killed him—who'd killed Konz. And he remembered his death in another lifetime. . . .

Dyzigi saw how the name of the War Lord made Constantine react. "You saw what and who you were, Constantine?"

Coggins was pacing, looking at Constantine and Gatewood and again at his watch. "I get that you had a reason to keep this one alive. . . ." He nodded at Constantine. "But why the other one? They're problem people, they should be eliminated. We've only got thirty-eight minutes before the targets are in place. I say we kill these two."

"Interested in bringing about the apocalypse, are you, squire?" Constantine said. He shook his head. "Whatever these others have in mind—it isn't your Christian fantasy ending. And you know it, too. . . ."

He sensed grave doubts working in Coggins. Another influence on him . . .

Coggins stared at him in angry shock. Then he

backhanded Constantine, making his nose bleed. "You work for the Father of Lies, you Brit sleaze. That's obvious as all hell. Keep your yap shut!" He turned furiously to Dyzigi. "You heard what he said—he's trying to psyche-op me, dammit! I say we kill them and fast!"

"You will not kill them," Dyzigi said calmly. "I had intended to use someone else besides Mr. Gatewood, but he is handy; I will need him in the ritual. And I have reason to believe that Constantine here will serve N'Hept quite willingly. It is in his blood and bones and soul. He knows how little this faulty, house-of-cards civilization matters—don't you Constantine?"

Constantine swallowed. Dyzigi had struck a chord with that one. "Know what you mean. Been to Hell. Been out of me body. Seen people melting into Nepenthe like they never were. Seen the dance of maya, like. After that, this world seems . . . temporary. Doesn't seem to matter much if you blot it out and start over. So much wrong with it—it's worth a try, innit?"

Coggins snorted skeptically. "That's all just talk. I don't want him alive, Dyzigi, that's my last word on it. He's dangerous to the cause. He's not a *real* believer. He's a loose cannon and he's a problem."

"It's you who's not a believer," said Dyzigi, amused. "It's you, General, who's a loose cannon, as you put it."

"What the hell are you talking about?"

"Do you think I don't know they've tainted your mind? The enemy? The angels and their ilk?"

Coggins stared at him. "The angels . . . the enemy?"

Constantine snorted. "Sounds like you've outgrown your usefulness, 'General Ripper.' You don't get it yet? You and Morris and all you lot've been deceived like a lot of retarded school brats. Revelations had nothing to do with our time. You suspected it to, yeah?"

Coggins licked his lips. "No . . . they—" He looked desperately back and forth between Dyzigi and Trevino, who was walking up, smiling sadly, hands clasped like the ex-priest he was.

Trevino shrugged expansively. "I gave up that dream years ago—another kind of kingdom will come. . . ."

"Strucken was my man, General," Dyzigi said, "and a valuable man. You shouldn't have killed him. You have been tainted by their dream sendings. You're dangerous. And we don't need you anymore. You gave us The Blossom; we had your logistical support in Carthaga. But Morris was of more use, esoterically. And that imbecilic 'Christian apocalypse' scenario. Constantine is right—that business in Revelations was all about the Romans, I'm afraid. It really had nothing to do with our time at all." Dyzigi was clearly enjoying twisting the knife of truth in Coggins's vitals. "You make your book of Revelations seem to predict anything you like—and we made use of that ambiguity. It was one of our little games." Dyzigi turned his nasty crooked smile at Constantine. "I tell him this now because I wanted *you* to hear. To know I labor under no illusions. I want you to know exactly what it is you're signing on for so that you can involve yourself immediately, once we begin the true Transfiguration."

"What does he mean—signing on?" Gatewood asked.

"Mr. Constantine is in fact one of us," Dyzigi said. "From another lifetime."

"I don't know," Constantine said. "I just fucking don't know."

"John—" Gatewood looked at him openmouthed. "You can't be thinking of having anything to do with these people."

But Constantine felt it in him, and strongly: a connection with N'Hept. A hunger to see the world burn. And what power they would have. . . . It might be used for good, eventually. After all the purging was done.

"What is it you intend—after?" Constantine asked suddenly.

Dyzigi smiled. He was after Constantine's soul—they both knew that. Constantine's soul was worth a great deal in the Hidden World. There were those who would pay a great price to have Constantine's soul on its way back to Hell. G'Broag's master, Nergal, would reward his servant with a subworld of his own, once he was restored to power. . . .

"We intend to initiate the destruction of most of humanity, so that we can rule what remains," Dyzigi said. "We will allow humanity to destroy itself. It has always given into its impulses, its appetites—the bestial urges that take shape as the dark gods in the Hidden World. Long ago humanity created N'Hept from the base clay, as it were, underlying the Sea of Consciousness. He never quite went away—he merely slumbered, as other kinds of warfare came about. We found a certain cave in Britain, near the sea; we found in that hidden place the very skull that John Constantine, in another life, created from the head of his dead companion. That brutal option has tainted all your lives since, Constantine. It meant you were always one of us. The War Lord has awakened, thanks to your seed skull, and others from Atlantis herself. The power builds exponentially, battle to battle, skull to skull, as war feeds on itself. And N'Hept arises, and reaches out to embrace the whole world . . . to create a Third World War, more destructive than any war that has come before now. Oh, we'll keep the nukes down to a minimum—but our war will make World War Two look like a skirmish."

Dyzigi looked around at the subway station. "It is a great big world, to be sure. There are six billion mortal maggots crawling on it. They have created a monstrous nest to squirm in. Monstrous vast, monstrous complex. Difficult to make it all consumed by N'Hept's power—it took preparation."

"What was all that business on Carthaga, then?" Constantine asked.

Trevino made an Italianate gesture of enthusiasm. "Carthaga was like a spring rain to make the seeds grow. War feeds war; that small war is the spiritual seed of the great one. It gave us more seed skulls, and it woke the War Lord! It will feed and grow and spread! We have charged the seed skulls with enough power to start a world war, with a persuasiveness no one can resist, once it is unleashed. Everyone in the world will undertake to destroy everyone else! True, they'll align themselves with factions, with their race, their nation, their religion. But it's all qute arbitrary, in the end."

Dyzigi nodded. "We don't need The Blossom, we have . . . what is that betting expression?"

"Covered your bets," Coggins said hoarsely, hardly aware he was saying it. Stunned by these revelations—the true book of Revelations.

"Yes. Constantine knows about that. We have covered our bets. We will summon N'Hept in London—"

Walking up, MacCrawley said sharply, "I don't think we should tell Constantine any more."

Dyzigi shook his head insistently. "I need him to know what he is doing."

He wants my soul thoroughly tainted, Constantine thought resignedly. *Too late. Tainted already . . .*

"A critical international conference is taking place in a room just two hundred feet above us," Dyzigi said. "NATO is meeting with representatives from the Middle East. There is amongst them a Middle Eastern prime minister who is destined to unite the Arab world against the West. He will ally himself with China and North Korea. A world holocaust will result. I have seen it quite clearly along the continuum of probability. . . . The bone powder has been spread through the room the meeting is in, in advance. They will become our angry little puppets."

Coggins was staring, shaking his head. . . .

"We will bring the Old Gods back," MacCrawley said. "The wonderful Old Gods! Now *there* were gods! Not these simpering jackals people worship today!" Smacking his lips with the appreciation of a connoisseur. "We will create a world of neo-pagans, not simpering neo-pagans, but a return to human sacrifice, to heaving squalling children into furnaces—oh yes, I glory in the thought! Because it means *commitment!* Commitment to a sane world! A handful of rulers over all the planet—submitting only to the great powers of the Hidden World . . ."

Coggins roared and turned to Simpson. "Kill these lying sons of bitches, they've been using us!"

MacCrawley was moving to stand behind Simpson. . . .

"You mean—Dyzigi, MacCrawley, Trevino, sir?" Simpson asked, MacCrawley was gesturing arcanely. His lips moving . . .

"Hell yes—fast! Shoot, dammit!"

"Yes sir," Simpson said, drawing a pistol.

And Captain Simpson shot General Coggins in the forehead with a single round from a silenced 9 mm. Coggins crumpled without a word.

"Yes sir," Simpson mumbled, looking down at Coggins's body. "Yes sir, they've been using us. But I'm signing on with them."

"Good choice, my boy. I can always use an enforcer," said MacCrawley. Constantine saw then a look in MacCrawley's eye he knew quite well. Simpson hadn't made a conscious choice at all; MacCrawley had taken him over psychically, made him think he was acting on his own, but he'd used him as a weapon. MacCrawley, Constantine realized, had a powerful will indeed.

"What about this one?" Trevino said, pointing at Gatewood.

"Oh," said Dyzigi. "We need him. I was planning to use the general to finish the ritual—but when it became clear he was tainted . . . well, I brought this man along. And I have a jar I want to put him in. His power is useful; once he's in the jar, like Mengele, he will be a wonderful tool."

"How are you going to do it?" Constantine asked suddenly. "I mean, why here, now? This spot?"

"They are directly overhead," Dyzigi said, looking at the ceiling. "We expunged all records of this old station before they did their security check. The NATO meeting is there, full of men who will shortly be planning to kill one another."

McCrawley was shaking his head, scowling at Constantine. "I must say, I, too, am nervous about trusting Constantine, Dyzigi. He's notoriously deceptive."

"I have arranged for him to be psychically interrogated," Dyzigi said. "My divided nature weakens my power. Nor will yours be enough. But this other will penetrate Constantine's mind without hindrance. John Constantine cannot deceive us. He must make a real choice." He turned back to Constantine. "Your talent will make you high priest under those of us who have divided the world into our own kingdoms. War will end! There will be sacrifice first, in a controlled way. There will be only a few hundred million people left in the world at first. Those you see before you are the stewards of the great purge, but there are some six thousand members of the Servants of Transfiguration—some in high places—some handily close to high places, all of them poised to take over. We will make the world over as we choose, and you can help guide it. Imagine! Justice at last—whatever justice you have in mind! And if you don't like our great plan for afterwards, you can propose one of your own, once the cleansing is done! You feel your connection to N'Hept; you have always had it. That is why you had a horror of weapons: you fled from your own inner savagery. But now with the release of that very natural fury you can see yourself as you are—and be at peace! A strange and paradoxical peace, but a real peace at last, John Constantine . . ."

Constantine nodded. He thought about the Congo. The thug militias who took thousands of children from their villages and made them kill their own family; the men who made these same children into sex slaves and who cut off the children's hands if they disobeyed. All done as part of the struggle to control African gold and diamond mines so that wealthy women in America and Europe could wear gleaming baubles to openings.

He thought about Darfur, and the mass murders, the rape camps sanctioned by the Sudanese government. He thought about Rwanda and he thought about the Holocaust and he thought about the Inquisition. He thought about the World Trade Center crumbling, people leaping from the high windows . . . people falling, falling, almost indistinguishable from the debris as they fell. . . .

Once, traveling in Korea, he had visited an old sorcerer and he had spoken of his own suffering. The sorcerer had laughed and said, "You scarcely are acquainted with suffering." And he had taken him to a nearby farm, to a stinking basement where he saw a large, shaggy bear stuffed into a cage that was deliberately made too small for it.

It was, and is, a common practice in Asia; the bear constrained all its life in a metal straitjacket so that it can be "milked" for bile and other substances shunted from its body by tubes shoved into its belly. The animals went mad, of course, with misery. They were in unspeakable torment all their lives.

Human beings did that to them, just so they could make money.

And it had seemed to Constantine that it was a metaphor for trapped people; for people caught in the implacable machinations of the new global society, tormented by fear of starving into producing something that a few other people used for their enrichment. Billions of people were all stuck together, thrashing madly in the cage; they were the bears in the steel straitjackets.

It was time to start over, wasn't it? He had thought so for ever so long. And if he joined them, he told himself firmly, he could divert them afterwards. Take over from within. Maybe ultimately make a utopia.

"Yes," he said. "I believe I'll throw in with you—just as Simpson here has. . . ."

"You understand, Constantine, I have in my power someone who can penetrate your mind better than our finest psychics. I have forced him, under pressure, to develop this ability. He will interrogate you and see whether or not you are sincere."

"When?" Constantine asked.

"Tonight. Here. Do not think it is like deceiving to a lie detector; that can be done, as we both know. It will not be like that. *This* mind will look into yours and see your intentions. You will not be able to deceive Dr. Mengele. If he finds that you are not really sincere, well, I have another way to use you. You will be less powerful—but still useful. You see I have a jar just right for you, too, Mr. Constantine."

16

POWER BENEATH THE THRONE

London, England

Constantine was locked into an old maintenance room, ten feet by thirty. There was a broken industrial vacuum cleaner in the far corner; gray concrete walls thick with dust; a vent too small to escape through, high in the wall; and the folding metal chair he sat on, which tipped out of balance, almost falling over when he shifted his weight. *This is the room I've ended up in,* he thought. *This is the room they store my soul in.*

He felt old and tired. But he had chosen his course. He couldn't turn back now.

He heard MacCrawley's footsteps outside the locked metal door. He knew it was MacCrawley, he could feel it. Funny, the connection he felt to MacCrawley, whom he'd only just met. It was as if they'd always known one another, always been adversaries.

"You should not have left him in there," MacCrawley was saying.

"He can do nothing. Here is the guardian, outside his doorway. Constantine cannot cast a spell with Mengele here," Dyzigi replied. "He asked for time to think alone. I have given him five minutes."

"Why do you want him so much? Yes, he has ability, but . . . he is treacherous."

"If he turns . . . but hush . . ."

The two men moved away from the door. But Constantine had understood. He had already guessed Dyzigi's real motive. Who was it, he wondered, who had put in the special order from Hell?

Nergal? Probably.

It didn't matter. Constantine was on another course now. . . .

He smiled to himself. *A new world.*

He must focus on that—a new, scoured world . . . which would begin with . . .

He stood up and walked to the wall, and used his finger to draw a simple, clear image of N'Hept in the dust. He stared at it.

A world which would begin with N'Hept.

He took the figurine of Zoroaster out of his pocket; tossed it up and down in his palm. *Reflection, words, deeds,* the Blue Sheikh had reminded him. Well, he had sat here and he had reflected. He would declare his intent with words. Then he would show it in deeds.

Objective and subjective. Reality and unreality.

He looked back at the image of N'Hept.

He must make the commitment. . . .

⇥⊙⇤

MacCrawley watched balefully as Dyzigi pushed the serving cart over to the door. On the cart, under a gray cloth, was the guardian—a gallon jar, with parts of a man forced into it. Absurd.

MacCrawley hated to be near the thing; it reeked of a hunger to induce torment in others, and it would do it psychically to him, too, if it could.

He looked at his watch; the time was close. But they had nothing to do as they waited, for the next thirteen minutes. . . . Dyzigi was setting a kind of spiritual trap for Constantine, he supposed. Let Dyzigi have his toys. The great—or perhaps simply the notorious—John Constantine, locked up in a cell, with a pickled monster; rather amusing really.

Dyzigi gestured, and Simpson unlocked the door. He pushed the cart inside, right up to Constantine.

Simpson followed him in, pointing the 9 mm at Constantine's head.

Dyzigi glanced at his watch. "The world will change in a few minutes. We just have time to see if you have changed, too. Mr Simpson—"

"*Captain* Simpson," the pilot said.

Dyzigi glanced at him in irritation. "All prior ranks will become meaningless. But you will be far more powerful than a captain, if you are loyal. You will shoot Mr. Constantine in the head if he tries to touch this jar. I advise you not to look at the jar yourself, *Captain* Simpson. Do not come any closer."

Simpson only nodded.

Dyzigi stepped back, drawing the cloth as he went, and said something gutteral—something in German.

Constantine stared at the exposed jar. At the

crooked eyes sliding around in the dreary ooze. He felt its hatred like heat from a radiator. He saw it slide, brain and eyes pressing against the glass. . . .

Where had Dyzigi learned to create such a thing? It was beyond Constantine's knowledge and he was glad of it. Still, he was now in league with Dyzigi—he was going to help him destroy civilization, a great part of the human world. He must remember that. He had really, truly made up his mind to do it. No tricks—he was going to destroy the vermin that made life miserable for him, for so many others. And the survivors would be happy slaves, he'd see to that.

The thing in the jar stared and waited. It seemed to be asking a question.

"Yes," Constantine said. "Yes. Come . . ."

His stomach gave a lurch. But he opened his mind to the thing; he dropped all his defenses.

"Go ahead, Pickles, walk on in," Constantine said. "Have a gander 'round."

The jar burst open and the thing in it leapt at his face—

But only in his mind. It leapt at him mentally, almost jovial in a kind of psychological freedom—getting out of itself and into him.

Constantine almost burst into tears when he felt the jar-thing's psychic tongue pressing between the two front lobes of his brain. . . .

He wanted to scream *Nooooo, get it away,* but it was important he finish this process. If he didn't, he'd end up in a jar like this bugger.

Only—he felt like there were cockroaches forcing their way into his sinuses; he felt like his head was being sucked into the mouth of a giant lamprey, and it was sucking his brain out his eyes; he felt like his skull was cracking under the pressure. He felt he couldn't bear it another moment.

Think about your objective. You know what needs to be done. You've made up your mind—let them see it!

He saw himself astride the world—bigger than the planet, with a flamethrower in his hand. He switched on the flamethrower and he laughed as it played over the continents and boiled the seas away. . . .

The thing probing his mind joined in his laughter. Its companionship was disgusting.

And then Dyzigi spoke again. The thing in the jar drew its mind back, returning to its own little glassy world, so that Constantine suddenly felt as if he'd taken a shower after a long day sweating in a sandstorm.

Dyzigi looked at the jar, and then at Constantine, and then he nodded.

"I am now informed that you are completely sincere in your new allegiances. I am gratified. I knew that once you saw your former self, you would reawaken your relationship to the War Lord. Once N'Hept becomes part of us . . ." He shrugged and smiled. He covered the jar and strode to Constantine, extending his hand. "Join us at the ritual. The time has come. They are all in place, just a short distance above us. You will remember the words to be spoken. . . ."

◆━◎━◆

"John, don't do this!" Gatewood begged as Constantine stood before the altar. "Mercury's here—Tchalai . . ."

He recognized the altar; it hadn't changed much, all these millennia later. They'd genuinely found the original cave, it seemed. The same carvings; the grooves where Barasa's blood had dripped. Runes had been incised into the concrete floor around it, as if radiating outward.

And a few yards away were two gurneys. On the gurneys, gagged, were Tchalai and Mercury. Kidnapped from Paris, left here by Dyzigi's thugs.

"Mercury!" Gatewood shouted. "John—look at them! Think!"

But it didn't really matter, what happened to them here, Constantine thought. It was here—or elsewhere. It would come to them all. . . .

"I'm ready," Constantine said calmly, taking his place at the other side of the altar; to the right and left, one man to each side of the square altar, were Trevino and MacCrawley. Simpson stood guard nearby.

"The powder has been distributed in the target room." Dyzigi gazed into the skull box fondly as he spoke and lifted out the first skull to place on the altar. "I've just had that confirmed. N'Hept will be pleased. It's not enough by itself. But . . ." He laid a bronze war club on the altar, stained with blood from some ancient battle. "The powder creates a *literal* atmosphere of war." He placed the second skull on the altar. "Our invocation will call the War Lord from beneath. He will rise amongst them and they will lose all capacity to reason. We could have done it without you, Mr. Constantine—but you will make it ever so much more powerful. . . ."

MacCrawley was looking at his watch. "Let us begin."

"John, this is seriously fucked up—!" Gatewood shouted.

"Shut your gob or I'll cut your throat," Constantine told him, not turning a hair.

Dyzigi smiled approvingly.

✦══◉══✦

In a certain room above, as the men gathered around the table for the meeting, there was none of the usual small talk and polite discussion of golf courses and hotels. They had all been advised that an attempt had been made to launch a dirty bomb against Paris, a missile with ground human bones packed against its warhead, for some unknown symbolic reason. They assumed terrorists; there were Farsi markings, as well as some unknown to their analysts, on the warhead. The Iranian ambassador refused to own up. The public did not yet know.

The men looked at one another, and felt a kind of imminence in the air. . . .

✦══◉══✦

"N'Hept, War Lord of the new world, set us free from the madness that invests mankind!" MacCrawley intoned.

Dyzigi nodded to Simpson, who went to Gatewood and unlocked the shackles on his arms and legs.

Constantine was aware of all this distantly. . . .

His mind was on the War Lord, who was beginning to take shape around them, though as yet he was quite unseen. But Cons... ering himself from within... and from the skulls arrayed... Consciousness: an identity ... ous parts, an amalgamation o... real supernatural, to create an ar... certain purposes. This identity wa... human world—once triggered, he ca... ...asily and willingly.

Simpson shoved Gatewood toward the altar. "What the fuck . . ." Gatewood muttered. "Yo, I'm not a virgin, you know."

Trevino turned to him, smiling beneficently, just as he had when he'd molested altar boys, and pressed an old bronze knife into Gatewood's hand. He stepped back and raised his arms, joining in the incantation. Words and names from Atlantean magic were spoken and seemed to echo impossibly far and long, reverberating down the old train tunnel.

Constantine knew his part, remembered the words from his previous incarnation, and it was all coming together beautifully. He eagerly chanted the incantation, wanting to get this thing done, get N'Hept summoned, the world transformed; what a relief it would be to finally act on the rage that he had locked up so long in his heart.

Gatewood turned to run by Simpson, who shoved his pistol against his head and forced him back toward the altar.

The incantation gathered power. . . .

Gatewood looked at the knife in his hand. "If you think I'm going to—"

ok his head. "Fight me."

knife?"

s. Or we'll torture those two to death. The Mercury chick—that French broad. Why do you think we brought 'em? You and that girl have a connection, right? You want her to die nicey-nice or not? Fight!"

He fired the 9 mm, deliberately creasing Gatewood's ribs.

Gatewood staggered; blood coursed, but the wound wasn't deep.

"Fight!"

Constantine waited, chanting. Gatewood would try to fight, and he would be shot down. His blood—the blood of a warrior in battle—would consecrate the summoning. . . .

Gatewood snarled and raised the knife—

And then MacCrawley came to a point in the incantation that Constantine remembered well.

The name of the War Lord shouted three times, in the intonations of the sea people . . .

"N'Hept! N'Hept! N'Hept!"

And Constantine looked down at the face of N'Hept painted on the altar's side.

The two things came together in his mind. The name chanted three times. The face.

And the posthypnotic suggestion was triggered. Constantine came out of the self-hypnotic trance he had placed himself in when he was alone in the maintenance room.

Gatewood slashed at Simpson—who cocked the gun. . . .

Constantine had made himself *believe* he was

going to take part in this ritual, this scheme, so that he could pass muster, so that a demonic being could look into his mind and see only commitment to that course and no other, because he had managed to believe it himself. He had used the power of the Zoroaster figurine in a self-hypnosis that fooled Mengele and Dyzigi, and in a sense Constantine had conned himself too. . . .

And as he'd planned before the self-hypnosis took effect, the sight of the image of N'Hept and a certain repetition of his name in the ritual triggered the posthypnotic suggestion that freed him from his commitment to the Transfiguration.

He shivered and gasped, as the posthypnotic trance left him—and he came back to himself.

"On the other hand," Constantine said, grabbing the bronze-headed war club and striding over to Simpson, "being in any kind of association with vile tossers like you lot would fairly turn my stomach, wouldn't it?" And so saying he slammed Simpson on the back of the head with the war club.

Simpson went down—but blood from his scalp spurted onto runes incised on the floor, and the very air roared with the arrival of N'Hept, his gigantic face shimmering into manifestation over the train tracks, beside the altar.

Konz . . .

Constantine could see the others were locked into the incantation, focused on N'Hept, afraid to break the spell. He tossed the war club aside, jerked the black pendant from Gatewood's neck with one hand and with the other plucked the mummified hand from his coat and handed it to Gatewood. "Just reach out inside yourself and let them out. It's in you to do it, Bob's your uncle! They're the opposing force here— come on, nippy like!"

Gatewood stared down at the saint's withered hand. "I don't know . . ."

"Get it done, Gatewood! Now!"

MacCrawley and Trevino and Dyzigi seemed paralyzed—caught up in the presence of N'Hept. But Constantine had broken free of it—and now he smiled nastily at Dyzigi. "Right. 'Fraid I'm going to have to cry off world war, yeah? It's all about to fall apart . . . ought to be bloody entertaining."

But again N'Hept called out:

KONZ!

Constantine turned defiantly to N'Hept. "Here, you! Bugger off! I'm John Constantine! I'm no more Konz than an old man is a toddler! I've grown some since I called you up last—but not you, you don't change! You're just a blood thirst and a rage and that makes for piss-poor company, Sunshine! Now FUCK OFF!"

If a god could register astonishment, it might've been there for a moment. Which is all Constantine hoped for.

In the room overhead, men were shouting, threatening, phone calls were being made, demands pounded into the table. . . .

And then Gatewood moaned, and the saint's hand clutched and opened wide, and a spiraling ectoplasmic mist emerged from it, twined about with faces, issuing voices, and in seconds a crowd of ghosts stood on the platform.

N'Hept stared at them. **What are these rabble! Such are nothing to me! They are leavings for the demonic vultures! Take them from my sight!**

"Not likely! Then we'd only have you for company, you great lummox!" Constantine shouted.

He saw Futheringham stepping forward from the crowd, stroking his mustaches. Constantine pointed upward—and Futheringham nodded.

The ghosts swirled again, and the vortex of souls swept up through the ceiling, through tunnels and pipes and street, through floor after floor and at last to the room where power-possessing men gathered, and made themselves known. . . .

Gatewood gripped the mummified hand, as if holding hands with the saint, concentrating, moaning—his power, the reason he'd been brought here all along— was *making the ghosts visible to the men in the conference room.*

Not a word was spoken. No speeches were made. There was only a gentle psychic reaching out.

So that, in that moment, the men in the conference room—the men shaping the future of the world—saw these spirits in death as they had never been able to see them in life. They saw innocent victims of war— their wars. They saw scores of tragic bystanders. They saw refugees.

They saw in them every baffled, horrified child who'd ever screamed when strangers had ridden into the village, killing her parents; they were every kid who was shot in a gang drive-by intended for someone else; they were people blown to pieces by a car bomb because they'd applied for a job with a new government that someone else didn't like; they were children herded like goats in the Congo and slaughtered like lambs in Rwanda; they were women raped till they died in Darfur. They were nude, screaming children frying as they ran through a rain of napalm in Vietnam.

They were the ones with no interest in the wars. They were the ones caught in the crossfire.

Their lives and deaths poured through the minds of the men in the conference room.

The men saw these ghosts and their lives so clearly that for a moment they forgot their own rigid, squirting egos; for a moment they saw things as these innocents did. For a moment *they saw themselves* as their victims saw them.

They saw themselves concerned only with a great financial chess game, the struggle for political advantage, for oil and money and power, that defined the world. They saw a bestial, ancient face, apelike and reptilian at once, quivering in the air behind them, seen but unseen, dominating them; they saw themselves caught up in the emanations, the mindless influence of N'Hept. They saw themselves.

They shouted in horror and covered their eyes, and they rejected that vision of themselves. Seeing it, they no longer felt so much a part of it. They turned away.

And far below, in the abandoned London Underground station, N'Hept began to shrink.

"Off you go, then!" Constantine said, grinning despite himself, enormously relieved.

I cannot go . . . I can only become invisible . . . I will bide my time.

MacCrawley and Dyzigi stared, aghast. Trevino

was shaking, whimpering. MacCrawley looked toward the exits . . . as the angry words of a repudiated god boomed in all their minds.

It is well that I retreat, for a time, from this world. It is not the world of real warriors, Konz. It is the world of smart bombs and guided missiles and armored vehicles! The world of poison bombs and nuclear weapons! Yes, I have been watching—from within you! I know how your warriors have disgraced themselves with this cowardice! This is not war! It has no purity! It is the war-making of cowards!

Dyzigi fell stunned to his knees, muttering, trying to find the right incantation to bring the god back under control. MacCrawley slipped off into the left-hand tunnel, through a gap in the debris. . . .

And N'Hept raged on.

This is the war of scheming women and frightened old men! I am glad to turn my back on it until you should become warriors once again!

"Here, take one of these bastards with you, old boy!" Constantine said. "I hate for you to leave without anything for the road!"

So saying he shoved the nearest of the magicians toward the great head of N'Hept—Trevino, flailing, shouting in terror. N'Hept grinned at Constantine, and opened its mouth wide, sucking Trevino's soul in like smoke from a crack pipe. Trevino fell dead—his body a shell, his spirit trapped forever in N'Hept.

And the War Lord shrank in on itself, spiraling to nowhere, gone and never quite gone. . . .

Constantine pushed a serving cart up to Dyzigi, on his knees beside the altar.

On it was a gallon jar.

Dyzigi looked up at Constantine, shaking his head, imploring.

Constantine smiled sunnily. "Just felt you should be reunited with your old mates, Sunshine!"

And with that he picked up the gallon jar containing all that remained of a human monster, charged with the pure essence of evil. He opened the jar, and upended it over Dyzigi's head.

"Time to empty the slops jar."

Constantine expected that both of them would die from the toxic content, but he had not reckoned on Dyzigi's true nature. He was not exactly a human being. And not exactly a demon. He was a man so thoroughly possessed by a demonic spirit, it had actually altered his physical substance. What Constantine expected did not happen.

Instead, Dyzigi began to shrink. It was as if the glass jar was opening its mouth wide for him, and he was shrinking to enter it, and in moments he was compressed into it along with Mengele . . . the two of them trapped together, in viscous living ooze, gray and drab and banal and always on the edge of disintegrating and never quite falling apart.

Constantine turned the jar over—being careful not to touch the fluids—and hastily screwed the top back on.

Then he went to untie Tchalai. Gatewood was already setting Mercury free. She threw her arms around Gatewood in a particular manner that was not lost on Constantine.

"Christ, I thought we were going to die in those

sodding gurneys," Mercury said, hugging him. Then she sensed something—a tension in him. She looked up at his face curiously.

Gatewood stepped back from Mercury and looked at the ceiling.

"Yes," he murmured. "Now . . ."

⊷⊨◉⊨⊶

In the room far overhead, the men who'd come for the conference were weeping—embracing one another—while their guards ran to get doctors, sure that someone had introduced some kind of mind-altering substance into the coffee. They couldn't see the ghosts, though they were crowded all around the room.

Futheringham turned to the others and said, "Right, we have changed things, a little. We made a difference, my friends. It won't last—but it will help. And that means we can all go on to the next world."

Two spirits appeared in the room, visible to the ghosts alone.

They appeared as bearded men in long robes. One of them had appeared to Gatewood, in Baghdad. The other was the Blue Sheikh.

They gestured, smiling broadly, toward the window. A ray of light shone through, and formed itself into a glittering solid thing—a road that vanished with straight and perfect perspective into an infinite point.

The ghosts bade good-bye to Gatewood, and they took the starry road.

One of them hesitated, hung back a moment. He had been a young man from California, in life, calling himself Spoink. He took a long last look at the world—and then followed the others up the starry trail, and into that infinite point: infinitely small, infinitely large, the Ground of Being, the Sea of Consciousness, beyond the River of Forgetfulness.

⤙═◎═⤚

"Rabbi Hivel?" Constantine said. "You here?"

"Yes, yes . . . what is it, that John Constantine, come to bother me about the Kabbala? You know nothing of the Kabbala, you are a dancing fool, a vaudeville jokester, you are not a Kabbalist, you come back when you're serious—"

Constantine nodded gravely. "Yes Rabbi—right-o. Listen, I've got something here in a bag—it's a jar with something nasty in it. Wanted you to have it."

The old man scowled at the canvas bag and pulled at his beard. He was as Constantine had last seen him: wearing a black frock coat, the Orthodox Jew's broad-brimmed black hat, palises of white hair curling on either side of his shaggy old head. He leaned, a little unsteadily, on the counter of his curio shop, pushing the dusty bric-a-brac aside with his elbow. "I saw this in a dream. It's real?"

"It is . . . too real. Too objectively real. Rabbi, take this and—you still have those fish you keep? You always loved fish."

"My aquariums are a beauty, they are, yes."

"And you have the piranha?"

"I do. Oh, I see!"

They went into the back room, bubbling and bright with aquariums. Thousands of brightly colored fish darted behind dozens of panes of glass. Constantine handed over the jar and, ceremoniously, calling out thanks in Hebrew, Rabbi Hivel opened the jar and fed the remains of Dyzigi and Josef Mengele to Brazilian piranha.

They snapped them up eagerly, their little eyes glowing.

<hr>

John Constantine smiled and lit a cigarette when they got in sight of The Cutter, that misty evening. He and Tchalai and Mercury and Gatewood. "Wonder if they've got anything to eat, just now."

"John—talk him out of going back to Baghdad!" Mercury said. She was walking along just behind Constantine, holding hands with Gatewood. The destruction of the thing in the jar had set her mind free—and being with Gatewood seemed to keep the errant psychic impressions at bay. She was sheltered from the psychic winds in the lee of his love, Constantine supposed.

"Got to go back," Gatewood said. "Just the way I was raised, I guess. Finish my duty to my country— even when it's full of crap. Maybe they'll send me to Afghanistan—I still believe in that one."

"Tchalai and I spoke to the CIA station chief at the American embassy," Constantine said. "I cut a deal with him. You still mad enough to want to go to

Afghanistan, mate, they'll send you after you go back to Baghdad. It's either that or the CIA kills us all—and the French secret service wouldn't like that."

"How'd you do it?" Gatewood asked. "Reinstating me—a guy who 'went AWOL.' Tall order, man."

"Amazing what you can do with a little blackmail," Constantine said, shrugging. "When I told them about my close acquaintance with Norm the chopper pilot and his little trips sneaking secret prisoners into Abu Ghraib—well, it was either kill me or accommodate me. And they decided to accommodate me. The gits would've been smarter to kill me, of course. . . ."

"It is all thanks to me!" Tchalai said. "I got us into the CIA! Everyone owes me a great debt!" Then she laughed.

"Maybe they've got bangers and mash," Constantine said, as they walked up to the pub.

Tchalai snorted. "They can't have food worth eating at this pub, John! You should come back to Paris with me!"

"Come on in, love. I'm not going anywhere till I have a pint."

"Oh, *d'accord,* very well . . ."

But Constantine hesitated outside the door a moment. He had the irrational feeling that he might yet realize he wasn't actually here, that this was a dream, or another astral wandering from some cell in Iran.

Right on cue the door of The Cutter opened and Rich stood there, grinning. "Con Job! Saw you through the window! You're back! Come on in and buy me a drink! I'm flat broke, mate!"

Constantine nodded to himself. This was the real

thing, all right. "Right you are, Rich. I've come all the way back here just to buy you a drink."

"Where you been, John?" Rich asked, scratching his groin.

"Oh—Iran, mostly. North Africa some. Catacombs of Paris. You know."

"What—all this time, wandering about them places? When you could've been here, buying me something wet?"

"Spent a lot of time in a monastery, believe it or not, mate."

"A *monastery?*" Rich hooted in mock outrage. "Someone let *John Constantine* stay in a monastery?"

"Yeah. Funny old world, innit?" Constantine said, as he ground out his cigarette and went into the pub.

About the Author

JOHN SHIRLEY is the author of numerous novels, including *Crawlers, Demons, and Wetbones,* the recent motion picture novelization of *Constantine,* and story collections, including *Really Really Really Really Weird Stories* and the Bram Stoker Award–winning collection *Black Butterflies.* He also writes scripts for television and film, and was coscreenwriter for *The Crow.* The authorized fan-created website is www.darkecho.com/JohnShirley and his blog is www.JohnShirley.net.